Frisbee Ball Rules

By
William P. Bahlke

Debbie & Mike

First published by Dog Ear Publishing
4010 W. 86th Street, Ste H
Indianapolis, IN 46268
www.dogearpublishing.net

ISBN: 978-1-4575-2973-3

Library of Congress Control Number: has been applied for

This book is printed on acid-free paper.

This book is a work of Fiction. Places, events, and situations in this book are purely Fictional and any resemblance to actual persons, living or dead, is coincidental.

Printed in the United States of America

This book is dedicated to my wife, Meda, whose constant encouragement and gentle guidance have made this lifelong dream a reality. Thank you, sweetheart, for your love, for your support, and, most of all, for being my best friend.

CHAPTER ONE

*I*t was a hot, stagnant summer morning. Reagan Davis, sitting on the third step of his Murphree E dorm entrance, lacing up his black Converse All-Stars, could already feel the moisture dripping from his every pore. The relentless heat and humidity were the culprits. The large quantity of beer he had consumed the night before while touring fraternity rush parties certainly wasn't helping matters.

Reagan squinted upward toward the bright blue sky. *Damn!* He had been hoping for at least a little cloud cover. Rising to his feet, he watched as two freshmen co-eds, standing in the center of the complex's courtyard, hoisted Old Glory up the flagpole to its flaccid terminus.

The scene, the setting, and his circumstances brought a broad smile to Reagan's face. It was bright and early on a Saturday morning. The year was 1973, and the Vietnam War had recently ended. The drinking age was eighteen, and Reagan was away from home for the first time in his life. Since arriving in Gainesville one week earlier, he hadn't seen a single schoolgirl wearing a bra, and that was all right with him.

He had an afternoon's worth of homework ahead of him. His classes were going to be tougher than he had expected. His head was throbbing, and his mouth was dry. He had already gone through most of his first month's allowance.

Despite it all, he had never been happier, and he couldn't seem to wipe the smile from his face. It was what he had been dreaming about for as long as he could remember. *Life just might not get any better than this.*

Reagan looked up one more time at the sky and swatted the sweat from his forehead. He turned, glancing back over his shoulder at the two girls, and then whispered under his breath, "This is going to be one hell of a hot run!"

Reagan chose the shade of the tunnel, which connected the five-hundred-plus student housing facility with the main body of the campus, to do his pre-run stretches. The corridor contained a water fountain, a garbage can, a bulletin board plastered with announcements, including one advertising next Friday night's *Beatles Night at the Ratheskellar*, and a mirror. Through the scratches on the mirror, including frat insignias, love messages, cuss words, and a brainstorm that simply read, "Ban the Bomb," the incoming freshman conducted a personal assessment.

Gazing past his six feet four inches, 185-pound frame, dark blue eyes, and dirty blonde hair hanging as long as his father would allow, his chiseled handsome face badly in need of a shave, and his bright smile, and tanned complexion, his stare came to rest, disappointedly, at his biceps.

* * *

Reagan's high school football coach, Coach Shanahan or Coach Shanny, as he was affectionately known, had broken the rules and allowed his "favorite second-stringer" to work out with the varsity team during the summer. And work out, Reagan had. Some days for two hours, he lifted weights and did push-ups, sit-ups, and pull-ups. Coach Shanny had even speculated that if Reagan would have put as much effort into his conditioning during the previous two years, he might have been a starter. But being a starter was never Reagan's top priority.

Despite his somewhat inward personality, Reagan was very popular in high school, especially during his senior year. His good looks always managed to get him dates, oftentimes to the dismay of his more outgoing buddies.

But now he had a real reason to add bulk and definition. He had an overpowering desire to look his best. He'd gone from being a top-dog senior to a lowly freshman, "the freshman curse," and he fully understood that he would need every advantage to get what he so desperately wanted. And what he wanted, and what now was his number one priority, even if he wouldn't admit it openly, was . . . *girls!*

* * *

While taking a break from his pre-run routine, and after looking both ways and seeing no one, Reagan flexed first his right arm and then his left. *Not bad!* Certainly bigger than they had been, but not big enough, not for what he was up against. Earlier that morning, he had read about the college's gym in the school's student-run news publication, *The Alligator*, and had promised himself that he would find the weight room and do some lifting the following day.

He was finishing up his stretches when a tall, slender brunette with hair down to her waist and a perky bounce in her blouse walked by the entrance of the tunnel and glanced his way for just a split second. The look in her eyes, and the expression on her face, was one he was getting used to, but not one he enjoyed. It was the *Oh, you're just a freshman* look. Reagan Davis glanced one more time in the mirror, shook his head, reconfirmed his promise to himself, and then set out on his first run as a Florida Gator.

The run, which he had mapped out the night before, would cover about six miles. From the tunnel he headed down Fletcher Drive, took a right on Stadium Road, and then ran past Alligator Alley, a structure that housed both the basketball facilities, numerous classrooms, and, as it turned out, the gym.

While making a mental note about the gym's location, he continued in front of the football stadium and next reached a building with a placard that read *ROTC Headquarters*. Behind that building was a large field where a number of army formations were marching in full uniform. Reagan paused at a nearby bench and, while tightening up his left shoe and loosening his right, admired the precision and crispness of the students who had chosen this method not only to pay for their education but also to serve their country during these very troubling times.

Looking up once more toward the sun, and then to his left, he saw a group of six shaggy-haired boys about his age sitting under a large oak tree, smoking pot. The dichotomy of the moment fascinated him, and Reagan looked around to see if anyone else was sharing the scene.

It was early Saturday morning; the Hippies had probably been up all night, and the marchers had most likely received reveille at 6:00 AM. The rest of the student body was seemingly still sound asleep, and Reagan was all alone to take in the moment.

* * *

During this past year at home, the dinner-table debates had grown more intense, sometimes lasting several hours. Eventually, someone in the family would have had more than they could handle and would storm out of the front door.

The subject had almost always been the same: the Vietnam War. Reagan, who had sat second-chair on his high school debate team, could take either side of an argument with great skill. Knowing his parents controlled the purse strings, however, he would always back down just before losing his allowance, driving rights, or, worst, his late-night-out privileges. His older sister, Alice, who had lost a boyfriend *over there* and had had several other buddies come back in bad shape, would often excuse herself from the table early and retire to her bedroom, weeping.

Mom and Dad were totally convinced that the Communists were trying to take over the world and needed to be stopped . . . in Vietnam. They were also sure that the United States would ultimately win the war because "we always do."

At the time, Reagan wasn't totally sure where he stood. He certainly didn't want to be governed by the Chinese or the Russians, but he also had no desire, as he approached his draft eligibility age of eighteen, to pick up a rifle and start shooting at people. As a matter of fact, he had already privately decided that he would not be going. Canada sounded much better than the hot, swampy rice paddies of some faraway land. Luckily, the draft ended that year. If the contingency draft, which was held in its place, had been the real thing, he would have been standing alongside those third in line . . . or not.

* * *

Looking up once more at the marchers, he realized that with the passing of time, he now knew exactly where he stood. He also believed that he had a decent handle on the country's place in history and also a good picture of what the future might hold.

The Vietnam War, which started for the United States reportedly with a single torpedo being fired at a PT boat in the Bay of Tonkin and resulted in 58,000 casualties, had recently ended. With it also ended the student riots that had rocked the nation to its core. America had lost the war, a fact that, although rarely discussed openly, was understood and, at least privately, acknowledged by most.

Disgraced, our country would take out its embarrassment and frustration on the backs of the returning soldiers. Few of them had volunteered for this journey, but most had gone willingly, fought unselfishly for its citizens and for what our country stood for. Some never returned. Some came back in body bags. Some came back wounded, physically or mentally. None of them would ever be the same.

They all, however, would face the humiliation of an unwelcoming nation. For several years to come, the men and women in uniform, including college ROTC students, would be scorned and treated as if they'd individually caused the war and had been the reason for America's defeat. These unforgivable injustices would be one of the largest scars on the body of our nation's history. Any effort of future reconciliation would prove to be lame and unsuccessful. This would be a wound that would never heal.

For Reagan's generation, this was a time of rebirth and newfound freedoms. They'd been right; the establishment and their parents had been wrong, dead wrong. And if their parents had been wrong about the war, what else had they been wrong about? Everything! No sooner had the rioters retreated, than, suddenly, the "sex, drugs, and rock-n-roll attitude" that swept every college campus in the country stepped in. There were streakers, sex parties, burn-the-bra bonfires, no rules, and no responsibilities.

As Reagan continued his run, which took him next past Fraternity Row, the pounding in his head reminded him of the fun he had the night before. "There is nothing better than fraternity rush," he muttered out loud. *Especially if you are a decent-looking guy who can turn on the charm when you need to.*

* * *

Every frat house, every year sets out to replace their graduating seniors. They all want to do so by attracting the cream of the crop from the freshman class. This is done through their rush, bid, and initiation process. The beginnings of this process are the rush parties that take place the first week of school and are open to the entire freshman class, and all other uncommitted male students, for that matter.

Reagan realized at his third house that their methods were all quite similar. The brothers whom the frat has chosen to be their facemen greet you at the front door. These are the fraternity's best-looking guys who happen to also be blessed with the most outgoing personalities. Within seconds of entering the house, you are visually assessed, evaluated, and categorized. If the rushee is a potential keeper, through some sort of a codified communication system, the top faceman is assigned to the candidate and is the first to approach him. This had been the case for Reagan at every house he had visited.

You receive a strong welcoming handshake along with a soothing smile, and then the interview begins. Where are you from? Have you chosen a major? What sports did you play in high school? What do you think about all of the good-looking girls at the University of Florida? Without knowing it the rushee has just been tested, graded, and put into a slot for further interrogation and review. If you pass the first test, the next few will be conducted with increased vigor and interest. After meeting the other facemen, one by one, and upon completion of all of "the tests," you are then seamlessly passed to a younger brother, usually a sophomore. He will give you all the reasons you should consider this particular frat and let you know how much he enjoys being a brother, as he walks you through the house and into the party room.

5

By this time, all of the brothers know pretty much everything about you, right down, most likely, to the cup size of your jock strap.

The candidate will then be offered a beer, dropped off, and introduced to one of the several groups of brothers gathered in the room listening to the music and watching people dance. If it has been determined that you are the scholastic type, you will find yourself surrounded by the chemistry majors and pre-law students. If you are a jock, you will be introduced to the head of the frat's intramural teams and probably one or two of the brothers who play a varsity sport for the university.

In every house, Reagan had been categorized as a ladies' man and found himself blushingly talking to the gorgeous girls from the frat's sister sorority who were there for just that purpose. For those few minutes, the freshman curse was neutralized by the fraternity's growing desire to have him pledge their house. He had even walked away with a few names and phone numbers.

God, where did I put those? Yes, there is nothing better than fraternity rush!

* * *

While realizing that the sweat-gushing run was quickly clearing his cobwebs, Reagan took a right onto Museum Road, another right onto Hull Road eventually reaching SW 34th Street. He was leaving the campus boundary and entering the city streets when he paused momentarily to review his planned route. He was also trying unsuccessfully to block his worst childhood memory from resurfacing.

* * *

There was another 34th Street that Reagan knew very well, but it was about 350 miles south of this one, in Miami, where he had grown up. In the final five months of his senior year, Reagan had dated, exclusively dated, Barbara Ann Withers. They were in love. He knew it. She knew it. Their parents knew it. The whole school knew it. Everyone knew it.

They had dated off and on for a year before deciding to go steady, a commitment that needed to be made before Barbara would . . . well, before Barbara would do what every boy Reagan's age wanted his girlfriend to do. Before Barbara would do what neither of them had done before.

It was this other 34th Street that he would take to her house the night she, with trembling hands, gave him the bad news. It was this other 34th Street that they would take to get to that building. That darkened awful building where they had met that man and had given him the money, where Reagan had heard those God-awful screams. And it was this other 34th

6

Street that he had driven home on the night he and Barbara Ann decided that it was too painful to continue their relationship and had broken up.

* * *

Back in stride, Reagan, thinking that he was glad to be on this 34th Street, felt his tears, the tears that were blending with the sweat as both dripped down his face.

The runner's pace quickened as he crossed over Archer Road and noticed the broken-down marquis that read "Shady Oaks Mobile Home Community." The sign was marking the southeast corner of what was a large plot of land covered with trees and underbrush. Through breaks in the foliage, Reagan spotted what looked to be hundreds of portable homes of all shapes and sizes: campers, travel trailers, Volkswagen busses, and even some pop-up tents. It made him shiver to imagine how spooky this place must be at night. *It is like something out of a horror movie.*

Reagan was returning his attention to his stride when he first saw it. He was sure that around here they called it a hill, but to him, it looked like a mountain. His regular run around the Miami Springs Golf Course was also about six miles in length, but it was as flat as a pancake.

He could sense that he was already well behind his normal pace because of the heat of the day and the rolling Gainesville terrain, but this was really going to slow him down. At the foot of the hill, he took a deep breath and looked straight ahead, concentrating on the spot. The spot was the top of the hill and was marked by a wooden light pole. For some reason, at that moment, the vision of the brunette in the courtyard earlier flashed into his head and started to piss him off. Getting closer to the spot, he was completely out of breath, his legs were burning, and the sweat was pouring out of him even faster than before, but he was determined to make it to the top without stopping, and he did.

Jogging in place, Reagan turned around to assess his accomplishment. *Wow, maybe I'm in pretty good shape after all.* He felt the confidence building inside of him as he reasoned out loud, "And by the way, any girl at this university would be damn lucky to have a date with Reagan Davis." He had a mission now, and nothing was going to stop him. *To hell with the freshman curse!*

It was downhill all the way to Williston Road, where he took a left and started looking desperately for water: a garden hose, a water spigot, even a stream or a lake would work at this point. *I am thirsty.* Then he saw it coming up on his right, a park. Not much of a park, actually. It was more like a large clearing amongst the trees: a flat field with several people throwing a Frisbee around, a bench, and, yes, a water fountain.

Reagan didn't remember water ever tasting so good. He bent over the fountain for the longest time, feeling the moisture as it trickled down his throat, rejuvenating his entire body. He washed his face and let a full scoop or two run over his head and down the back of his neck. He would certainly remember this moment, this park, and, most importantly, this fountain.

Just before getting back to his run, he pulled from his pocket the bandless gold-plated watch his father had given him, and checked the time. He'd been running for forty-six minutes, which really didn't mean anything to him, not knowing how far he had gone or how much farther he had to go. Just a point of reference for future runs.

As he was turning to go, Reagan felt something lightly tap his right shin and heard it fall to the ground. Looking down, he saw that it was a Frisbee. He was bending over to pick it up when he heard her voice for the first time.

"Hey, preppy, are you planning on giving me back my Frisbee, or didn't they show you how to toss one of those at that expensive high school your parents sent you to? Round here, they teach young men manners. Seems like you might have skipped that class. Probably off in the bushes with one of your girlfriends, trying to get it up."

If Reagan realized that he'd been insulted at least a half dozen times in one breath, his expression wasn't showing it. What he had looked over to, and what now commanded his full attention, was the most beautiful girl he'd ever laid his eyes on.

"Hey, are you listening to me? What are you staring at? Haven't you ever seen a real woman before?"

Reagan flicked the Frisbee back in her direction but was otherwise frozen. She stood about five and a half feet tall, with golden blonde hair, and a sparkle in her bright blue eyes. He'd never seen a woman's body with so many curves . . . so many gorgeous curves. The crooked smile on her face gave away the fact that her cutting sarcasm was just part of the package and not meant to be hurtful. She was wearing a white, grass-stained terry-cloth shorts outfit that was barely covering her assets. Yes, he was frozen. His mouth was open. His legs wouldn't move, and when he tried to answer her, only gibberish came out.

She was obviously charmed by his infatuation. Her smile broadened, and her eyes blinked twice before she turned, walking away with an exaggerated wiggle.

"Wait! Hold on." Reagan had quickly regained his composure and was walking after her. "What are you all playing? Do you need another player?"

He froze again. What he was certain had to be a figment of his imagination, or a wonderful dream, had done a quick turnaround and was staring him down with a look of dismay.

"We're playing Frisbee ball. God, you did just get off the bus from Mars. And, yes, we could use another player. Can't you see that there are just five of us? Here, let me help you. Hold out your fingers; one, two, three, four, five." As she turned and was heading again toward her obviously impatient friends, Reagan quickly caught up with her.

"Okay, so it's called Frisbee ball. What are the rules?"

This stopped her in her tracks once more, and her look suggested that she was about to withdraw her invitation. "Okay, preppy, if you are going to join us, you need to talk less and listen more . . . a lot more. I am the boss. Do you hear me? It's Frisbee ball! There are no rules. There are plenty of games out there with rules, hundreds of them. People have been playing those games and following those rules for years. If you have to have rules, then go off and play one of those games, but if you want to play here, now, and with us, then you better get used to the fact that we have no rules."

Despite her obvious disappointment, Reagan continued, "But if it's a game, there has to be rules. Otherwise, how would you know who wins and who loses? How would you keep score? If there's a foul, how do you know what the penalty is? How do you know when it starts and when it's over?"

His rambling tickled her and was taking her out of character. She flashed a now genuine smile, shook her head with a giggle, and paused before responding in a softer tone. "I think you are missing the point. Like I said, I am the boss. At the end of the game, and I will tell you when the game is over, you will know the score. You will be both a winner and a loser, and if you commit a foul, your winning days will be over sooner than later." Their eyes locked in a serious stare. "Now, any more of your lame-brained questions?"

He was still deciphering her latest response and had no more questions.

"Fine then." She was sporting a sly sexy smile now. "We're playing shirts and skins. Your team is skins, so off with that shirt."

Reagan glanced over the girl's shoulder at the other four people on the field, two men and two women. They all had their shirts on. He looked back at her now inquisitive smile, paused for a moment, and then pulled his shirt over his head, all the while thinking, *God, she is beautiful.*

It was now her turn to stare, and Reagan noticed it. He was enjoying her obvious admiration, and he let the moment linger before asking one final question. "So, if there are no rules, why do you need teams?"

They started walking side by side. Her response was muted and somewhat serious. "Because, preppy, when there are no rules, sometimes you need someone on your side to help you understand the game. By the way, I'm Charlotte . . . Charlotte Summerland. You can call me Charley. Everyone does."

CHAPTER TWO

Reagan didn't bother to check the time on his watch before setting out for his run back to campus. Following two hours of the most ridiculous, and possibly the most enjoyable, game he'd ever played, every muscle in his body was yelling at him. After turning left on NW 13th Street and making sure he was out of the sight of his new friends, especially Charley, his run turned into a jog, and then eventually, he was walking, limping along.

Coming up on his left, he noticed a sign perched proudly above what appeared to be a charming gingerbread home that had been converted into a restaurant. He immediately recognized the name, Hoggetowne Pizza and Suds, remembering that this was where the Sigma Chis were having a social with Kappa Delta Sorority this coming Thursday night. He couldn't remember—was it the redhead with the fire in her eyes, or the curvy brunette who had invited him to be her date? *I really need to slow down on the beer consumption. It's fogging my memory and getting in the way of my top priority.*

Near the front door of the restaurant, Reagan noticed a phone booth standing beside a cigarette machine and a newspaper box. Reagan always carried spare change when he went for a run. He paused, briefly thinking about using a dime to call Dan, his roommate. He could tell Dan where the keys were hidden, where his car was parked, and ask Dan to come pick him up.

Coming to his senses, and remembering that Dan was Dan, Reagan turned back toward the street just before hearing the door to the restaurant unlock and a man's voice call out, "Hey, are you here about the job?"

* * *

On the previous Sunday, Reagan had met Danny Miller for the first time. Reagan had been in the room for two nights by himself, beginning to wonder if anyone would be sharing his eight-by-twelve-foot room—a room that held two single beds, two three-drawer dressers, two desks, one working lamp, a tiny closet, and a sink with a constant drip. There were no pictures hung on the walls and no curtains. There was only one window, and Reagan, having been the first to arrive, had already claimed the bed next it. The place looked like it hadn't been painted in quite a while. The community phone, the bathroom, and the showers were down the hall, and the kitchen was two flights down, on the second floor.

There were no parents and no curfew, and visitation by members of the opposite sex was allowed until 11:00 PM Sunday through Thursday and until 12:00 AM on Friday and Saturday. No one seemed to care about there being alcohol or drugs in the rooms, and stereos could be cranked until someone complained. With his time alone to think about it, Reagan had concluded that he had found paradise. He had never felt more freedom in his life.

Then, that afternoon, while he was sitting quietly at his desk, staring out the window, and working on a list, there was a loud knock on his door that nearly jolted him out of his seat.

Reagan had a list for everything. He even had a list of his lists. The one he was working on when the knock came was the most important of all and was entitled "How to Stay in College." Staying in college was paramount to accomplishing his number-one priority. There were already eight items on this list, four of which he had written down before leaving home—the four commandments, his parents had called them:

1. Cs or better.
2. Stay away from the student riots.
3. No drugs.
4. Don't get a girl pregnant.

The first three were not a problem. Reagan was a pretty good student, and although not a brainchild, he was always willing to put in the hours it took to make the grades.

He was very curious about the rioters. On his second night in town, he had, from a distance, watched them march down University Avenue. But he knew that this was his dad's number-one no-no, and he would definitely avoid the riots.

Drugs had never really interested him. He didn't mind being around them, but he would much rather have a beer. Drinking beer was a restriction his parents had not placed on him, knowing their son too well.

The pregnancy thing, however, was a concern. Although it seemed like every college-age girl was on the pill, there was still a risk, a big one. Not a bad idea to have a backup plan—a plan his father had helped him with two nights before they'd loaded up the Ford station wagon for the six-hour drive north.

After a few scotches, Reagan's dad would often visit him in his bedroom before lights-out. Usually just to say goodnight, maybe letting Reagan know how proud he was of him, or just wanting to smooth things over from whatever dinner-time debate had gotten out of control. This particular night, however, had been different. His dad was carrying a paper bag, he seemed to be tiptoeing, and he was sporting a sinister smile.

"Son, the best thing to do about those college girls up there is to steer clear. You know, be friendly and all, but don't . . . There's nothing good that can come from sleeping around with a bunch of floozies."

With that introduction he had practiced with Reagan's mom out of the way, his dad seemed more relaxed. He sat down on the bed and continued, "Now just in case you find yourself in a situation that's gotten . . . well . . . anyway . . . here." In the bag were three boxes containing twelve rubbers each. Reagan had seen them sold individually in the men's bathroom at the gas station but had never imagined that they came . . . a dozen in a box.

"Now, here's the deal." His dad continued. "You promise me you'll keep this little secret from your mom and sis, and I'll mail you more of these whenever you need them. You just call me, even if it's every week. You hear me?"

The every-week offer brought a big smile to his dad's face. He stood up, told Reagan how proud he was of him, turned off the light, and shut the door behind himself, still smiling on his way out. Reagan was guessing that they had just had "the talk." It was a shame that it had not come sooner.

Nonetheless, Reagan would keep the three boxes tucked away, in his bottom dresser drawer . . . just like every other freshman boy on campus.

* * *

The door of his dorm room cracked open just enough for Reagan to see two peering eyes studying him curiously up and down for what seemed like several minutes. Finally, as the door slowly opened, he got his first glimpse of his roommate, Danny Miller.

"Thank God you're not one of them. It's all I've been able to think about. What if my bunk buddy is one of them?" The door closed behind him, and Danny did a quick assessment of the room, pausing at the window, before continuing, "You're not one of them, are you? 'Cause I gotta tell you,

I like to sleep in the nude, and if I gotta sleep with one eye open, and wearing a butt plug to bed every night, I'm not gonna be very happy."

Danny Miller was tall and skinny. He was wearing jeans that were skin-tight. His eyes were a light brown, and his hair was so short that it was hard to tell what color it was. He wore a white tucked-in t-shirt and cowboy boots, and his belt buckle resembled a large gold medallion. His country accent was a bit muffled by a mouthful of shiny silver braces. He had a curious look on his face and wanted an answer but continued anyway.

"On the other hand, if you're a ladies' man, we're gonna have some fun, you and me. With your good looks and my personality, we're gonna churn more chum than a charter boat on a hot run. Have you seen some of the meat walking around this rodeo? They are hot and horny, and they all came here for one reason. Don't let yourself be fooled by their attitude. They want to be pinned back and rolled around in the mud like a hog in heat. Why do you think they are wearing close to nothing? You just got to have the bags to ask them. No shot, no goal. No tick, no tock. Are you listening to me, or have I lost you? Where are you from, anyway? What you working on there? Looks like a shopping list. Only women go shopping. Wait a minute, you're not one of them, are you?"

Reagan stood up and walked slowly toward Danny. After the many times he had rehearsed the lines he wanted to use to greet and impress his first roommate, standing there at that moment, he couldn't think of a single one of them. The only thing he could come up with was "Do they really make something called a butt plug?"

* * *

The fifth item on Reagan's list had nothing to do with him staying in college, but he really didn't want to have a list lying around entitled "How to Get Laid," so he had added the directive to this list after his first night in Gainesville.

5.   Get a part-time job.

Over dessert one evening at home, using every angle he could come up with, Reagan had tried unsuccessfully to convince his parents to increase his monthly allowance. From their perspective, however, everything was paid for: tuition, books, supplies, and meals. He had all the clothes he would need, and it was his idea to take along his car, despite the fact that freshmen were not allowed to have cars on campus. Paying for parking and gas were going to be Reagan's problem. Other than that, his parents had reasoned, thirty dollars a month should be more than enough for anything else that might come up.

On his first night in Gainesville, Reagan had happened into Big Daddy's Lounge and had forked over $12 buying drinks, trying to impress a cute Santa Fe Community College co-ed. All he had received for his generosity was a kiss in the parking lot. Not even a phone number. If he was going to get laid, he needed to find a job.

* * *

Reagan was studying the man at the door when the question was asked again. "Are you here about the job?" There was something about the knowing smile on this man's kind face. He looked a little like Santa Claus and had a twinkle in his eyes and a chuckle that made Reagan feel immediately at ease.

"Yes, sir, I am. I apologize about the . . ." Reagan was looking down at the grass stains on his legs, the blood that had now dried on his right knee, and the sweat marks on his shirt.

"Not a problem, son, come right in. Have a seat over there at the bar, and I will get one of those applications for you to fill out. Have you ever worked in a restaurant before? Ever made a pizza?"

Little did Reagan know that he had just walked into what would become his home away from home for the next four years. The man locked the door behind them. The restaurant, which opened every day at four in the afternoon and stayed open until the city-mandated closing time of two in the morning, was empty except for the two men.

A perfect college hangout, the place had a bar that stretched from the front door to the back wall, picnic-style tables arranged in rows, neon beer signs everywhere, and posters on the walls that ranged from pictures of half-naked girls to University of Florida sports heroes. In the back, next to the bathrooms, were three pinball machines, a jukebox, and a pool table. The restaurant had the sour smell of stale beer, somewhat offset by the sweet aroma of Italian sauces and spices.

"Pour us a cold one. I don't know where Pam put the fucking applications. Aw, to hell with it." Hiram Schmidt, who had disappeared into the office, was back. "The glasses are in the cooler over there. We have three beers, all on tap: Miller, Old Milwaukee, and Schlitz. They all taste about the same, so you chose. When you work for me, the beer and pizzas are free, there's no borrowing from the cash registers, and you must keep your paws off of the female help. I don't need the competition." *The chuckle.*

Reagan, who had made his way behind the bar, was pouring his first beer as a bartender and was feeling good about it. Hiram settled onto a barstool and, following the formal introductions, looked deeply into his new protégé's eyes before continuing.

"Here's the deal. I can teach you everything you need to know about the restaurant business. I will need you to work four nights a week. You will be making pizzas and clearing tables. When things are slow, you can do your studies at the desk in my office. I usually only hire girls." *The twinkle in his eyes was back.* "But the three I've got working for me now are driving me fucking nuts. If they weren't so damn good-looking, I'd fire every last one of them. They just don't know how to treat their boss, if you know what I mean." *The knowing smile.* "Not like the last group I had in here . . . My wife doesn't care, she's just glad to have me out of the house while she watches the boob tube. I'll get them broken in. You just wait and see. So are we set? I gotta run by the bank, so I'll give you a ride back to campus. You look like you need a shower, or maybe an ambulance. Pour us a couple more for the road."

The new hire waited in the car, and when Hiram came out of the bank, Reagan received a twenty-dollar advance from his boss. The smile on the young man's face told Hiram all he needed to know about his choice for a new assistant, at least for the time being. They discussed the job in a little more detail and agreed that a week from Sunday would be Reagan's first day at work.

If you could call it work, Reagan thought, *free beer and pizza, working with hot girls. I've already made money and haven't tossed my first pie.*

Hiram seemed excited after hearing that his new employee might be coming to the Sigma Chi party on Thursday. It would give him an opportunity to meet "the girls."

* * *

After being dropped off by Hiram and hobbling up the four flights of stairs, Reagan made sure to check the sign hanging on the doorknob before entering his dorm room. He and Dan had concocted a secret code. One side of the sign read, "Class in Session," the other, "Open for Business." Reagan saw that it read the latter, so he knew there was no girl in the room—"No hot sauce being cooked," as Dan had put it. In other words, the coast was clear. Upon entering, Reagan breathed a sigh of relief. The room was empty. His roommate must be out stirring up trouble.

In the past couple of days, Dan had taken up with Dusty Collins, a red-headed, goofy-looking sophomore transfer from the University of Georgia whose room was just down the hall from theirs. Those two had become partners in crime, which was all right with Reagan.

16

Earlier that week, Reagan had spent an evening with Dan at the Ratheskellar "trolling for chicks," and Reagan had had enough. It wasn't that he questioned Dan's pickup theory or doubted its effectiveness; he was just embarrassed by it.

Dan had no shame. He would talk to, actually flirt with, every girl who walked by. The first twelve "cheesecakes" who had the misfortune of coming too close to the gawker had looked back at him with a scowl. Reagan was about to crawl under the table.

The next girl, on the other hand, had offered up a smile and a wink, which was what Dan had been waiting for. He was going in for the kill. As she sat down, Reagan noted that she was a little short and pudgy, but as he would soon find out, Dan didn't cull, his motto being, "If it wiggles, it giggles."

Shortly afterward, a smiling Dusty Collins strolled into the Rat and joined them at their table. Reagan, seeing an opening, quickly took advantage of it and excused himself to go to the library to study.

Later that evening, when he got back to the room, class was in session, and Reagan had to wait in the courtyard for two hours until the coast was clear. The following day, Reagan peeked into Dan's bottom drawer and there were two missing rubbers. Reagan's three boxes were still intact.

* * *

6. Find a study partner.

In the right pocket of the blue jeans he'd worn the night before while visiting fraternity houses, there were three pieces of paper, each containing a name and a phone number. Two of the three were so badly smudged that he couldn't read them. *Damn!* The third read, "Molly Turner—Pre Calculus—Library West—3:00 Saturday."

The worrisome thing was that Reagan didn't remember meeting anyone named Molly Turner. He figured that she had to be one of the knockouts he'd met at the Sigma Chi house, or maybe some other good-looking girl he had come across the previous night. It didn't really matter. It appeared that he had a date, a study date, nonetheless.

After taking a shower and tending to his bruises and scratches, Reagan threw on those same jeans, grabbed a t-shirt, tied up his shoes, and was out the door and down the stairs.

Reagan hid behind a tree in the plaza just outside of the entrance to the library. It was just past three. He was hoping he would recognize Molly and then might recall at least part of their previous conversation. Unfortunately, the only person waiting at the door was a girl he did not recognize. She couldn't be one of the girls he had met at last night's rush parties. She was short, wearing glasses, had shoulder-length brown hair, was carrying a stack of books, and looked like she was actually wearing a bra. He took a second look. *Yeah, a bra.* Trying to figure out his next move, Reagan looked over again and saw that the girl was headed his way with a suspicious look on her face. *Crap!*

"Hello, Reagan," she said, standing in front of him, looking up at the top of the pine tree he had been hiding behind. "Did you lose something, or does your admiration of this particular type of foliage have you at a loss for words?"

"Well, hello, . . . um . . ."

"You don't recognize me, do you? Molly Turner. We are in pre-calculus together: Monday, Wednesday, and Friday, first period. I sit right beside you. You said you would help me with math if I would tutor you in humanities. Is any of this ringing a bell, or do you need to ask your friend the tree?"

"I'm sorry. I was just . . . "

"Yeah, looks to me like you've forgotten all about it and was hoping I was . . . Anyway listen, if you have other plans, I totally understand, but I'm trying to get passing grades, so I'm gonna go inside and study. See you later."

Molly was through the door, into the library, and out of sight before Reagan could figure out what to do or say. The hurt look on her face as she turned to walk away bothered him, but not enough to make him chase after her.

Passing grades. That comment was also bothering him. He did need to study. Just not with Molly Turner.

7. Don't fall in love.

Reagan had already been in love once. He seemed to be prone to it, and at least that time, it hadn't turn out well. He knew there was nothing that could screw up his college career, or interfere with his number-one priority, any faster than falling in love.

Following his confrontation with Molly Turner, Reagan had headed straight to his dorm's study hall. After reading a chapter and a half of *Moby Dick*, he just couldn't take it any more. In an effort to stay awake, and realizing that he wasn't a big fan of Herman Melville, the author, he cracked open his political science textbook for the first time. That didn't help. The real problem was, he was having trouble concentrating on anything. He felt bad about how he had treated Molly Turner. It wasn't like him to be rude or standoffish, and he was afraid he had hurt her feelings. In truth, she wasn't that bad-looking. She was just not what he was looking for. But that was not an excuse, and he would apologize to her Monday morning in class.

The only thing that could bring him out of his funk was the thing he hadn't been able to get off of his mind all afternoon: Charlotte Summerland. *God, she is beautiful!* And, as it turned out, she was also quite a handful.

Amongst the other Frisbee ball players that morning had been two exchange students from China. Ye and Yang (Reagan couldn't begin to pronounce their last names) spoke very little English and were obviously very much in love. In actuality, the couple didn't seem to realize that there was a game going on at all. They spent most of their time following each other around, tickling and tackling, never once attempting to chase or catch the Frisbee.

Ye and Yang were very excited when introduced to Reagan and were all smiles and bows. Ye had bounced up and down like a bunny, saying something in Chinese that Reagan found himself pretending he understood. They were delightful, and Reagan somehow felt a little relieved. If the Chinese did take over the country, at least they were nice people—the first two he'd met, anyway.

The other female player was Terri Spencer, whom Reagan had immediately labeled a tomboy. At about five feet tall and a solid 130 pounds, she didn't appear to have an ounce of fat on her. She had sweat running down her forehead, and the skimpy outfit she was wearing was covered in dirt. With short black hair, dark blue eyes, and a serious look on her face, she was obviously very competitive, a fact that was already concerning Reagan, her new teammate.

Gary Glaser sported a forced smile and a very firm handshake. Of the five, he was the only one who seemed a little annoyed by the arrival of the newest participant. Polite nonetheless, Gary gave the rookie a welcoming pat on the back that almost sent Reagan stumbling. Noticing the disapproving look that Charley shot Gary, Reagan tried to defuse the moment, pretending like the slap had been welcomed, even appreciated. Gary was tall and slender, and he had jet-black hair and darting hazel eyes. He seemed much older than the others, and as it turned out, he was quite the athlete.

In reality, Frisbee ball was a little like sandlot football. The two sides line up opposite of each other, and the quarterback, so to speak, hurls the Frisbee in the general direction of his or her teammates, who are running aimlessly, down the field. The disk is then tossed back and forth, handed off, sometimes intercepted, until one team or another finally makes it to the opposite end of the field. No score is recorded, and then the process starts all over again.

There is a lot of grabbing, pushing, and tackling involved, and the banter and bragging that passes back and forth, although sometimes ruthless, is for the most part good-natured. Charley's comments to Reagan were often flirtatious, which by design was getting under Gary's skin. Gary would sneer at her, and she would give him her *you'd better back off* look, which would temporarily calm him down and quickly put him in his place.

Charley and Terri went after each other aggressively, sometimes even when the Frisbee wasn't in play. At one particular point, the Frisbee flew well over Charley's head, but Terri tackled her anyway, quickly pinning her to the ground, holding down both her legs and arms and straddling her. Charley struggled, but couldn't move under Terri's strength. Both girls were panting, and Terri's sweat was dripping onto Charley's face.

"If you're gonna do it, do it," Charley's inflection was both strained and inviting.

Terri slowly lowered herself, pressing her lips against Charley's, in a deep lingering kiss. Reagan had never seen two girls kiss before, at least not like that, and he couldn't take his eyes off of them. Gary, upon reaching the scene, was yelling encouraging words, obviously enjoying the excitement himself.

With a burst of energy, Charley rolled her captor over, and quickly assumed the advantage. In the process, Terri's blouse flew up, exposing her solid, milky-white breasts. Charley pressed her lips down against Terri's, driving the tomboy's head into the dirt. The others had all now gathered around them, wondering what would come next. Even Ye and Yang had stopped their frolicking and were curiously watching the show. When the second kiss was over, the two girls collected themselves. Terri gave Charley a firm smack on the butt, and the game resumed.

After a time, and without any formal announcement, the game was over. Reagan had kept an unofficial score in his head and knew that his team had lost seventeen to eleven. As they were walking off of the field, Charley grabbed Reagan's hand, pulled him toward her, and whispered into his ear, "Hey, you're not bad for someone who's so clumsy and slow. We play every week. Don't be late next time." Then, without the sarcasm she continued, "I really did enjoy meeting you, Reagan. Need a ride back to school?" She was pointing to a white Stingray parked next to the water fountain.

"Uh, no, that's okay, thanks anyway. I want to finish up my run."

Charley looked him in the eyes and shook her head. "Yeah, you're not bad, but you do have a lot to learn." She was giving him a seductive smile. "You'll have to come over to my place sometime for a lesson or two." She had said that loud enough for Gary to hear, and the stare between Charley and Gary lingered uncomfortably.

As the Stingray roared out of the parking lot, Reagan was kicking himself in the butt.

Gary, not happy with Charley's flirtation, gave Reagan a stern warning. "You can look, but you cannot touch. Charley's off-limits. Get it?"

* * *

In the study hall, Reagan packed up his books and promised himself he would study again later. He couldn't get Charley out of his head, and he needed a beer. Later that night, when he got back to the dorm room, for emphasis, he would add it to the list, one more time:

7.   Don't fall in love.

CHAPTER THREE

$\mathcal{S}$ ometime in the middle of the night, it had started to snow. By the time Walter Collins and his wife, Martha, got out of bed and were sipping coffee at the kitchen table, it was almost a whiteout. It was Saturday, and also Walter's first day in retirement. He'd put in thirty years with the transit system and at fifty-nine years old was still in good health. Martha had retired a year earlier from the phone company. They both had good pension checks to rely on, and together, they had accumulated a healthy nest egg.

Their house in Garden City, New York, and their red Chevy Bel Air sedan were paid for. Martha had been unable to have children, so they had no dependents. The year was 1955, they had a wonderful marriage, they were best friends, and they had no idea what they were going to do with the rest of their lives.

As usual, Martha's breakfast was delicious, and, as usual, Walter helped clean up. "I better get ahead of this," Walter said, finishing up his coffee and heading out the front door with a snow shovel.

"Be careful, old man. I need you to help me move some furniture around later."

Walter caught Martha's smile as he closed the door behind him. It warmed his heart, but the rest of his body was soon shivering from the blustery wind and drifting snow.

Inside, Martha, a little ball of energy, looked for a project to do. She loved projects. In the past year, amongst other things, she had rearranged the furniture in the entire house twice, repainted the bedrooms, sewn new curtains for all of the windows, and wallpapered the kitchen. She was out of projects and was about to go stir-crazy. That afternoon, she was going to have Walter help her move the furniture in the living room, probably back to where it had been two weeks earlier.

Walter wouldn't mind, and he would never say a word in protest. He loved to watch his wife flitter around, all excited about one of her projects.

Outside, Walter was sweating underneath four layers of clothes and was short of breath from his labor. Working hard, however, was something he was used to. He had worked ten-hour days as the head mechanic for the regional bus line. He had also been the president of the 1500-member labor union and represented his men with ruthless vigor. The big bosses had tried three times to promote him into a management position, a level that would have required him to forfeit his post, but Walter would have nothing to do with it. He was loyal to his guys, and they loved and admired their leader. Walter Collins had many friends.

At the end of the sidewalk, he looked back at the house and laughed out loud. The pathway he'd scraped clean a few minutes earlier was once again covered in snow.

Inside a few minutes later, Martha helped her husband get out of his snow boots and winter gear. She had made hot chocolate, and he started a roaring fire. They sat on the sofa, holding hands; they did that a lot.

"What do you think about us moving to Florida?" Walter was only half kidding.

They sat there thinking to themselves for a good minute, not saying another word. When their eyes finally met, he had his answer.

"I'll start packing." Martha Collins was quickly on her feet and scurrying around the house. She had a new project.

* * *

Walter's best friend, Bob Taylor, owned a large moving trailer. For years, Bob had used it to cart around his stock car from weekend race to weekend race. Sometimes Walter had gone along and was there the day Bob hit the wall. The trailer had come back empty on that Sunday, and at Bob's wife's insistence, it never carried a stock car again.

Walter and Bob were packing the last piece of furniture into the trailer when Martha came out of the house with the iced tea. Twenty men had been there to help with the move. The hardest good-bye was saved for Bob.

It was June 1st and everything that Walter and Martha owned was either following them in the trailer or crammed into the trunk of the Bel Air. Walter and Martha Collins didn't look back as they pulled away for the last time from the home they'd lived in for over thirty years.

On their third day on the road, they were well into Florida, and it was starting to get dark. They decided to pull off of US Highway 301 and drive toward a little town called Gainesville. They had never heard of it but were hoping to find a decent place to spend the night, and they really needed a good meal. The Chevy, which until now had been running like a champ, had started to sputter a little, and Walter was concerned that it might be overheating under the weight of the trailer and the ninety-degree temperature. And overheat it did.

At the crossroads of SW 34th Street and Archer Road, steam started spewing out of the hood, and Old Red came to a jerky stop along the side of the road. It was pitch dark, and Walter and Martha felt like they were in the middle of nowhere. There wasn't another car in sight. Off to their right stood a sign that read "House and 60 acres for Sale." Martha noticed a porch light shining through the woods. They look at each other; neither one of them had a better idea.

Seventeen days later, Walter and Martha Collins were the proud owners of what the seller had called "a prime piece of Florida real estate."

* * *

The tall skinny man came calling every Thursday at about 1:00 AM. His motorcycle turned into the park and drove slowly past the house and the first three motorhomes. The rider killed the lights and the engine, then the bike glided quietly toward the fourth trailer on the right. The sound of the leaves crunching under the tires wasn't loud enough to wake her up.

Stephen Crain was in the fifth trailer and was there to watch. He watched this scene unfold every Thursday night. Watching it turned him on beyond belief. He'd been in the fourth trailer himself. As a matter of fact, he went there on the first day of every month to collect the rent.

Tonight the tall skinny man was a little late, but that didn't matter. Crain would wait up all night if he had to. He was prepared with his tube of petroleum jelly, towels, binoculars, and camera. He had smoked exactly two bowls of Gainesville Green and was in the perfect mood. He had one candle lit, the smell of incense filled the room, and the bottle of Jack Daniel's was uncapped and close by. Stephen Crain was not wearing any clothes.

The tall skinny man leaned his bike up against the white car that was parked just outside of the fourth trailer on the right, took off his leather jacket, and snuffed out his cigarette on his boot heel. He was a good-looking man, and this turned Crain on even more.

The door to the fourth trailer was open. It was always open on Thursday nights. The tall skinny man went in and locked the door behind him. He reached into the refrigerator and took out a beer. The popping sound echoed through the otherwise quiet night. The tall skinny man lit one of the three joints on the table and smoked it. The fourth trailer on the right, as usual, was lit by candlelight, and Crain had the perfect view of the man as he stripped naked and walked toward the bed where the woman slept.

* * *

The house on sixty acres was a little larger than Walter and Martha's home back in Garden City, but it had not been maintained properly. Walter and Martha settled on a budget, and she had the time of her life fixing it up.

Walter had never been much of an outdoorsman but had found that he enjoyed tending to this beautiful piece of property. It was covered with oaks and pines and had its share of wildlife, including deer, squirrels, and gopher tortoises. He even boasted that he'd seen a panther down by the creek. While his wife was submerged in her project, he spent his time mending fences, clearing underbrush, trimming trees, and even planting a garden.

Their first visitors were going to be Bob Taylor and his wife, Alice. They had purchased a used Airstream camper and were itching to come to Florida on a vacation. Martha had seen the excitement in her husband's eyes as the visit drew closer. Walter was busy clearing a plot of land adjacent to the house where their friends would park. He had brought in gravel, extended the driveway, and hired an electrician to pull a power hookup.

Walter by then was enjoying an occasional beer or two in the evenings. Martha would even join him from time to time, but just for one. They loved sitting and sipping their drinks on the front porch while looking over at the spot where their friends would soon be camping. Martha had finished her project; the house looked beautiful, and she was anxious to show it off. Walter was dying to hear all about the goings-on at the old shop.

The Taylors arrived on a beautiful blue-sky day in October. The Airstream fit perfectly into its spot, and the four friends took to catching up, talking about the old times, and drinking beer.

During the days, the men enjoyed walking the property, target practicing with Walter's new rifle, and, afterward, pulling crawfish out of the stream. In the evenings, they sat on the porch, smoked cigars, and sipped on a bottle of Irish whiskey that Bob had brought along just for the occasion.

The ladies stayed mostly inside, working on a puzzle spread out all over the family room table, cooking, and talking. Martha had never really had anyone she could open up to. Of course there was Walter, but there were some feelings best discussed between two women. The more she got to know Alice, the more comfortable Martha felt talking to her. As they spent time together, Alice showed pictures of her four grandchildren and Martha talked about her much younger sister, Janet Crain, and her mischievous, always-in-trouble, late-in-life son, Stephen.

* * *

On the first day of each month, Stephen Crain would come to be with her, come to be with her in the fourth trailer on the right. He was there to collect the rent, the rent he knew she couldn't pay; he prayed she couldn't pay. He always brought her two bags of Gainesville Green, enough to last her for a while. She had made it very clear that she would pay rent only once a month.

It had been ten months since her man had left to fight in the war, five months since she had received the telegram. They hadn't been married, so there would be no military pension, no savings account, and no property, nothing except the car. She had loved her man and he had loved her, but now he was gone. She felt so sad, so alone, so lost, but no one would know. She wasn't going to let them see her cry. She would get by somehow. She had been paying her rent this way for several months now.

After two joints and three beers, she would crawl into bed and face the wall. She would think about anything she could to forget the moment.

Crain would savor every second. This would have to last him until the rent was due again, or at least until the following Thursday night.

*   *   *

It was a sad day when the Taylors packed up and headed back to New York. The friends had truly enjoyed their time together, and Bob and Alice were already planning their next visit. Walter had convinced them to leave the Airstream in Florida rather than tow it all the way home. Alice hadn't taken well to camping anyway, having been spooked by a snake on their first night, and she and Bob had stayed the rest of their visit in the guest room. They weren't going camping again anytime soon.

When Bob got back to work, he told the whole gang about "Camp Collins." Over the next few years, Walter and Martha had a dozen or so visitors. There were soon ten campers being stored on newly carved plots on their property, and the man from Alachua County Code Enforcement wasn't too happy about it.

"You all are operating an illegal mobile home park. This infraction comes with a retroactive $100-a-day fine, and all of these campers need to be off of this land by sunset tomorrow . . . unless . . ."

The "unless" cost the Collins $200 and a guaranteed trailer space for the man from the county, but soon, their property was zoned for up to 250 mobile homes and they were getting calls from folks interested in leasing spaces. A picture in the *Gainesville Sun* showed the proud, smiling couple next to a newly erected cornerstone. The Shady Oaks Mobile Home Community was open for business.

The man from the county, along with a friend, visited his trailer a couple of times a month. His wife would never see or know about the place.

*   *   *

The tall skinny man was very well equipped, something else that excited Crain, and the girl in the bed was suddenly awake and following instructions. She was doing something that she didn't do when she was paying her rent, and she was doing it with an enthusiastic attitude. She was kneeling in front of the man, her voluptuous naked body illuminated by the candle flickering behind her. Crain grabbed the lubricant and the towel. It wouldn't be long now.

The girl followed her visitor's instructions with precision and was soon on all fours. She was facing the wall and was savoring everything this man was doing to her. She was not trying to forget the moment. He had her filled up, as usual, and she was about to reach the point of no return. She didn't necessarily like the tall skinny man, but she wouldn't give up his Thursday-night visits for anything.

* * *

The news about Janet Crain's passing came to Martha and Walter by way of a telegram from the Coroner's Office. Their desire to perform an autopsy would need to be approved by a relative of legal age. Janet's husband had left her years earlier and was nowhere to be found. Martha gave her authorization for an autopsy. The results were inconclusive.

According to her closest friend, Janet's symptoms before she died had included high fever, vomiting, blood in the urine, and dehydration, and they were likened to the symptoms of a serious intestinal virus. There was no such virus in circulation anywhere in the country that year.

At the funeral, after a lengthy discussion and some serious soul-searching, Walter and Martha decided to invite seventeen-year-old Stephen, their last living relative, to come and live with them at Shady Oaks. He could finish his high school studies, maybe get into a nearby college, and, as Walter had mentioned to Martha, "At my age, I can sure use the help around the park."

At first, it had all worked out fine. Stephen went to school and even got decent grades. He was a big help clearing property and preparing new trailer sites. He was also an excellent auto mechanic and loved working on Old Red. He soon took a liking to collecting the monthly rent checks, which was a major relief to Martha, who hated the job.

But as time went by, things had deteriorated. Stephen moved out of the house and into one of the many vacant trailers. He started hanging around with the wrong crowd, smoking pot, and drinking large quantities of whiskey. Some of the park residents claimed that he was abusive and demanding. Martha and Walter had lost control, and were getting ready to send him packing. Stephen Crain had another plan.

* * *

More than eight hundred people attended a memorial service for Martha and Walter Collins that was held at the First Presbyterian Church in Garden City, New York. The church could not handle the crowd and had to set up overflow seating on the front lawn. The testimonials went on for two hours and were cut short only because of a wedding scheduled later in the day. Stephen Crain was not in attendance.

The police report had simply stated that the vehicle, one red Chevy Bel Air sedan, had lost control on a curvy road after its brakes had failed. The two passengers had been dead when the officers arrived, a fact that was soon verified by the attending paramedics. A footnote to the final report read, "The occupants of the vehicle were holding hands."

* * *

The tall skinny man, having had his way with the girl, popped open another beer and lit a joint. He pulled up his jeans and put on his boots. He was in no hurry. He carried the rest of the joint over to the bed and handed it to the girl, who was lying there, listening to soft music. He bent down as if to kiss her but did not.

Stephen Crain, after finishing his business and failing to achieve another erection, was ready to go back to the house—the house that he now owned, along with the rest of the Shady Oaks Mobile Home Community.

The tall skinny man drained his beer, left the empty can on the table, and walked out the door without saying a word. He lifted his motorcycle carefully off of the white Stingray, hopped on, pushed his left foot down, and fired it up. He was not careful about the noise as he left the park. Everyone heard him, just like they did every Thursday night.

CHAPTER FOUR

*G*raduate assistants (GAs) taught most classes taken by freshmen at the University of Florida. Students saw their real professors, most likely PhD's, from time to time, but otherwise, had very little contact with them. The real professors, the majority of whom were men, usually didn't know their students' names or anything else about them unless, of course, they happened to be knock-out co-eds.

GAs were simply postgraduate students enrolled in the master's program of the classes they taught. They were also the real professors' grunts, performing any and all tasks for the "gods of higher learning," including doing research, writing papers and theses, holding office hours, and even fetching dry cleaning, if that was what it took to gain favor. For the most part, GAs were very intelligent, thought-provoking individuals who could relate better to the students than the professors could and often had a flair for extravagance.

Reagan's political science GA was Marty Schemer. He was a tall, lanky, hippyish-looking fellow with long, already graying hair, and a beard that would have looked better braided. Everything about life excited Marty Schemer. He brought a level of energy to the classroom that, whether a student liked political science or not, was hard not to enjoy. Marty was a basketball player in high school, but, as he had explained, he gave that up to spend his time uncovering the true meaning of the "cosmic intellectual forces." "Why waste time and effort," he expounded, "throwing a round ball at a stationary orange hoop when you can make better use of your life answering the question, why does anyone truly care if it goes in?"

Current-event topics were one of Marty's passions, and the last fifteen minutes of every class, which for Reagan was Monday through Friday, third period, was spent discussing something new going on in the world. On their first Wednesday, Marty had been all excited about a recent occurrence in New York City. Apparently, a man named Martin Cooper had invented a wireless telephone, a portable cellular phone, Cooper was calling it, and while standing on 6th Avenue he had made a phone call to a similar phone in a building close by.

"Can you imagine, telephones with no wires or cords, not mounted to the wall?" Marty was pacing the classroom, his face red with excitement, the veins popping out on his neck. "What a change that could bring to our society. I'll tell you what; for extra credit, I want you all to write a two-page opinion on how cellular phones could affect our future. Papers are due on Friday. Class dismissed."

Reagan really enjoyed Marty's class and always sat near the front. Marty's enthusiasm was contagious, and Reagan decided to spend substantial time thinking through and preparing this extra-credit assignment. After careful consideration, he decided that this invention, if it ever made it into the mainstream of American culture, was destined for failure. *Who in the world would want to lug around a portable phone?* People didn't really like to talk on the phone anyway, and this would turn out to be nothing but an expensive burden. Especially for the younger generation, he would conclude, "We have more important things to do, to see, to explore. You will never see one of us with our faces buried into some sort of electronic device."

Reagan was proud of his paper, and all weekend had anxiously anticipated the results of his labor. On the following Monday morning, at the beginning of class, Marty had tapped twice when he laid Reagan's C-minus result on his desk. A note on the top of the paper read, "Reagan, please come by and see me in my office this afternoon."

Later that day, in the basement of Peabody Hall, in a tiny cluttered office, Reagan stood waiting for his GAs ranting to subside.

"Do you realize how many men we lost in that war, and how much money we spent fighting it? It left us a wounded country with nothing but egg on our face. Are you aware that there are still people out there who think it was a good idea to send our troops to the other side of the world, and amongst other atrocities, slaughter women and children with napalm bombs? These same assholes believe we never should have left there; they think we should go back . . . for Christ's sake."

When Marty was finally finished, he pushed a stack of papers two inches thick off of his chair and sat down. He was breathing hard, and his face was still contorted from the frenzy he had worked himself into.

"Anyway, I'm sorry I just get carried away, and you brought it up, didn't you? No, I guess not. Where were we? Ah, yes, Reagan Davis, third period."

There was no place else to sit, so Reagan was leaning against a bookshelf, wondering what he would be confronted with next. His legs were a little shaky, and his mouth was dry. He'd been summoned to the graduate assistant's office. This couldn't be good.

"There, sit over there." Marty was pointing to the opposite side of the room.

Reagan looked over and noticed for the first time a sofa so covered with books and papers that it was hardly recognizable.

"Just push some of that crap out of the way and have a seat. Now, I asked you to stop by and see me . . . um . . . hand me your paper and let me remind myself . . . ah, yes."

Marty's expression turned serious, and he looked deeply into Reagan's eyes. "It's not just that you made the worst grade in the class." *Ouch!* "Or that your handwriting and spelling are a mess. I see that all the time. By the way, you might want to think about buying a typewriter and a dictionary." *Double ouch!* "All of that can be corrected, and I recommend you do so. You have an excellent writing style, but you have one major problem, man. You gotta let your mind go. Let it float into the universe. Turn that engineer want-to-be inside of you off, and use your imagination. Just as important, always play to your audience. Do you think I wanted to hear you say what you could've said in seven words? 'The cell phone thing ain't gonna work.' Hell no, I didn't, and I don't think you truly believe that, either. Let me guess. You were on your high school's debate team? Always arguing the other side, whether you believed in it or not. You need to free your mind, man. Figure out what you think, not what everybody around you up 'til now has been telling you to think.

"Now, this morning, I noticed you were eyeing that hot brunette with the short skirt in the back row. I think her name is Beverly McNamara . . . Anyway, how are you gonna get in touch with her, huh? She probably lives in a dorm with no phone and wouldn't know the number to give it to you anyway. Out of luck, so sorry.

"Let's assume for a second that she wants you to call her. Fat chance, but like I said, use your imagination. Now, close your eyes and envision that she happens to have a portable phone in her purse. She slips you the number after class, and you use the phone in your pocket to make the call later that day to ask her out. Still think the cell phone thing ain't gonna work? Do you have a question?"

"Uh, no . . . no, sir."

"Please don't call me sir. I'm not that much older than you, and in some ways, you remind me of me when I was a freshman. That's really why

31

I asked you to come see me today. And the question you should have asked is whether or not I will give you an opportunity to rewrite the paper. And the answer is yes. Bring it back by my office on Wednesday. Now, come on. I'll buy you a beer at the Rat."

* * *

Gary Glaser, Sergeant Gary Glaser, had risen within the ranks of the Gainesville Police Department much faster than most. His good-ol'-boy personality and tough-guy attitude were admired not only by the rank and file but also by his superiors. He was considered a natural leader and was always the life of the party. His few critics pointed out that his promotions might have been facilitated by the fact that his wife happened to be the daughter of the police chief.

Amongst his peers, Gary was considered the bad boy of the department, and they all loved to hear about his latest conquests over beers at the end of their shifts. With a rather mundane Monday behind them, Gary and four of his cronies were finishing their third pitcher at the Red Lion Pub. Gary, as usual, was dominating the conversation.

"I couldn't believe the bitch was stupid enough to leave the bag and pipe sitting right next to her. She had every opportunity to toss them under the seat while I was pulling her over. But there they were, in plain view, along with those mountains she was sporting. I gotta tell you guys, I've never seen a slant-eyes with tits that big. They were popping out of the top and bottom of her tube top. I had no choice but to pull her out of the car and frisk her. At least she had the brain cells to be cooperative." Gary had his buddies' full attention. They could already tell that this was gonna be a good one.

"There wasn't enough pot to make a good bust, but I knew I needed to teach this cunt a lesson. When I told her that I was bringing her in, she started to squeal like a stuck pig. She asked me if there was anything she could do and begged me not to arrest her, something about caring for her sick mom. That's when I knew I had her where I wanted her. I told her to pull her heap onto the dirt road and sit tight while I went back to the squad car and decided what to do with her. I let her know that when I came back, she was only going to have one shot at convincing me not to lock her up."

When the fourth pitcher arrived, interrupting the story, Gary pulled the petite brunette waitress onto his lap and wrapped his arms around her waist. She didn't resist but instead smiled and wiggled.

"That's not my pistol you're feeling, sweetheart, but it is a dangerous weapon. Of course, you already know that. It's been way too long since we've gotten together. You want Uncle Gary to come visit you tonight?"

As the waitress walked away, her smile answered his question, and the guys, now more impressed than ever, leaned back in for the continuation of the story.

"Anyway, where were we? Ah, yeah. So, after giving her plenty of time to think about it, I come back to her car carrying my cuffs. I look in, and the bitch is completely naked, lying down on her seat, fingering herself. Can you believe it? I think she was actually turned on by the whole thing. She sees me and gets on all fours with her head out of the window, and before I know it, she has my pants unzipped and has me in her mouth, all the way in her mouth. That's not an easy trick; you guys have seen me in the shower." All heads were nodding in agreement.

When a group of sorority girls walked into the Lion and past their table, smiling and giggling, Gary's story was interrupted once again. The sergeant motioned to the brunette waitress, who gave him a dirty look. Before long, two pitchers were delivered to the girls' table, and Gary was on his way over to introduce himself. A few minutes later, Gary was back with his buddies, boastfully carrying two napkins inscribed with several names and phone numbers. He sat down and slowly looked around at the anxious eyes staring back at him.

"So, you gotta tell us, Sarge, did you send her on her way? I mean after the blow job?" one of them finally asked, hoping along with the rest that there was more to the story.

"That's the funny thing," Gary said, flashing his big smile, "when I told the slut she was free to go, she didn't want to leave. She asked me to bring my cuffs and walk her into the woods. She had me strap her up against a tree. I think she must have cum fifteen times. I'm meeting her back at the same place tomorrow afternoon. Any of you guys want to come along? I'm sure she would love it."

* * *

Molly Turner hadn't sat next to Reagan the next morning in their pre-calculus class. As a matter of fact, she had sat in the far back of the room and had never made eye contact with him. He had turned around, looking her way several times, hoping to get her attention. He still felt bad about their meeting and wanted to apologize, but there was also something else. She had on tight jeans and a loose-fitting halter shirt. She was wearing makeup and somehow didn't look like the same girl he had confronted at the library.

When class was over, Reagan had to literally run down the hall and outside of the building to catch up with her.

"Molly, hey, wait up. I wanted to—"

She didn't slow down or look back as she interrupted. "Well, if it isn't the world's rudest tree lover? Imagine my great pleasure in seeing you again. Don't you have someone else's day you can ruin, or am I just the luckiest girl in the world?"

"Molly, please stop for a second. I know I deserve that, but I wanted to apologize for the other day. I don't know what got into me. I'm sorry. Is there any way we can start over? I could really use your help with humanities, and my guess is that you had a hard time with that pop quiz this morning. Am I right?"

"Okay, Reagan." She had turned and was suppressing a smile. "Your apology is accepted, but let's get something straight. What's gotten into you is the same thing that's gotten into every other freshman guy on campus. You're away from home for the first time, and you have a one-track mind. That's fine, and it's none of my business. I will study humanities and calculus with you, but I'm not going to be your biology lab partner. Get it? Besides, I have a steady boyfriend who is a sophomore at FSU. He's on the football team and doesn't take kindly to other guys trying to get into my pants.

"Now, if we're square, you can buy me a cup of coffee at the student union. We'll walk through those trees to get there. That is, if you can make it past them without getting overstimulated."

* * *

"Hey, Reagan, don't look now, but that girl, the one behind the bar, pouring beer, is checking you out . . . I told you not to look."

"Which girl?"

"The good-looking one right over there, the one with the curves, and that look in her eyes. You know the look I'm talking about." Marty Schemer was raising his eyebrows and smiling. He'd been smiling since halfway through their fourth pitcher. Reagan glanced over toward the bar again. *Indeed, it does look like I might have an admirer.*

He knew that Marty had a lot of energy and a brain full of opinions, but their time together this afternoon at the Ratheskellar had brought this realization to a higher level. They seemed to have covered every topic imaginable, from the war, to music, politics, and, yes, girls. Marty had warned him to put girls into perspective.

"Don't make the same mistake I did. I spent most of my freshman year and part of the next so wrapped up in the chase that I missed out on the rest of what was going on around me. You have to feel the vibes, check out your place in the universe, and stake a claim. Do you get where I'm coming from? There is nothing wrong with . . . well, you know . . . but it's not every-thing. Reagan, stop staring at her. You're going to scare her off.

"Anyway, think of them like they're an appetizer. You don't go to a restaurant and order a whole tray of appetizers, do you? Save room for the main course and the dessert. Don't fill up too soon, or you will miss out on the rest of the menu. Life has a lot more to offer than you might think at your age. You've got to get through the smoke to find the fire. By the way, she is heading our way."

Sherri Miles indeed had fantastic curves, along with a killer smile and a sparky attitude. She had beautiful dark blue eyes and dirty blond hair that hung almost down to her butt. She was tall—very tall—almost as tall as Reagan, and yes, she had that look in her eyes.

"Hey, guys, I noticed that your pitcher is almost empty. Can I get you another, or do you want to wait until seven? There's a special that starts at seven."

Reagan, who about fell out of his seat, was obviously tongue-tied, so Marty took control and decided to play matchmaker. "Thank you for checking on us. My name is Marty. This is Reagan Davis. Do you have the time to join us? Please have a seat. I need to be heading out in a few min-utes, and I'm sure my friend here would enjoy the company."

"I would love to, but I'm working. You all don't want to get me in trouble with the boss, do you?" Her smile lit up the room. "I can get into all kinds of trouble on my own, and usually do." Sherri was talking to both of them but looking directly at Reagan, who was finally gaining his composure.

"That's a shame. I would really enjoy the company," he said. "By the way, your special, the one that starts at seven, what is it?"

"Seven's when I get off work. I'll bring you another pitcher in the meantime . . . on the house. Don't you go anywhere, hear me?" Her look had him frozen in his seat. He wasn't going anywhere.

Marty chuckled and said something about enjoying the appetizer before shaking Reagan's hand and heading out.

* * *

Sergeant Gary Glaser had been assigned as the department's liaison with the University of Florida's private police department and, as such, had access to any and all records he so desired. Bright and early Tuesday morn-ing, he had been to Tigert Hall, the school's administration building, and had been granted access to a file of interest to him. The file contained all available information in the school's possession regarding one Reagan Davis.

Making careful notes, the sergeant added more details to his list that already contained information he had gathered through the Florida Department of Motor Vehicles. Before he was finished, he would have everything he needed to keep a close eye on his newest nemesis. Gary Glaser protected his turf with a vengeance. If he took one step out of line, young Reagan Davis would have to face the music. He wouldn't be the first man to cross the sergeant, and there was never anything pretty about the consequences.

* * *

With Marty gone, Sherri Miles had been over to Reagan's table several more times to check on him. With each round, her flirtatious comments became more suggestive. In her most recent visit, at 6:40 PM, she had told him that she lived at the Pointe West apartment complex on SW 34th Street and that her roommate was out of town for a couple of days. "If you would like, you can come over tonight. I'll serve you my house specialty . . . and Reagan, I don't cook."

At this point, he was just sipping on the beer she had brought him. He didn't want to have a problem with— *Crap!* A realization jolted him out of his seat. *My rubbers! They're in my bottom drawer. Shit . . . damn, what am I supposed to do, carry them around with me all the time?*

He checked his watch, 6:45 PM. His dorm was only five minutes away. If he ran, he could get there, up the stairs, and back in plenty of time. But what would he tell Sherri? *Certainly not the truth.* He was panicked but thought clearly enough to lean his chair against the table. *Maybe she'll think I went to the bathroom.*

If Reagan hadn't been in such a hurry, he might have noticed the man sitting on his motorcycle while smoking a cigarette. He might have noticed that the man was wearing a leather jacket in the summer heat. He might have noticed that the man had on sunglasses after sunset. But Reagan was in a hurry and didn't notice the man . . . the man who was watching him very carefully.

Reagan made it to the entrance of Murphree E in two minutes and up the four flights in a flash. *Unlock the door. Turn on the light, a funny sound coming from the far end of the room. Crap! I forgot to check the sign!*

Reagan was having trouble believing his eyes. There, braced spread-eagle against the desk, facing the broken lamp, completely naked, sweating, and breathing hard was Danny Miller. Behind him, in pretty much the same state, was Dusty Collins, whose arms were holding tightly to Danny's shoulders. Their heads slumped in embarrassment, not a word was said, and Danny Miller was not wearing his butt plug.

"I'm so sorry. I should have . . . I just need to get into my drawer for a second. This is really none of my business. I will be gone in a . . . I'll lock the door behind me. I'm so sorry."

Reagan stopped for just a second on the landing at the second floor after he had left the room. *Holy crap!* He was still having a hard time registering what he had seen. *Men really do that?* He had heard rumors about two of the guys on the baseball team in high school but had never thought much of it. They hadn't mentioned this sort of thing in his sex-ed class.

He checked his watch. It was 7:00 PM. No more time to think about it now. He was in a hurry again and had, in his right hand, what he had come for.

Reagan hopped down the four stairs of the dorm entrance in one leap. He would be back to the Rat in two minutes. The big smile had just returned to his face when he heard a faint sound coming from the tunnel to his right. Someone was crying, and it sounded like a girl. He stopped and was walking slowly toward the sound when he heard a faint voice in the darkness, almost in a whimper, say, "Reagan, is that you?"

CHAPTER FIVE

Stephen Crain used his key to unlock the door to the fourth trailer on the right and went inside. He had keys to most of the trailers in the Shady Oaks Mobile Home Community but used this key most often, sometimes several times a week.

He was alone inside of her trailer, just like he had known he would be. He knew when she left for work and when she came home. He knew where she worked and had been there many times to watch her, watch her dance at the Pleasure Palace, Gainesville's only topless bar.

She worked the day shift Monday through Friday. She had never noticed him when he came in and paid his cover fee, or spotted him watching her. He always slipped into the dark, dingy bar that smelled of stale whiskey and Lord knows what else, then quickly slid into the pitch-dark booth to the left of the bouncer's perch. He could see her perfectly from there, but she couldn't see him—just the way he liked it. The Pleasure Palace was his kind of place, and she was the most beautiful thing he had ever laid his eyes on.

Stephen Crain closed the door of her trailer behind him, locked it, looked around, and took a big whiff. He already felt the excitement buzzing through his body like an electric current. *How can she live, how can anybody live, in such a tiny place? Even when I lived in a trailer, it was twice this size. Now I live in the big house, the one that my aunt and uncle left for me, the fools.*

Her place was small, but it was cozy and decorated with a woman's touch: brightly colored pillows scattered throughout, frilly window treatments, fresh flowers in pots and vases, a bright pink tablecloth, and paintings that she had painted herself hanging on the walls. Her bed was covered with a baby blue comforter and had stuffed animals all over it.

Stephen Crain was very familiar with this bed, the one he was now lying on with a pillow wedged behind his head. He once again took in the room's aroma, a combination of perfume, incense, and the lingering smell of marijuana.

From her top dresser drawer, he grabbed a pair of silk purple panties. He would need those in a couple of minutes. Under the rest of the underwear, he found it. He found why he was really here, the reason he came by himself to the fourth trailer on the right. He pulled it to his chest, opened it, and started to read. He started to read Charlotte Summerland's diary.

On some days, he read just the last entry or two, but on this day, he was not in a hurry and would start at the beginning—not at the very beginning, where she used to write as a little girl, but from where she had resumed writing as a young adult several months before. He particularly loved the parts where she mentioned him. She despised him, and this turned him on beyond belief. No matter how much she hated him, the rent was due at the beginning of the month, and he would be back here to collect.

* * *

June 6th, 1973

Dear Diary,

I'm sorry that I haven't written in such a long time. I don't have an excuse other than to say that things for me haven't been that great. I just couldn't face sharing my difficulties with you. I felt like putting all of my troubles down on paper might keep me from wishing them away. My wishes never came true, and I never wrote, but three things happened to me today that made me think of you.

The first thing that happened was that I heard a bird singing for the first time in weeks. That might be because I haven't been outside, outside of this trailer very much, since the telegram arrived.

I guess I should back up a bit, and fill you in on what's been happening in my life. Everything was going along great, right up until my mom died suddenly on my fifteenth birthday. Dad took it very hard and was never the same after we buried her. He took to drinking, became angrier by the day, and by the time I turned seventeen, he was just sitting around the house, coming up with one excuse after another to yell at me.

I tried so hard to be mature, to help him, to do all of the things Mom would have expected of me. Nothing worked, and I became frustrated, lonely and yes, concerned for my own safety. He never hit me, or anything like that, but he was having trouble controlling himself. That's when I met Ronnie. That's when I met the man I will love forever.

Ronnie was the mechanic at the corner service station where Dad had his car worked on. One day, because Dad was too drunk, I walked down to pick up the car, and there he was, covered from head to toe in oil and grease. I'd never seen a more handsome man in my life. He asked me out that night, and within three weeks I had moved in with him, into this trailer. He was older than me, almost twenty-one.

He told me from the start that he planned on enlisting in the Air Force on his birthday. He wanted to become a pilot, make something of his life, and serve his country, just like his dad had done. I was too naïve at the time to understand what all that meant. I know what it means now.

Ronnie wanted to marry me before he left for overseas, but I wanted to wait until he came home. He promised me he would come home. That's the only promise Ronnie ever broke with me. Then the telegram arrived. It was from Ronnie's sister in Omaha. It was a cold and cruel way to find out, but that was before I had a phone in the trailer, and it was the only way she could get in touch with me. It was a sweet note, and she wrote that Ronnie had told her how much he loved me, and that he was going to marry me when he got his wings. He told her that if anything happened to him he wanted me to have the Stingray, his pride and joy. That's why I went outside today. I wanted to check on the car. That's when I heard the bird singing.

The second thing that happened to me today happened while I was at the grocery store. I was completely out of food, and with roughly thirty dollars left in my kitty, I was standing in front of the mac and cheese boxes looking for the best bargain when I heard a man's voice say, "That stuff will kill you if you eat too much of it. As a matter of fact, buying ten boxes like you're getting ready to do could just be illegal. I might need to haul you in."

I turned around, and there was a police officer standing right behind me. My heart nearly stopped. He looked so serious at first, but then a big smile came over his face, a very broad smile with gleaming white teeth and a happy glimmer in his eyes.

"Hey there, Officer. Yes, you are probably right, but I am on a budget, and with some added milk and butter, I can eat off of one of these boxes for a couple of days."

He took a step backwards. His smile folded into a look of sympathetic curiosity as he studied me up and down. You know, diary, like policemen do. They have such keen observation skills. It's like they can see right through you, into your soul.

He said, "The name is Gary Glaser, and if you'd like, I can help you shovel the rest of the boxes from the shelf into your basket. There're only about twenty or so left up there."

I could tell he was flirting and decided to give it right back to him. "That won't be necessary, Officer, or should I call you Gary? I think I'm okay with just these ten boxes. I still need to buy some bananas and maybe some creamy body lotion. And, by the way, I'm sure you probably want a few boxes for yourself. Where is your cart, anyway?"

As quickly as he had appeared, and after another smile, along with a firm handshake to say goodbye, he was gone. I wasn't even sure he had heard me when I had called out my name to him. I have to admit that I was disappointed when he left. He was the first real person I had talked to in weeks, and something about Gary Glaser made me feel at ease, relaxed, and maybe even a little happy. I haven't felt happiness in a long time.

I had a grocery bag tucked under each arm when I saw the flat tire, the back right. I thought to myself, What am I going to do now? Dad had taught me how to change a car tire years ago, but not on a car like this.

Then, there he was, Officer Gary Glaser, coming to my rescue. As he pulled up alongside of me and rolled down the window to his squad car, I tried to wipe the tears that had started to trickle down my cheeks.

"You're in luck, Charley; tire changing is my specialty . . . one of them, any-way. Put those bags in the passenger seat, hand me the keys, and we will have you on your way in no time flat. Pardon the pun."

He was out of his car, flashing that smile, and bending down to look at the tire when I noticed how handsome he was, in a rugged athletic way. I also noticed the ring for the first time, a wedding ring. Damn!

Gary insisted on following me home to make sure I got here safely. On the way, we stopped by a service station. The mechanic there, Teddy, I think his name was, who's a friend of Gary's, fixed my tire for free. Before I knew it, we were ready to go and pulling into Shady Oaks.

I asked Gary if he wanted to come in and wash his hands. After taking a quick look around at his surroundings and then curiously at my trailer, he said he did.

We sat and drank a beer and talked for a time. For some reason, I felt so com-fortable around him. I found myself opening up and sharing things with him that I haven't told anyone, not even Ronnie.

After a while, Gary stood up to leave. That's when the third thing happened, the thing I <u>really</u> wanted to tell you about.

When he bent down to give me a peck on the cheek, I turned to him, looked him deep in the eyes, and kissed him passionately on the lips. I don't know what came over me. I've never done anything like that before. I'd just met him. I didn't know if he even wanted to kiss me, he's a cop, and he is married!

As it turns out, he did want me to kiss him, and he wanted a lot more. I wanted a lot more too. That's when it came over me. I'm tired of all of these rules and restrictions. I'm tired of living my life like I've been told I'm supposed to. I'm tired of men getting away with anything they want while women have to be prim and proper, double standards. I'm an adult, a free woman, and ready to have some fun. And from now on, I'm going to have fun—lots of fun, damn it!

And have some fun we did. Gary was both gentle and powerful. He filled me like no man has ever filled me before. He took me to a place I've never been. And when it was over, with both of us still panting and dripping with sweat, he held me and talked to me, whispering sweet words into my ear.

We smoked a joint together, and when we were finished, he asked me what I needed more than anything else. I could think of a lot of things, but what I told him was that I would really like to find a job. What I didn't tell him was that after my shopping today I am down to under five dollars, and the rent is past due. I could soon be without a place to live.

"Well, do you like to dance? You definitely have the body for it." Gary was standing, putting his uniform back on, and giving me that inquisitive look. "Are you nervous about being around men without your top on?"

"I love to dance. I took several dance classes while I was in high school. And no, I guess not. I'm laying here completely naked in front of you, aren't I?"

Gary looked down with admiration in his eyes before asking, "Where's your phone?"

When Gary came back over to me, I was wearing a pink nightie and sitting on the edge of the bed. He bent down and gave me a deep kiss before saying, "Well, you now have a job. I've written the information down, and it's over there on your table. You start tomorrow. Be there at two o'clock and ask for Chuck. He will take very good care of you. Chuck's the owner. Bubba's the bouncer. They are both good friends of mine. Bring along exactly what you are wearing." His admiring look lingered.

"How can I thank you? That is the sweetest thing anyone has ever done for me."

"Well, Charley, to be honest with you, I would like to come see you again sometime. As a matter of fact, Thursdays, I am allowed a boys' night out." He continued, glancing down at his wedding ring, to offer explanation, "You could thank me by allowing me to swing by, after I leave my buddies, just to say hi, of course, and to check on you."

"Officer Gary Glaser—I mean Sergeant Gary Glaser, you can come by and check on me anytime you want. Thursday can't get here fast enough as far as I'm concerned."

As his car pulled away, I watched from my window and thought of Ronnie. Gary Glaser was not a replacement for him and never could be. I couldn't deny the fact, however, that I felt better, a lot better, than I had in a long time.

That's all for now, diary. I will write again soon. I promise.
C

* * *

Stephen Crain was still lying on her bed. He had taken off his clothes and pulled the sheets and blankets up around him. He was very excited and wasn't going to last much longer. He especially loved the part where she described how the tall skinny man filled her up. That's something that Crain knew he could never do, but that didn't matter to him at all. He grabbed the purple panties and then skipped a couple of entries to get to his favorite, the one about the first time he had come to the fourth trailer on the right to collect the rent.

* * *

June 16th, 1973
Dear Diary,

I knew it was going to happen sooner or later, and it happened today. I've made some good money at the Pleasure Palace, but not nearly enough to pay the rent. I was smoking a joint and wearing just a tee shirt when I heard a knock at the door. It was him: Stephen Crain, my landlord, the worm.

I heard him through the door say, "Miss Summerland, this is Stephen Crain, the owner of the park. You have been ignoring the notices I've been sliding under your door. You are seriously behind on your rent. I know you are in there. I need to come in. We need to talk."

I opened the door, and there he was, the slimy little bastard. He had a shitty grin on his gruesome face as he studied me up and down, undressing me with his eyes. Yuck!

"Please come in, Mr. Crain. I'm sorry about the notices. I wasn't ignoring you, I promise. I just got a new job, and I've just been so busy."

He closed the door behind him and started his rant. I didn't listen to most of it, but it went on for at least ten minutes. Something about eviction, how he had another renter wanting to move in, needing to have my stuff cleared out by tomorrow night, or he would call the police. What he said next I did hear, loud and clear.

"Unless we can make other arrangements. Come to some sort of an agreement."

After some more threats and a longer rant, I agreed to his terms. I lied there on the bed facing the wall. I couldn't believe what I was doing. At least he agreed to wear a rubber. I couldn't even feel him inside of me, what a worm. He only lasted about a minute, and then he was gone.

"I'll be back to collect next month's rent in about two weeks."

I watched the disgusting smile on his face from my window as he skipped away. I am so ashamed of myself, but what else was I going to do? I won't move back in with Dad. Hell, I don't even know if he is still alive. I need to work harder and make more tips. I've got two weeks to come up with the rent.

That's all for now. I need to go take another shower.

C

* * *

Stephen Crain, holding the purple panties, was finished with his chore. The part where she called him a worm always did it for him.

Hoping to get it up one more time, he flipped to another of his favorite entries. He remembered the occasion very well. It was one of his favorite nights watching her from the trailer next door.

* * *

August 2nd, 1973
Dear Diary,

Last night I had sex, or made love, I'm not sure what you call it, with another woman for the first time in my life. At first I wasn't sure I would ever want to do it again, but after sitting here thinking about it all day, I'm now sure that I do.

Yesterday was the day the rent was due, so I had been sitting around all afternoon, waiting on the worm to come collect. I'd made enough to pay it this month, but last week, the car broke down. Gary's mechanic friend, Teddy, gave me a good deal, but it still cost me almost all of my savings to fix it. He said something about water in the fuel line, it needing another carburetor, and a tune-up. Hell, I don't know. Gary says he trusts the guy, so that's good enough for me.

By the way, Gary and I had our first fight last week. He came over as usual, and we had fun just like we always do, but afterward he started warning me about some of my customers at work. I told him that he shouldn't be the jealous and possessive type, which he is, and he got very mad, which made me mad. When I told him that he didn't own me and that I could go out with anyone I wanted to, his face got really red. He just stood there, staring out the window, drinking another beer, and not saying a word.

I started to feel bad. After all the kind things he has done for me, and even if he has not been as caring lately, I still owe him. This was no way for me to be to treating him. I got up, kissed him, and told him that I was sorry. We edged towards the bed. He threw me down and pulled off my panties. He said he loved me, and then climbed on top. He has never been that aggressive. I didn't want it to be over.

Anyway, all of that went out of my mind when I heard the knock on the door. I was sure it was him, the worm, but it wasn't. Standing at my door, with tears running down her face, was Terri Spencer, the girl I play Frisbee ball with. I've told you about her. I asked her to come in, and we sat at the table. We drank a beer, and she told me how she'd caught her boyfriend with another girl, two other girls, actually.

I thought that after sitting and talking for a while I had cheered her up, but out of nowhere, she started sobbing again. I leaned over and gave her a hug, and she hugged me back. She asked me if we could lie on the bed for a while, and I said sure. We hugged some more. The first time she kissed me, I could taste the tears from her face. I asked her if she had ever done this before, and she said no. I've never felt so much tenderness in a lover's arms.

Terri spent the night, and when we woke up, I made her coffee and breakfast while she lay there in my bed, just watching me. She stayed around most of the morning, and we made love again. I think she was feeling much better when she left. I know I was. And, yes, I do want to do that again.

Will write again soon.

C

* * *

Stephen Crain was frustrated. He was trying so hard to get it up again, but he couldn't. *The tall skinny man never has this problem.* He turned to the latest entry, the only one written since his last visit.

* * *

August 25th, 1973
Dear Diary,

I started dating one of my regular customers at the Palace. His name is Robert. I don't know his last name, but he comes in a couple of times a week, and to be totally honest, maybe I shouldn't call it dating. He is always very generous and always selects me for his private dances. After I dance for him he pays me for one extra dance, but he only wants me to sit and talk to him. It's embarrassing to admit, but he is older, much older, maybe even Dad's age.

He asked me to go to dinner with him after my shift was over one day. I told him that seeing a customer outside of work is strictly prohibited and if we were seen in public I would lose my job. What I didn't tell his was that if Gary caught us he might kill us both. Gary is becoming a bigger problem. I might need to break that off, but I would sure miss his visits.

Anyway, Robert asked me if I wanted to come over to his hotel room and said we could order room service. He comes to Gainesville two nights a week and stays at the fancy place down the road. I'd never had room service before, and he seemed like such a nice man, so I said yes. I've had dinner with him three times now. The first two times we ate, drank the bottle of wine he had ordered, and talked for hours. He is very intelligent and tells such funny stories. He has traveled all over the world. He's never said it, but I can tell that he is a very lonely man, even though he is married. What's up with me and married men these days?

After dinner on our third date, I did something very naughty. I'm not sure what got into me, maybe the wine buzz, but when Robert excused himself and went into the bathroom, I took off all of my clothes and crawled under the covers of his bed. When he came out, he almost fell over. I thought he was mad at first, but his expression was more of a worried one. I don't think he has been with a woman for a long time. He was very gentle and a good kisser.

When I was getting ready to leave he walked over and kissed me on the forehead. He thanked me with both his lips and his eyes, and put something in my right hand. He explained that he had meant to tip me more the last time I danced for him at the Palace. I didn't look at what it was until I got out to my car. It was a fifty-dollar bill! I almost took it back to him in his room, but I didn't. It's under the spare set of sheets in my bottom drawer. I now have enough money to pay rent this month. Yeah! Isn't the worm going to be surprised?

We had a new player at our Frisbee ball game today. His name is Reagan Davis and he is very cute. He is too young and naive for me. I think he might even be a virgin by the way he acts around girls. When I asked him if I could give him a ride home, his face turned red and his legs started to shake.

He is a pretty good player, and I enjoyed flirting with him. It really pissed Gary off, and I loved every second of it. I know that this Thursday, Gary is going to take that aggression out on me. Something must be wrong with me, because I am really looking forward to that.

I'll write again later.

C

* * *

Stephen Crain was very proud of himself. The last entry had gotten him excited again, and his second explosion had been even more impressive than the first. He wiped himself off with his t-shirt and carefully placed the diary and the purple panties right back where he had found them. He looked out the window and, seeing that the coast was clear, stepped out of the trailer and locked the door. This, of course, was after he had confiscated something very important from under the folded sheets in Charlotte Summerland's bottom dresser drawer.

CHAPTER SIX

*W*hen Reagan finally returned to his dark dorm room around midnight, Danny Collins was gone, along with all of his belongings. Reagan wasn't surprised. Not after what he had walked in on earlier in the day.

Reagan never made it back to the Ratheskellar that evening. The crying sound coming from the tunnel, at first distracted him. Then when he saw the sobbing girl's face, and what a state she was in, he knew instantly that his date with Sherri Miles was going to have to wait. That is, if Sherri Miles would ever talk to him again. The thing that surprised Reagan was that he wasn't disappointed. He would much rather spend the evening with the crying girl in the tunnel.

Barbara Ann Withers was on the last leg of her prospective college tour and heading back from Atlanta to Miami when she saw the sign along Interstate 75 that read "Gainesville Exit - 2 Miles." Her favorite prospect so far had been Emory University, and she had called her parents earlier that day with the news. She hadn't planned on touring the University of Florida, and certainly, stopping there on this day had never crossed her mind. For some reason, however, her car just steered her in that direction.

She hadn't seen or spoken to Reagan since their decision to go their separate ways a year earlier. Her life had since gotten somewhat back to normal, and she was now dating a fellow senior at her high school and was very fond of him.

After asking around on the University of Florida campus, she found out that Reagan's dorm was Murphree E. She sat outside of it and waited for a good part of the afternoon. She knew deep inside that she really needed to see him, and she was hoping he would understand.

"Barbara Ann, is that you? What in the world are you doing here? I mean . . . it's so good to see you. Why are you crying? Are your parents alright?"

"Reagan, I'm so sorry. I don't know why I am here. I hadn't planned . . . I would've called if I had . . . It's just that this thing . . . sometimes it eats me up inside. You're the only other person who knows. I was hoping we could spend a few minutes together. You look so skinny. What's that in your hand?"

After quickly slipping the rubbers into his pocket, Reagan responded, "Oh, it's nothing, and I am so glad you came by. How in the world did you find me? It's really great to see you again, Barbara Ann. Let's go into the courtyard and sit on a bench. Please stay as long as you want. I've been wanting to talk to you, too."

Reagan reached down, pulled her up from a sitting position, and used his thumb to wipe away the tears that were flowing down her cheeks. Minutes turned into hours, and the much-needed talk and shared crying time made them both feel a little better, at least for the time being.

When they were finished talking, Reagan snuck Barbara Ann up the four flights of stairs and into his room. It was too late for her to finish her drive, and he wasn't going to let her spend the night in her car like she had volunteered to do. She slept under the sheets on his bed, and he slept on Danny's old bed. Things between him and Barbara Ann would never be the same, but the two of them would always share a secret. As painful as that secret was, they now shared it with the promise that they would always be there for one another, if and when the need arose.

* * *

Only a few of the posted dorm rules were actually enforced with any level of severity. The enforcers were supposed to be the resident assistants. For their efforts, the RAs lived in single rooms, rent-free, and received small salaries. Every dorm had an RA, and everybody wanted to be an RA. Murphree E's RA was Lou Rollins, a heavy-drinking prelaw junior who was dating the best-looking girl in the Murphree complex, Karen Stein.

Two rules that were actually enforced and that could lead to a student's eviction, were

1. NO MEMBERS OF THE OPPOSITE SEX IN THE DORM AFTER VISITATION HOURS.
2. NO PETS ALLOWED IN THE HALLS OR ROOMS AT ANY TIME.

Early the next morning, Reagan found himself in apparent violation of both of these rules, and he realized he had a couple of more things he needed to add to his list.

Their plan had been for Reagan and Barbara Ann to wake up early in the morning, say their good-byes, and then she would quickly slither down the stairs and out the dorm's front door. If somehow she were caught, she would simply say that she had entered the dorm building by mistake and was just leaving. She wasn't a student at the university, so she couldn't get in trouble.

Reagan and Barbara woke up as planned and spent a couple of minutes talking, but just about the time she was ready to make her escape, they heard a dog barking loudly just outside of their door.

Reagan cracked the door open, and sure enough, a German shepherd was standing there looking up at him, wagging his tail and breathing hard.

"Scoot. Go away, boy. Get out of here."

Every time Reagan shut the door, the dog would bark. It was 6:00 AM, and the entire dorm would soon be awake, wondering what was going on.

"Crap, then come on in, if that will keep you quiet."

"What a beautiful doggie, Reagan. Is she yours?"

"No, she's not mine! I've never seen her before."

"Well, she sure acts like she knows you."

The shepherd was turning circles, licking Reagan in between loops, with her tail wagging so hard, it was making a loud whacking sound against the desk chair.

"What's going on in there?"

When Reagan looked up, he saw Lou Rollins peeking through the crack in the door. His heart started pounding, beads of sweat started forming on his forehead, and he felt like he could throw up. His whole life flashed in front of him. Less than two weeks in, and he was about to be kicked out of his dorm. How was he going to explain this to his parents? And he hadn't used a single rubber.

"I don't know where this dog came from, honest, Lou."

Lou was in the door, kneeling down, petting the licking dog behind the ears. "Hey, Heidi, how have you been? You haven't come to visit us in a long time.

"I'm not concerned about the dog, Reagan. His owner, Tyrone Miller, lived in this room three years ago but flunked out and lost his deferment. Heidi lives with Tyrone's mom, east of 13th Street. Every once in a while, she jumps the fence and comes here looking for Tyrone. No, I'm not concerned about the dog, Reagan. What I am concerned about is whoever that is, under the sheets, in your bed."

After the introductions were made and Lou Rollins had spent a couple of minutes reading Reagan the riot act, he turned off his RA persona and sat down at the desk. He started rubbing his temples, obviously nursing a hangover. "Okay, here's what we're gonna do." Looking at Barbara Ann, he continued, "Miss Withers, you really need to have better control over your dog. You should walk him on a leash. He got away from you this morning, wandered into the dorm, and you came in after him. I understand that, but dogs are not allowed in here. Are you following me?"

"Yes, sir."

"Good, then I will escort you and your dog out of the building and over to the plaza. Reagan, you give us a couple of minutes, and then meet us there. You get to take the puppy back to his home. Any questions?"

The relieved and appreciative looks on the faces of Barbara Ann and Reagan gave Lou Rollins his answer. Turning to Reagan with his RA face back on, Lou concluded, "You only get one of these, do you understand me? I could lose my job, and it's six in the morning, for Christ's sake."

Lou was rubbing his temples again as he and Barbara Ann left the room and headed down the stairs. Heidi followed close behind, still wagging her tail.

* * *

Reagan was running a little late for class, so he grabbed a seat in the back of the room by the door. Marty Schemer was already ranting about something when their stares locked for a second. Marty's eyebrows jumped upward, and an inquisitive smile flashed across his face. Reagan was not looking forward to confessing that he had missed out on the appetizer.

"Just because the race riots have simmered down doesn't mean we have equality in this country, not even close. Equality won't happen because of a new law that Congress passes, or a government-sponsored program. It has to come from deep within a society's gut. The people need to rise up and demand it. It's got to come from the heart. To hell with the bigots who don't get on that train."

Reagan looked curiously over at the boy seated next to him who wrote something on his note pad and passed it Reagan's way.

"He's reading Malcolm X's autobiography."

Reagan flashed him a *that explains it* look as he handed back the pad.

"Did you know that more than forty percent of our frontline combat soldiers in Vietnam were black? How do you explain that when they made up only twenty percent of our army's population? And that's our own government discriminating against them, for heaven's sake."

Reagan took a moment away from Marty's lecture to think about how his morning had gone so far. He glanced down at his hands, which were all scratched up and blistered. He couldn't remember having worked so hard in a long time.

* * *

With Lou and Barbara Ann safely out of sight, Reagan slid on his blue jeans and took the rubbers out of his pocket. He returned them to the box so they could rejoin their nine lonely buddies. Before heading out, he grabbed his list from the desk drawer and added

7.   No girls in the dorm after curfew.
8.   No pets.

His heart was still beating wildly from the encounter with his RA. It felt as though his world had almost come to an end. He put the pencil down and saw that his hands were shaking. He had a sick feeling and felt like he could pass out. *Crap, I really need to be more careful. I owe Lou Rollins big time!*

Reagan waited another five minutes and then dashed down the stairs, and over to the plaza where Lou was waiting with Heidi. Lou explained that Barbara Ann had left for her drive home to Miami and had asked him to say good-bye for her.

"Heidi's home address is right there on the tag attached to her collar. Tyrone Miller's mom's name is Rita Mae. She is a sweet old lady, and if she asks you to come in for some banana pudding, you should take her up on it. It is the best I've ever had. You better watch out, though; she'll probably try to put you to work. You might want to have your excuses ready. And Reagan, watch your back. It's a tough neighborhood, if you know what I mean."

Reagan would know what Lou meant soon enough. A half block after turning right off of 13th Street onto 6th Avenue, he felt the neighborhood start to change. It was a black neighborhood, and from the stares and comments coming from the front porches, it was obvious to Reagan that he was not welcomed there. He held tightly to the rope that Lou had attached to Heidi's collar. He didn't necessarily feel protected by his companion, but possibly, Rita Mae's neighbors would recognize the dog and realize that a good deed was being done.

Reagan felt as if he had been holding his breath for the last block and a half before finally reaching the house. He climbed up the two rickety wooden steps onto the porch and tapped on the screen door, which rattled with each knock. Heidi slumped, cowering, as if anticipating the scolding she was about to receive. Reagan glanced backward and counted at last a dozen eyes locked and loaded, like shotguns, watching his every move. His hands were shaking even more than they had been earlier that morning.

Rita Mae Miller approached the door cautiously with what looked like part of a broomstick in her right hand. She stared straight into Reagan's eyes with a look that could have melted a rock. Reagan subconsciously took a step backward as Heidi let out a deep moan causing Rita Mae to look down at the dog for the first time. The woman looked back up at Reagan, who watched her carefully, as her eyes softened into a gaze of appreciation.

"Get yer sorry ass into this house before I beat you with a stick," Rita Mae said.

Reagan took another step backward as he looked down at Heidi, who was now crawling on her haunches slowly across the threshold of the one-room house. "You be damn lucky to have a home at all, you sorry mutt. If it weren't for Tyrone, I'd send this no-good excuse of a guard dog hikin' down the block for good."

Rita Mae's eyes returned to Reagan's cautious stare, and sensing his discomfort, she softened her tone. "Now ain't you a fine-looking young man? You remind me a little of my youngin'. There's a picture of him in uniform right over there on the table. Come yourself on in, and have your-self a look. He's 'bout ta make sergeant, over in Germany, ya know. He's fightin' boredom, best I can tell, figurin' by his letters. Now, he ain't really my blood, but I been havin' him since he's two years old, so he's mine . . . sure enough. You fancy banana puddin'? Cuz if you does, I got a fresh batch in the fridge. Now make yuz self at home. Sit ya right on down over there. Do ya enjoy yard work? Cuz I gotta few things 'round here need doin'. Hear me? I can't pay ya, but I'll send ya away with some fresh oatmeal cookies."

Lou Rollins had been right. It was the best banana pudding Reagan had ever had, and his grandmother Alice made some really good banana pudding. As Reagan sat at the table next to the ten or so pictures of Tyrone, Rita Mae talked nonstop. Reagan was guessing that she hadn't had a visitor in quite a while, at least not one who reminded her of her "youngin'."

Looking around, Reagan noted that the home was about the same size as his dorm room. With a single mattress pushed against the back wall, he wondered where Tyrone had slept growing up. The stuffing on the worn-out easy chair was spilling out onto the lime green shag carpet that had lost a good part of its shag. The chipped and stained coffee table, next to the chair, held a lamp, the room's sole source of light, reading glasses, and a bible that was folded open upside down. In the far corner of the room, Heidi had curled up into a ball and wasn't about to make a move.

The kitchen area consisted of a sink, a stovetop oven, and a small countertop where Rita Mae was now standing, mixing up a batch of what Reagan guessed were cookies. Watching her move gracefully, and noting how quickly they had relaxed into the moment, he realized for the first time that without even opening his mouth, he had somehow volunteered for yard work duty.

"Your home is so cozy. How long have you lived here? Thank you for inviting me inside. This banana pudding is delicious." Reagan took advantage of a momentary pause in the story Rita Mae was gushing to speak for the first time. "And your son, I mean Tyrone, you must be very proud of him, Mrs. Miller."

Rita Mae suddenly stopped the mixing motion of her right hand and looked over at Reagan, studying him for what seemed like a minute before saying, "Ya never been in a home like this before, young man, have ya?" She paused again, looking even deeper into his eyes. "And even so, ya seem so comfortable here, and ya have such nice manners. Your parents done brought ya up right.

"Now . . . you can call me Rita Mae. I've never even been married. Ya hear? Never saw much use in it. Lived in this house since I was a little girl. Grandmama raised me. Taught me how ta read right there where yer sittin'. And Tyrone . . . he is my son, praise the Lord! And, yez, I'm very proud of him, just like I'm a sure yer mama and daddy is proud of you."

Tears had formed in her eyes, and Reagan watched her as she returned to her cooking. For the first time since he had walked through the door, Rita Mae was quiet, except for a song she was humming softly. It was a gospel song, similar to some that Reagan had heard while flipping through the channels on his car radio. Every once in a while, she would sing a couple of words and then return to a hum. She had a beautiful voice, and when Reagan looked over at the dog, he saw that Heidi was sitting up straight, listening along.

An hour later, with his chores complete, and holding a paper bag overflowing with cookies, he looked at his gold watch and realized that he had less than half an hour to shower and get to class. Rita Mae walked him out onto the front porch, and in clear sight of her closest neighbors, she put her hands on his shoulders and kissed him gently on the cheek.

"Young man, I wanna thank ya for yer help this morning. I enjoyed getting ta know ya. Yuz welcome in my home, anytime."

Reagan pet Heidi on the head, turned to leave, and then stopped in his tracks.

"By the way, Miss . . . I mean, Rita Mae, my name is Reagan . . . Reagan Davis. I'm afraid I forgot to introduce myself. I am so sorry. And thank you. I enjoyed meeting you also, very much so."

"Oh, I done already knows who ya are, young man. Lou Rollins, he stopped by 'bout a week ago ta say hi and ta get him some of that puddin'. He told me to be expecting ya. Now, don't ya be a stranger, ya hear?"

Reagan was somewhat relieved to see a Gainesville Police Department patrol car pass by as he walked quickly back toward 13th Street, but something seemed different—or was it his imagination? The people on the porches weren't paying as much attention to him now. He even thought he saw a lady sitting in a rocking chair with a big gray cat on her lap smiling his way.

Just then, he saw them a half block ahead, standing square in the middle of the sidewalk that he would need to cross. There were three of them. They were big, muscular, black boys, a little older than him, Reagan guessed. They were talking to each other in loud voices, and he couldn't understand a word they were saying. They were obviously standing where they were for a reason.

Reagan weighed his options. He could turn around, or cross the street, or maybe head back to Rita Mae's house for a while. Possibly, he could outrun them, although he seriously doubted that. But something inside of him said no. He had done a good deed this morning, and if he was going to get the crap beat out of him for that, then so be it. For whatever reason, he decided to keep walking, straight ahead, not slowing down or showing hesitation.

As he approached, the three young men stopped talking and turned toward him in a formation that blocked his path. Each had a serious yet curious look on his face.

"Good morning. How are you all today?" Reagan asked trying to hide his anxiety.

The largest of the three put his hand in the center of Reagan's chest, stopping him in the middle of the sidewalk. The other two circled Reagan, close enough that he could smell their breath.

"Yuz leave that young man alone, ya hear me?" a woman's voice said. "He be a friend of Tyrone's, and I know you ain't gonna want ta be answerin' to that boy when he gets back home."

Reagan looked behind him and saw Rita Mae in full stride, broomstick in her right hand, Heidi in tow, and with that rock-melting look back in her eyes.

If the circumstances hadn't been so volatile, Reagan wouldn't have been able to control the smile trying to make its way onto his face. There, sprinting toward them like a bulldozer in high gear, was a woman with skin the color of coal and a girth as big around as her five-foot-tall frame. She had shoulder-length curly black hair, wore a yellow dress, obviously home-made, and still had on the stained light blue cooking apron that she had been wearing earlier while making cookies.

Everything on Rita Mae jiggled when she walked, from the extra flesh on her legs to the jowls on her face. She had a few teeth missing and was growing a pretty thick black mustache that Reagan was just now noticing for the first time. She was out of breath by the time she reached them, but she was not out of spunk.

"Is that yuz, Jamal Spikes? Yuz might a gotten a lot bigger, but yuz ain't a gotten no smarter. And if ya ain't a-thinkin' I won't whack ya upside the head with this stick, then yuz be as crazy as yer daddy. Ya hear me?"

"Yez-ums, Miz Miller. We's just havin' fun, sayin' hi and all, ya know? We's be meanin' 'im no harm."

The three boys unfolded from around Reagan and started walking slowly backward across the street, their eyes shifting between Rita Mae and Heidi, who had managed a pretty convincing growl.

Reagan looked back again at Rita Mae and nodded as she gave him a smile that told him to be getting on his way. Halfway down the block, he turned to see Jamal Spikes, along with his two foot soldiers, standing in the middle of the street, facing him. They were not smiling.

* * *

"Did you read about the black high school senior in Mississippi last month who was beaten within an inch of his life just because he talked to the school's white prom queen after class one day?" Marty Schemer had worked himself into such a frenzy that his veins were popping out of his neck and forehead. "And do you know what happened to the three white star football players that did it? Nothing! Case closed due to lack of evidence, and the black boy's not talking. For heaven's sake, when will this end?"

The boy next to Reagan was scribbling something on his pad again, and Reagan leaned in to read it.

"When is this guy gonna get off of his soapbox?"

Reagan stared with intense curiosity at his new friend. His stare was answered with another scribble.

"We're not all Malcolm X fans."

The two smiled at each other. It was a smile that turned into a giggle, which caused them to look away from one other so it wouldn't get out of

55

control. When Reagan finally turned back to his neighbor, he took notice for the first time that his scribble buddy was black.

"Now, for extra credit, I want you to tell me what little thing you have done, or are going to do, to make a difference, to help turn this damn injustice around." Marty glanced Reagan's way before continuing, "And I want it to come from the heart: one thousand words, papers are due Monday. Class is dismissed."

Reagan, who looked down again at the scratches and blisters on his hands, would take this extra credit assignment seriously, just like he had the last one. Only this time, the result, and the subsequent visit to the graduate assistant's office, would bring praise, admiration, and congratulations for the class's highest grade.

"Hey, Reagan, hold up. Have you got a minute? Sorry about making you laugh in class. I hope I didn't get us into any kind of trouble. I'm Gerald Jackson, but people just call me Jackson."

The two were walking toward Library East, where Reagan had a study date with Molly Turner.

"Oh, I'm sure you didn't. How do you know my name?"

"That doesn't matter. I've got something to talk to you about. I wanted to thank you."

The two stopped and faced each other.

"Thank me? For what? We just met."

"I saw you in my neighborhood this morning, bringing Tyrone's dog back to Rita Mae. Tyrone is like a big brother to me and a lot of others on the block. So, thank you . . . That took a lot of guts."

Jackson extended his hand, which Reagan shook as he looked deeply once again into his new friend's eyes.

"I was just glad I could help out."

Jackson was looking at Reagan's hands. "Looks like you helped out quite a bit. Did you get any of that banana pudding?"

"Sure did, and some great cookies. Want one? They're in my book bag.

As Jackson took a cookie from him, Reagan asked, "You still live at home?" He had been told that all incoming freshmen were required to live in the dorm.

They were walking once again, Jackson enjoying his cookie.

"I'm on a waiting list. As soon as a dorm room becomes available, I'm moving onto campus."

Reagan glanced over and smiled. "I just might know of one that just opened up. Let me talk to my RA and see what I can work out."

Chapter Seven

*I*t had been two weeks since Reagan's introduction to the Frisbee ball gang, and his right calf muscle was still a little tender. Nonetheless, as he and his running partner approached the spot and started up the hill, he wasn't about to use his sore leg as an excuse, or show any other signs of weakness, for that matter. Their pace was considerably faster than what Reagan was used to, but glancing over, he noticed that his new roommate wasn't breathing hard and had barely broken a sweat.

Jackson had the muscular body of an athlete, and he wasn't wearing a shirt—a detail Reagan knew Charley would enjoy. Inviting him along to play today would prove to be a bad idea for several reasons, not the least of which was because Reagan would be assigned to cover him and Jackson was as fast as lightning.

* * *

The previous Tuesday, after his study session at the library with Molly, Reagan had gone straight to Lou Rollins's dorm room. He wanted to thank Lou for his leniency that morning, tell him about his visit with Rita Mae, and talk to him about his roommate situation. Lou wasn't there, but Karen Stein, Lou's girlfriend, was.

Reagan already knew that Karen was a knockout. At about five and a half feet tall, she had short black hair, ocean blue eyes, a Playboy magazine-ready body, and a fabulous smile.

What he didn't know about Karen was that she was a sophomore physical education major, had gone to high school in Miami (attending Reagan's high school alma mater's archrival, Hialeah High), and had something else in common with Reagan. They both worked at Hoggetowne Pizza and Suds. According to Karen, Hiram had called the three girls together Saturday night and had told them of his new hire.

"Reagan, you're going to enjoy working at the Hog, and we're going to love having you. Another man around, thank God! Hiram is quite a character and fancies himself a lady's man. He's always hitting on us. It bothered me at first, but now I realize it's all for show, at least as far as I'm concerned. He knows I'm in love with Lou. As for the other two girls, well, I'm not sure where that's going.

"By the way, you're in for it. Both Sharon and Pam are boy crazy. When I told them that I had heard of you, they wanted to know everything about you, right down to your shoe size, which, of course, I didn't know." Karen paused for a second, looking down at Reagan's size-fourteen sneakers before continuing. "They've already had two fights over you, and they haven't even met you yet. You're gonna have your hands full with those girls, that's for sure. By the way, why did you need to see Lou? Is there something I can help you with?"

Later that afternoon, Jackson would receive a phone call from the university's housing office. An opening was now available in Murphree E, and he could move in immediately.

To celebrate their first night as roommates, Reagan and Jackson purchased four bottles of Pagan Pink Ripple at the Magic Mart and sat under the moonlight, in the plaza, drinking until the last drop was gone, at about three in the morning. They became fast friends, telling stories about themselves, discussing personal beliefs, and sharing confidences.

Through the grogginess of the next morning, three things stood out in Reagan's mind about Jackson. First, he was truly girl crazy, maybe even more so than Reagan himself. Second, there was a lot to him, and third, he had not had an easy life up to this point.

* * *

On a hot August afternoon, Brenda Montgomery was walking barefoot along the dusty dirt road that led from the town square to her family's home out in the woods. Brenda was a fifteen-year-old firecracker who had always given her parents fits. With naturally curly, strawberry-blond hair, hazel eyes, curves much too pronounced for her age, and an untamable attitude, she was a force to be reckoned with.

The year was 1955, the town was Speckle Creek, North Carolina, and her strict Catholic upbringing had done nothing to calm the upheaval Brenda felt churning at the core of her every thought. She had two dreams. One was of the day she would be old enough and would have saved up enough money to get out of the one-horse town forever. The other was to escape the life she had created for herself trying to make her first dream come true.

It had started innocently enough, selling kisses behind the schoolhouse shed for five cents, but that had been five years earlier, and things had changed. Boys were no longer interested in just kisses, or even the twenty-five-cent feel-ups they had stood in line for back then. Now they wanted it all. And Brenda Montgomery would willingly give them what they wanted and more . . . for the right price.

In a funny way, Brenda's enterprise had had a positive effect on the little town of Speckle Creek. There was never a shortage of young men anxious to perform chores for the local businesses, the mayor's office, or even elderly widows. As long as there was money to be made, there were always hot-blooded boys ready, willing, and able to get the job done.

Another interesting phenomenon was the fraternal closeness that had developed amongst Brenda's regular patrons. They had formed a pact. Nothing would ever be discussed that would have gotten Brenda in trouble or would have exposed their well-kept secret.

Of course, there were the suspicions, as well as the occasional gossip and giggles from the other girls in the schoolyard. Brenda handled these herself. She was as tough and headstrong as she was pretty, and no one wanted to cross her.

So, for the most part, Brenda and her customers went about their business right under the noses of the entire town: parents, religious leaders, teachers, and the boys who had not been lucky enough to get in on the action.

One of those boys who had not been included in the fun for many reasons, not the least of which was the color of his skin, was Monroe Jackson Jr. He was the only black student at Speckle Creek Community School, and he had heard the rumors.

As a senior, Monroe had already reached a higher level of education than anyone in his family, with the exception of his aunt. He had recently been awarded a full scholarship to Ohio State University as a result of his achievements on the track team. His speed on the track, however, was not the only reason Monroe's widowed father was proud of him. Monroe was a straight-A student, a fact that angered and bewildered many in the township, who were not inclined to accept his type or their achievements.

Just before turning right off of the dirt road and onto the rocky driveway that led up to her house, Brenda Montgomery heard a car coming up from behind her. It was a pickup truck, actually, and from the flaking yellow paint job and the sputtering engine, she knew exactly whose it was. The driver stopped alongside her and waited for the dust to drift by before leaning over and winding down the passenger-side window. He and Brenda talked for a few minutes, and then the much older black man pulled a twenty-dollar bill out of his wallet as an offer of proof. Brenda looked at the cash, flashed a smile at her newest customer, hopped into the truck, and off they went.

Seven weeks later, a hysterical Brenda Montgomery, accompanied by her fuming, red-faced father, was sitting in the conference room at the Sheffield County Courthouse in front of Sheriff Wilson and his deputy, Dallas Hawk. Brenda was barely able to get the words out of her mouth: "He raped me . . . black man . . . too embarrassed to come in before now . . . pregnant."

Presumably too upset to continue, Brenda left the room to join her mother who was waiting in Sheriff Wilson's private office. Dallas Hawk shut the door behind her, and the three men held court.

"Ain't nothin good ever come from mixin' our good folk in with those kind. They shoulda been left out in the cotton, where they belong. They ought notta be takin' up space in our schools, comin' into our restaurants, or tryin' to use our toilets. Now, you got a bull's-eye example of what happens when they get too close to our women."

Dallas Hawk, a mountain of a man with a balding head and bulging arm muscles, paced the floor. He had finished his rant and was waiting for direction. The sheriff leaned back in his chair and lit up a cigar. Brenda's father, Jim, the town's auto mechanic, was sitting motionless at the table with his fists clenched, staring at something on the other side of the room.

"Reckon we oughta pick him up and bring him in for questioning, Dallas?" The sheriff asked while looking up at the ceiling and blowing black smoke rings into the air.

The three men's eyes locked before Dallas answered his boss, spitting out the words, "I'll round up some men. It might take us a day or two to track him down. You know, word's out, and he's probably on the run by now. But we'll find him. Don't you worry 'bout that. And when we do—"

The sheriff quickly interrupted the big man, giving him a stern look, "Just take care of it, Deputy. You heard the young lady. The boy raped her. Any questions?" There were none.

The town's hanging tree was about a mile from the square, down Main Street to Reynolds Road.

Monroe Jackson Jr. was genuinely confused at the sight of twenty men standing in his front yard, wearing white robes with hoods. He was glad that his father, who had left hurriedly to visit a friend in a nearby town, wasn't there to witness this.

At first, Monroe was certain that this visit was some sort of a scare tactic or warning. It was only after the men approached him, formed a circle around him, pushed him to the ground, and started punching and kicking him that he finally realized his plight and had started to put up a struggle. He was quickly overpowered and begged to know what he had done to deserve this. No one said a word in reply.

With his hands and feet tied with rope, Monroe looked around at the hate in their eyes and the sly, anticipating smirks on their faces. He recognized two of them, Dallas Hawk, who was tying the knot, and his high school track coach, who was about to give the command. Neither of these men realized that they are about to hang the wrong man.

Brenda Montgomery spent the next eight months "away at a private preparatory school," living with her aunt in Pittsburgh, Pennsylvania. She gave birth to a healthy baby boy, whom the nurses named, at his mother's request, Gerald Monroe Jackson before they sent him off to the first of many foster homes.

Brenda Montgomery would never return to Speckle Creek and would spend the rest of her days drifting from one place to another, looking for something that she could never find.

Monroe Jackson Sr., having heard about his son's death, and fearing for his own life, slipped back into town in the middle of the night and gathered his belongings. He packed up his truck, and preferring warm weather to cold, he decided not to head north to be with his younger sister, a third-grade schoolteacher, living in the Northeast, but, instead to drive south to a small town in central Florida where he would live with his older brother.

A broken man, he would often think about his deceased son, Monroe Jr. He would never shake the heavy burden of grief and guilt, brought on by having been the reason for his own son's death. He would reminisce about his beloved late wife and pray that she had been reunited with their boy in heaven.

Sometimes at night, in the darkness of his room, he would wonder about the child he had never met. The baby he and Brenda Montgomery had created in his moment of weakness. With a heavy heart, Monroe Jackson Sr., would get down on his knees and ask the Lord to bring him together with this child and grant his grieving soul just one more chance, just one more chance to be a father.

*　*　*

The runners had reached the field. Jackson was drinking from the water fountain while Reagan checked his watch. They had made it there in forty-three minutes, three minutes faster than Reagan's time last week. *How in the world am I ever gonna beat that?*

61

After seeing Charley and Gary off to his left, under the oak tree, in what appeared to be a serious conversation, Reagan decided to walk Jackson to the far end of the field, where the rest of the gang was sitting.

When Ye saw them coming, she jumped to her feet and started skipping across the grass with her hands up in the air. She was yelling out happy words in Chinese, but when she got close to them, she stopped and with a very proud look on her face said, "Hello, Mister Reagan. How is you tonight?"

A bright smile came to Reagan's face, which, he saw as he looked over at Jackson, was contagious. "Why, Ye, your English, it has gotten so much better in just one week."

Ye was jumping up and down like a bunny, obviously very pleased with herself, when Terri Spencer and Yang finally caught up with her.

"I'm helping them a little. Who do you have with you today?" Terri, who was carrying what looked to be a beginner's English book, was studying Jackson curiously.

"Oh, I'm sorry, let me introduce you all to my room—" Reagan stopped in mid-sentence and looked over at Jackson. It had been a while since he had bonded so quickly with another guy. None of Reagan's pals had decided to attend the University of Florida, and Reagan had been missing male companionship. Jackson was already more than just a roommate.

Jackson, who was becoming a little uneasy with the awkward pause, looked over at Reagan and was about to introduce himself when Reagan continued, "Let me introduce you to my friend, my good friend, Gerald Jackson. He goes by Jackson."

Choosing fair teams was not easy. The unspoken truth was that Ye and Yang were never much of a factor, and this day was not going to be any different. They were both so excited about the new English phrases Terri had taught them that they were having trouble concentrating on anything else.

Yang shouted out, "I go groozery store, buy some mike," which sent the two of them racing down the field, giggling, high-fiving, and turning cartwheels.

The rest of the group huddled and decided that Reagan, along with the two girls, against Gary, Jackson, and the happy couple would be the best combination. Gary had trouble hiding his disapproval, not happy with having been teamed up with the new guy. Earlier, he had also had trouble greeting Jackson with any sort of congeniality. The two girls, however, were smitten with Jackson and gathered together every few plays to compare notes.

As it turned out, the teams were not fair at all. Gary was a master at hurling the Frisbee, despite Charley's ferocious rush, and Jackson was much too fast for either Terri or Reagan to keep up with. Before anyone knew it—if anyone had been keeping score—it was seven to two, but even that hadn't made Gary happy. Every chance he got, he berated his teammate, calling him chicken legs and slippery fingers, and mumbling other names under his breath.

* * *

Jackson's youngest childhood memory was of getting off of a school bus in front of his new school on the first day he attended third grade. What he didn't remember was his four previous foster homes or the three other schools, scattered throughout Pittsburgh that he had attended.

His latest foster parents were Pastor Schmidt and his wife, Ann. They were a kind, generous, and loving couple who had fallen in love with Jackson after he started attending their church's Sunday school class a year earlier. When the Schmidts found out that Jackson was once again in need of a family, they jumped at the opportunity. They had never been able to have children of their own and wanted to adopt Jackson in spite of the ethnic differences.

There were twenty-three children in Mrs. Allen's third grade class that first day. Twenty-one were black, and two were white. But Mrs. Allen didn't see color. What she saw was a chance to make a difference in each of their lives, and in doing so, she had made a difference in her own. For thirty-five years, she had volunteered to be the only white teacher in her inner-city school, and she had helped shape the lives of over seven hundred children.

The current school year was to be her last. She was retiring and had mixed feelings. As she took roll call, she got to the name Gerald Monroe Jackson and paused to look curiously over her wire-rimmed glasses. In front of her, sitting in the first row, was a bright-eyed little boy with a beautiful smile, who had his hand sticking as high into the air as he could get it. Gerald Monroe Jackson. She glanced again at the name on the roster. It couldn't be. It had to be a coincidence. Nonetheless, she decided to mention it to her best friend, Patricia Jackson Highsmith, the school's other third-grade teacher, during their morning break.

* * *

Jackson's hearty belly laughing was keeping him from getting into any sort of a running rhythm as he and Reagan turned left onto 13th Street, heading back toward campus. "That's one hell of a shiner you have there, my friend. We should probably get some ice on that when we get back to the dorm. And by the way, I can stick up for myself; you didn't need to come to my rescue." Jackson paused, looked over at Reagan, and burst into laughter again, finally pleading, "Hey, man, I've gotta stop for a minute to catch my breath."

Reagan wasn't laughing, but he wasn't upset, either. A little black eye wasn't the end of the world. And besides, it might just be the attention-getter he would need to break the ice with the girls at the Rat later that night. He also felt certain that Jackson could handle himself with the likes of Gary Glaser, but that wasn't the point. The point was that Gary had belittled Jackson for over two hours, and his banter had gotten under everyone's skin. It hadn't been anything major, just teasing with a sharp edge, but it was still unnerving. Charley had scolded Gary three times about it, but not even that had stopped him.

And then, when a wide-open Jackson, running a perfect flank, dropped a beautifully thrown Frisbee, Gary let the words slip out of his mouth: "Stupid nigger!" Both Charley and Reagan had heard it. Charley shot Gary a look that caused his face to turn red with embarrassment, but he offered no apology. Reagan reacted without hesitation.

Coach Shanahan would not have been happy with Reagan's first attempt to get Gary Glaser to the ground. Despite all of the tackle drills he had endured, Reagan hit his target way too high and was easily cast aside. His second attempt, however, would have impressed his coach, as well as the entire varsity team.

Reagan's right shoulder made a solid hit, waist high. His arms folded around his opponent's legs, and within a split second, he was churning a surprised Gary Glaser into the dirt. The two were soon rolling around throwing punches and kicks.

Charley was screaming at the top of her lungs for them to stop. Yang was holding Ye, who was in total hysterics. Jackson saw the ruckus and was in full sprint toward it, but Terri got there first.

With pinpoint precision, Terri reached both hands into the heap and quickly grasped each of the brawlers by the balls, squeezing with just enough intensity to freeze the moment. "Now, if you two boys would like to keep these attachments, I would strongly suggest that you roll off of each other and go to separate ends of the field until we can get this sorted out. I'm not too happy with men in general right now, and I would enjoy nothing more than . . ." Terri's grip tightened like a vice grip, causing a combined yelp.

After the game was over, on their way back to campus, the runners passed the empty parking lot adjacent to Hoggetowne Pizza and Suds, their pace quickened on the downhill decline, which led them past the First Presbyterian Church of Gainesville. Seeing the minister's name on the placard reminded Reagan of the rest of the story Jackson had shared with him the night before.

*   *   *

The Schmidts had been successful in the adoption of a nine-year-old charmer named Gerald Monroe Jackson. The family spent the next six years living a peaceful life in the small two-bedroom home next door to the pastor's church. The Schmidts were loved and revered by the entire congregation, and although the elders had a difficult time with it at first, before long, Jackson was accepted into the church's extended family.

Patricia Highsmith followed Jackson's progress quietly, keeping her distance but making sure never to lose contact. She harbored a deep secret that she knew one day would have to be disclosed, but not until the time was right, not until he was old enough to understand. That is, if anyone is ever old enough to understand certain things in life. So, whether it was at a school play, at the neighborhood park, or while Jackson won a track team trophy, Patricia kept a close eye on him. She loved him as if he were her own blood, which he was.

According to the police report, the fire had started in the master bedroom, probably the result of drifting embers from the wood-burning fireplace. There was only one survivor . . . a brokenhearted fifteen-year-old black boy, looking more and more like a young man, who was once again without a place to live.

Patricia Highsmith went to the police station the morning of the fire. She sat down on the bench next to her nephew and looked deeply into his crying eyes. She reached out her hand and pulled him into a lingering hug. Ready or not, the time was right.

*   *   *

"Hey, Jackson, you never completely finished the story last night. Did you ever find your father?"

The runners had now reached the corner of University Avenue and 13th Street. Their pace slowed to a jog and then to a fast walk. Jackson turned to the question and looked carefully at his friend, black eye and all. Before he could answer, a smile came to his face and he tried hard not to start laughing again.

"Yeah, Reagan, I did find my dad. As a matter of fact, you walked by our house the other day, on your way to Rita Mae's to take Heidi home. Come on, let's go. I'll introduce you to him."

CHAPTER EIGHT

*R*eagan pulled his 1972 orange Opal GT, a car his mom bought him using money from her own savings account, into the parking lot of the Hoggetowne Pizza and Suds. It was two o'clock on Sunday afternoon. Hiram's car, the only other one in the lot, was parked way in the back by the lake, so Reagan pulled in alongside of it. Today was Reagan's first day at work, and his boss had asked him to get there early for a "pizza-making lesson."

The lesson started at the bar over three beers and a dissertation detailing the fifteen years that Hiram and his wife, Lucy, had owned and operated the Hog. They had worked together for the first few years, with Hiram making pies and his wife pouring beer. "After a while," Hiram explained, "Lucy lost interest in the place—and a lot of other things, for that matter—leaving me to take over the day-to-day operations."

With little to constrain him, if his stories were indeed genuine, he had turned the operation into "Hiram's Harem." He hired mostly women, willing women, and enjoyed the successes of being a sole proprietor.

Reagan got the impression, however, that Hiram's interest in chasing young co-eds around the bar might just be waning when the chuckling man said, "It's just not the same anymore. There's way too much effort for such little payoff. Girls these days are so damn independent. The world's changing faster than it's spinning. But every once in a while . . ." He gave a knowing smile. "You know, it's just in my blood. Now, let me show you how to make the best pizza in town."

* * *

That Sunday was the second day that week that the Orange Bullet, as Reagan's dad referred to the Opal, had made the trip from Sally Tindale's Nursing Home, where Reagan had made off-campus parking arrangements, to the Hog. The first time had been the previous Thursday evening, when Reagan attended the Sigma Chi/Kappa Delta social. That night, the parking lot had been overflowing with cars, but Reagan, after being recognized by a frat brother stationed at the front of the lot to direct traffic, had been waved over to a roped-off VIP parking area.

Standing at the entrance of the Hog were three of the facemen Reagan had met the previous Friday night at the fraternity house. As he approached them, trying to remember their names, he noticed what appeared to be nervous chatter, but as soon as they saw him coming, their chatter quickly melted into smiles, handshakes, and pats on the back. The three recruiters were soon crowded around their potential pledge, asking him how his week was going, if he was doing okay with his classes and, most importantly, if he'd had any hot dates.

Their conversation was interrupted when a fourth brother came out of the restaurant's door and, before seeing Reagan, asked with an edge, "Any sign of the Moose?"

Reagan couldn't help but ask, "A moose? You all are bringing a moose to your party?"

Reagan soon learned that the Moose was Anthony Mosul, a fifth-year senior and a 295-pound offensive guard who played on the university's varsity football squad. The Moose was also Sigma Chi's much-needed anchor on its beer-guzzling team. The Moose was late to the party, and the Moose was never late to a party.

As it turned out, the Delta Tau Deltas, or Delts, a rival fraternity, along with a scantily dressed contingency from the Chi Omega Sorority house, had crashed the party. After a lengthy discussion, the frats' presidents had made a bet. The losers of the beer-guzzling competition had to buy the victors a round of drinks and then vacate the premises.

The Delts were the university's beer-guzzling champs. The Sigs didn't stand a chance without the Moose. The contest was to take place at 7:00 PM . . . in a half hour. "Where the hell is the Moose?"

"I'm a pretty good beer drinker."

All eyes were suddenly trained on Reagan.

"Is it glasses or pitchers? Pitchers are my specialty!"

With that said, Reagan walked through the door. He couldn't believe his eyes. The Hog was packed wall-to-wall with people. Some of the crowd was drinking beer, and smoking cigarettes while standing on the tables. And the girls—*My God, I've never seen so many good-looking girls in one place in my life!*

The noise level was almost deafening. Reagan could hardly hear the jukebox, which was blasting out a Doobie Brothers song, over the hoots and hollers coming from the already inebriated and super-charged crowd.

Behind the bar were three girls, including Karen Stein, passing out pitchers as fast as the taps would pour them. Hiram hustled out of the kitchen, carrying two delicious-looking pizzas that were quickly swooped up and carried into the crowd.

The facemen at the door had seamlessly passed Reagan along to two brothers, who escorted him to the back of the room, where several other candidates, along with a horde of pretty girls were gathered. Before he knew it, Reagan had a beer in one hand, a slice of pizza in the other, and he was flirting with a top-heavy brunette.

* * *

About a mile down the street and several hours earlier, Sergeant Gary Glaser, in full uniform, walked into the Pleasure Palace with something on his mind. The short brunette up on the stage immediately recognized him, waved, and blew him a suggestive kiss. Gary waved back dismissively and then looked around the corner for his good friend, and the bar's bouncer, Bubba McGraw.

"Well, hello, Officer. To what do we owe this pleasure? Are you here to bust the place and shut us down? 'Cause if you are, get on with it. I could sure use a little time outside of these dingy walls." Bubba had come out of the dark booth to the right of the entrance and was approaching Gary from behind.

"Bubba, my friend. How the hell are you? You get bigger and uglier every time I see you. Aren't these girls giving you enough exercise, or have you started back as a regular, taking up space at the Krispy Kreme dough-nut counter?" The sergeant's smile was wide and genuine as he pulled his friend in from a handshake to a man hug.

"If you weren't wearing those stripes and carrying that piece, I'd take you out back and treat you to a big-time butt-whoopin'. You know I would. You know I could. You know I should. Don't you now?" Bubba's wide eyes, sparkling bright smile, and taunting head nod accompanied the tease.

Gary didn't doubt that Bubba would be a worthy opponent, but his thoughts were returning to the reason he was there. "Hey, buddy, it is really good to see you. We need to get together for a beer. Is Charley around? I need to talk to her."

"Sure is. She's back in the corner with a regular, probably flashing those pretty blue eyes and sucking the money out of his wallet at the same time. I'll go get her for you."

Earlier that morning, Charley had called the Gainesville Police Department and had gotten put through to Sergeant Glaser at his desk.

"Jesus, Charley, what in the hell are you doing calling me at work?"

"Where would you rather me call you . . . at home?"

The question had given the sergeant reason for pause before he continued, "What is it, then? Are you okay? Couldn't this wait until tonight?"

"Gary, I've been robbed. All of the money I've been saving for this month's rent . . . it's gone." Charley had been sobbing, her voice projecting both fear and outrage.

"Is anything else missing? Did you leave your door unlocked? Are you sure you remember where the money was hidden?"

After Charley convinced him that she had indeed locked her door and had known precisely where the money had been hidden, she continued, "Gary, I've got to get to work. Can you use the spare key I gave you and come over to check my place out? It's giving me the creeps just to be in here."

As soon as they hung up, Gary grabbed his fingerprint kit, hopped into his patrol car, turned on the sirens, and headed directly to the Shady Oaks Mobile Home Community.

He spent three hours checking out her trailer, walking the park, and interviewing as many of its residents as he could find. He even interviewed the park's owner, one Stephen Crain. He now had a theory and had come to the Palace for two reasons: first, to give his report to Charley, and second, to make a special request for his visit to her place later that evening.

* * *

At exactly 6:55 PM, a particularly somber-looking Brad York, Sigma Chi's president, walked up to Reagan and looked him square in the eyes before whispering into his ear, "How good?"

Reagan, who had been enjoying the attention of one Kappa Delta after another, turned and, after filling in the blanks, nodded before reaching over and filling his beer glass from a nearby pitcher. They were in the far back corner of the room, and very few people were watching when Reagan, with the speed of a gunfighter, drained the glass as fast as the beer would pour out of it.

Without changing his expression, Brad York turned to the table and said, "If you ladies will please excuse us, I need to borrow Mr. Davis for a minute."

As if in slow motion, the crowd started gathering around a table in the center of the room where Reagan joined the seven other fired-up contestants. Reagan was one of four on the Sigma Chi team, and he was sitting in the anchor seat. The stares between the competing sides reminded him of those between two boxers before a grudge match. The sorority girls were leading the chanting, which was picking up momentum from within the opposing camps.

The three bartenders came to the table carrying eight forty-eight-ounce pitchers filled to the brim. Karen Stein caught Reagan's eye, winked at him, and shouted, "Good luck!" The other two girls gave Reagan seductive looks that sent shivers down his spine.

Introductions were made between the contestants. The only name that Reagan caught through the crowd noise was that of Mark Glaser, sitting across from him. *Could it be? Sure looks like him . . . Gary's younger brother?*

Brad York, who was standing on the table next to the contestants, had his hand in the air, ready to start the contest. He looked over at the door once more . . . still no Moose. Later, he would find out that Anthony Mosul had been detained at a traffic stop by a Gainesville Police Department sergeant for an hour and a half before finally being issued a speeding ticket.

"On your mark . . . get set . . . go!"

Reagan was very impressed with the leadoff guzzlers. The Delts got off to a fast start, but by the time the first two empty pitchers were slammed to the table, everything had evened out. The lead went back and forth a couple of times, but the Sigs were a couple of ticks behind when the third Delt finished with a cowboy yell, jumping onto his chair, with his hands flailing in the air. All eyes in the room were focused on the two anchors.

His slight disadvantage gave Reagan a second to look across the table and size up his competition. He was already breathing a sigh of relief when the pitcher to his left was slammed to the table. But suddenly, Reagan was not in a hurry. He looked over at his anxious teammates, gave them a wink, and in a split second that seemed like an hour, mouthed the words, "Watch this!"

* * *

In the crowded living conditions of the Shady Oaks Mobile Home Community, everyone knew everyone else's business. Most of the dozen or so residents whom Sergeant Glaser had interviewed earlier that day knew exactly who he was. They also knew that he had been to their community many times, usually on Thursday nights. None of them, of course, brought that up or admitted that they would peer out of their windows and watch him come and go on his motorcycle.

They all, however, did have stories to tell about their landlord. None of their tales had been the least bit complimentary, and many had been downright disturbing. The investigating officer didn't like what he was hearing, and made careful notes.

It hadn't really been necessary to interview Stephen Crain, other than to see what the man looked like. The meeting was short and cordial, with the park's owner expressing shock and concern at the reported robbery.

"She oughta get the lock to that trailer changed out. That thing's been around here for years. Lord knows how many people still have the key to it. I'm pretty sure I don't, but I'm betting lots of people 'round here still do. Probably was one of them that went in and took that money. In the meantime, if you'll leave me your number, I'll keep an eye on the place and give you a call if I see anything suspicious."

Sergeant Glaser thanked Stephen Crain for his time, left him his contact information, got into his car, and drove out of the park. The sergeant was certain who had committed the crime, but he also knew that, under the circumstances, he would have to handle this matter off the books. Just exactly how he would handle it wasn't clear, but he would need to come up with a plan soon, real soon.

As his patrol car turned right onto Archer Road, toward the Pleasure Palace, to see Charley, Gary Glaser shook his head, smiled to himself, and muttered under his breath, "What an idiot. I never told the stupid shit what had been stolen or that the thief had let themself in with their own key."

* * *

Stephen Crain was sitting naked on a chair in the fifth trailer on the right. The tall skinny man, who had paid him a visit earlier in the day, was late again, really late, but that was okay. Crain was getting a free show, and he had been watching her dance naked in front of her window for the past fifteen minutes. It was almost as if she knew he was watching, and that was turning him on beyond belief.

He reached over and scooped a wad of petroleum jelly out of the open jar. He couldn't wait any longer. He took a drag from the joint, blew out the candle, and pressed his face to the window. She was moving so slowly, so seductively. *She must know I'm watching her. She must want me.*

His eyes were about to roll into the back of his head when he heard it. Was it something shuffling around in the leaves outside, or was it his imagination? She must not have heard it. She was still dancing, rubbing her hands up and down her body, reaching up, into the air.

Oh, God, she is beautiful. I'm so close! There's that sound again. Damn it! That's so distracting. Must be a squirrel or a raccoon or something. Forget about it. Concentrate. She needs me. She wants me. She knows the rent is due tomorrow, and she knows she can't pay it. She doesn't want to pay it. She wants to surrender herself to me. Oh, God!

This time it was a knocking or tapping sound, coming from the back of the trailer. Stephen pressed against the window again, looking right and left. Nothing. He turned his gaze again to the dancing girl. She wasn't dancing. She had on a t-shirt, and she was staring out of her window, shooting a bird at him. He heard her shout, "Fuck you, Crain."

And then, like a bolt of lightning popping from the sky, he saw him. The man's face was pressed against the outside of the window. His eyes were full of rage, sweat was pouring down his face, and his fists were clenched in anger. It was the tall skinny man. Dressed in all black. Carrying a knife.

"Open this fucking door, you slimy little turd, or I'm gonna break it down!"

CHAPTER NINE

*D*uring their freshmen orientation, which had been held on the Saturday before classes started, the newest arrivals at the university were reminded that they were not allowed to park their cars on campus. "You will receive one warning, and the next time, your car will be towed." Reagan, like many of his fellow freshmen, was certain that this ridiculous rule wouldn't really be enforced. Much to his surprise, however, he had received his warning on day one.

On day two, Reagan, never one to be outsmarted, drove the Orange Bullet into the residential neighborhood just north of the Murphree complex and found a perfect parking spot along NW 3rd Avenue.

On the afternoon of day three, Reagan was standing on the sidewalk adjacent to that perfect spot, studying the red-colored, city-issued traffic ticket for ten dollars, when he heard a chiding voice behind him say, "Don't they teach you young 'uns how to read before sending you off to college these days?"

The gray-haired, fragile-looking woman who had spoken, standing in a flower bed behind a white picket fence, was wearing a floppy straw hat and held a gardening shovel in one gloved hand and a wad of weeds in the other. She was looking at him curiously and pointing up at a sign directly in front of his car that read, "Residential Permit Required."

An embarrassed Reagan turned his attention back to the ticket but saw out of the corner of his eye that his teasing nemesis was laughing under her breath and shaking her head.

"Happens every year. First night, all of you smarty-pants whipper-snappers get your one and only warning on campus, and then thinkin' you've got it all figured out, move your daddy-bought gas-guzzlers into our neighborhood. Cops must've written more than two hundred tickets this morning. That's two thousand dollars into the city's coffers. At least y'all are doing your part to keep our taxes down. Park here as often as you like. That's what I tell 'em."

Reaching down, plucking another weed out of the flower garden, and emptying her collection into a silver bucket, she continued, "I'd tell you what happens every year on the third night, but I don't want to ruin the surprise."

Reagan looked down again at the ticket. *Damn. Ten dollars. And if Mom and Dad find out about this . . .* He turned back to the woman and, hoping to avoid additional humiliation, was about to plead for the third-night details, but she had already returned to her gardening, humming a tune and paying him no further attention.

The home Reagan was standing in front of, where the lady was so hard at work, had a rock facade. Its wraparound porch had been attractively decorated with potted flowers and ornate artwork. The furniture on the porch included a white wicker glass-top table, several wooden rocking chairs, and a swing that hung from the ceiling. Colorful pillows were scattered about, and a sign near the front door read, "Welcome Home."

It was a big house on an oversized lot, and next to it was a gravel parking area. Reagan was guessing that the area could accommodate at least ten cars. There was only one car parked there.

On a post in the garden, next to where Reagan was standing, was a placard that read, "Sally Tindale's Nursing Home." Up on the front porch, in one of the rocking chairs, an elderly man with a white beard was rocking hurriedly back and forth, and watching Reagan with harsh curiosity.

"Excuse me, ma'am, would you like some help weeding?" Reagan asked.

The little woman stood from her chore, stretching her back before saying, "Now why on earth would a young fella like yourself want to help an old lady with her yard work?" Her tone had softened a bit, and a grandmotherly smile along with deep dimples had folded into her face. "Don't you have better things to do with your time?"

Reagan glanced over at the parking area once again before responding, "Oh, I enjoy yard work. At home, in Miami, that is, I took care of our yard, and mowed and edged three of the neighbors' lawns to earn extra money."

"Oh, I can't be payin' you no money. So, if that's what you have in mind, then there ain't no need in getting your hands dirty."

"No, ma'am, it's not that, I just—"

"Well then, I'm not gonna turn down an offer of free help. I only look stupid. Get on in here." The woman pulled the gate open and waved him through, her smile becoming even more pronounced.

Sally Tindale stood belly button-high in front of Reagan, looking straight up at him. "Boy, they sure grow 'em tall in Miami." Her glance drifted down to his arms before she continued, "But they don't put much meat on a fella's bones, now do they?"

Ouch!

The pint-sized lady reached around, removed the extra pair of gloves she had stuffed in her back pocket, and handed them to Reagan along with the bucket. "There's iced tea in that pitcher up there on the porch. With this heat, we will take a break every half hour or so. That man up there in the chair is one of my residents. He's kinda grumpy, but he's loosening up. I actually heard him laugh, for the first time, at the dinner table last night, and that's after he's been with me for over two years." Leaning in now, and whispering, she continued, "We call him Colonel Sanders cuz a how he looks like that chicken-restaurant fella.

"Truth is, he was a New York City police officer. He also spent a lot of time in the army, fought in two wars. He doesn't have much to say 'bout that, but he has lots of them medals and all. Anyway, pay him no mind.

"When we're done, you can move your car into the lot. Yeah, I can see you've been eyein' it. Now, let's get to work."

Sally Tindale quickly turned her attention back to her gardening, humming once again as she bent over to pull out another weed. Using her usual tactics, she had found her yard helper for the year.

Colonel Sanders, having watched it happen the same way for three freshman orientations in a row, was now the one laughing under his breath and shaking his head.

* * *

Friday had finally arrived. The third week of classes had gone by in a flash. Reagan, who had weathered three tests and written four papers, was worn out and ready for the weekend.

The last paper had been optional, but, nonetheless, he had labored late into the night on Wednesday, finishing it up to meet Thursday morning's third-period deadline.

This particular assignment had actually been more like a contest. Reagan, who certainly didn't expect to be the winner, was looking forward to hearing the class's top paper being presented by its author Friday morning. He was secretly hoping that would be Beverly McNamara, the aloof brunette who always sat in the back row of his political science class.

But, first, he had to get to Friday's class. Heidi had paid her second visit to his dorm room that morning, and Reagan was running late. The good news was that he had a fresh bunch of oatmeal cookies in his backpack, and they smelled delicious.

* * *

The previous Monday, Marty Schemer had been as animated as ever. Only, on that particular morning, it wasn't in one of his rants; it was more like he was hosting a party. That weekend, Marty had caught a flight and, along with three of his high school buddies, had attended the Summer Jam at Watkins Glen.

Marty explained in his opening segue that although only 150,000 tickets had been sold, the Jam, which shared some striking similarities to the Woodstock Festival held four years earlier, had been attended by more than 600,000 pot-smoking, whiskey-drinking, out-of-their-mind partiers. "One person out of every 350,000 people in the country was there, with me, listening to the hottest music you can imagine." Marty had trouble containing his excitement.

Because of his excitement, on that Monday morning, the class had arrived to the sound of rock 'n' roll blasting from the record player that Marty had brought in for the purpose of recreating the Summer Jam for his students. First, he played a couple of songs by the Grateful Dead, including "Box of Rain" and "Eyes of the World." Next came the *Rock of Ages* album, with the Band performing "Chest Fever." Before the class was over, the captive audience had heard several songs off of two Allman Brothers albums, including "Whipping Post" and "Statesboro Blues."

While the music was playing, Marty bounced around the room, showing off a dancing flair that could only be described as a combination of jumping jacks with a hula-hoop swivel. He would throw in an occasional head bob and a barefooted karate kick for emphasis.

His enthusiasm was so contagious that several students joined in, each of them offering his or her own fascinating moves. Jackson looked like he was having a hard time staying in his seat, but Reagan was scared to death that someone might ask him to get up and dance.

Between songs, Marty recalled the details of his trip, including how his gang had to park along a dirt road and hike five miles in one-hundred-degree heat to get to the venue. He and his buddies hadn't been able to get close enough to the stage for a good view of the performers but had sat next to one of the huge amplifiers instead and had heard the music just as if they had been up front. He went on and on about all of the "groovy people" they'd met and the great conversations they'd had. "The people, that's what it's all about; that's what makes it all happen."

When the last song was over, and with five minutes left before the bell, Marty paused at the front of the room and appeared to be deep in thought. After a moment, he looked up at the class and, with his first serious facial expression of the day, said, "So, one thing I hope you will take away with you today is that you need to get out there. Experience life. Meet new and interesting people. Get to know them. Hear what they have to say. Listen to their words carefully, and consider their circumstances and perspectives. Decipher those thoughts and learn from them. Classrooms and books can teach you a lot, but life's lessons are better learned in the real world. A nut trapped in its shell can never produce a tree.

"So, to prove what a good mood I'm in, I'm going to give you—one of you, anyway—a gift. And this assignment is optional. Conduct an interview with someone you otherwise would not have routinely met or talked to. I'm not talking about your sister, or your roommate, or the goofy guy who lives in the dorm room down the hall from you. Step out of your comfort zone. Escape from your normal circle.

"Write it all down, including what you've learned from it. And here's the kicker. The best paper, and I will be the sole judge of that, gets a pass, an automatic A, on this class's midterm exam." There was a collective gasp from the room. "Papers due Thursday. The winner will be announced Friday and will get to present his or her paper, front and center."

* * *

That Friday, Reagan walked into his third-period class about two minutes late and saw that Jackson had saved him a seat up front.

After looking down at his roommate's scratched-up hands, Jackson scribbled on his note pad, "You really need to get your own pair of gloves, but the cookies smell great!" Reagan smiled his way and saw Jackson's head-nodding gesture toward the front of the room.

Marty was back in his normal persona and on that day had worked himself into a rage about the Watergate break-in. "If we can't trust our own president, then who the hell can we trust?"

Reagan looked curiously back at Jackson, who was continuing his gesturing motion. That's when Reagan saw them, two words written on the blackboard: "The Twilight."

Oh, my god!

* * *

In the previous couple of weeks, Reagan, time permitting, would do a little yard work each time he dropped his car off at the nursing home: pull a few weeds, rake up some leaves, trim a hedge, or take the mower out of the shed and cut the backyard. He really didn't mind the work, and he loved having a safe place to park his car. When he was there, Sally Tindale would usually come out of the house to chip in and chat.

Reagan learned that the rock house had been in her family for close to ninety years. Both of Sally's parents had passed away peacefully in the home. After her mom died thirty-five years earlier, Sally, being the only child, had inherited the big house along with all of its furnishings.

Sally had been an army nurse in World War II. She and her beloved husband, John, a bomber pilot who was stationed in the South Pacific, had gotten married two weeks after the war ended. They became cattle ranchers, living on a two-hundred-acre tract of land ten miles west of Gainesville, but after John had suffered a minor stroke, managing the herd had become too much for them, so they had sold that property and moved into town.

They'd had ten blissful years together in the old house raising their family, but then, on a cold January night, John suffered another, and this time fatal, stroke. Soon after his death, Sally, not one who enjoyed being alone, started showing signs of depression.

It was Sally's daughter who had suggested that her mom take in a roommate to keep her company. When Sally's best friend from growing up, Betty Clark, started having health issues, Sally invited Betty to come live with her in the rock house. Betty insisted on paying her way, and with that, the Sally Tindale's Nursing Home, now with the proper zoning approval and permits, came into existence. The nursing home had six guest rooms and through the years had accommodated fourteen residents, the latest being the grumpy man on the porch, Colonel Sanders.

* * *

On Wednesday, the day before the interview paper was due in his political science class, Reagan, having finished up his last test for the week, decided to take his car to the self-wash. Although he had no prospects at this point, he was hoping to find a date for Friday night and wanted the Orange Bullet to be at its shiny best.

After racking his brain, Reagan had not been able to find anyone to interview and had pretty much given up on writing a report. Having thrown in the towel, his plan now was to drop the car off at the nursing home, do a little yard work, round up Jackson, and head to the Rat for a pitcher or two.

Reagan was a half of a bucket into his weeding when Sally came out of the front door, pitcher of tea in hand, and explained that she was a little under the weather and wouldn't be helping out today. When Sally went back inside, the Colonel resumed what had become his role as yard work inspector.

For the past couple of weeks, the gray-haired man would, from his perch on the porch, point out a weed missed here, a blade of untrimmed grass there, or part of the sidewalk that needed further sweeping. Reagan would dutifully oblige the man's every demand, but he had to admit to himself that he wasn't comfortable with this military-like oversight. It was taking him out of his comfort zone. *Out of my comfort zone?*

Reagan had put his gear in the shed and was about to start his walk back to campus when he looked once more at the man rocking back and forth on the porch. *The paper is due tomorrow. I don't think I have enough time to write it now, even if the old guy would agree to talk to me. But a pass on the midterm . . . On the other hand, an ice-cold beer right about now would really taste good.*

Reagan was remembering the first, and most important, item on his list, "Cs or better," when he retrieved the notebook and pen out of the back of his car and started toward the porch. "Sir, I'm sorry I've never introduced myself. My name is Reagan Davis. Would you mind if I joined you for a couple of minutes and asked you a few questions? It's for a paper I'm working on in my political science class."

* * *

William Tyler Moore
An American Hero, An American Treasure
William Tyler Moore, Willy to his few friends and acquaintances, spends his waning years rocking in a chair on the front porch of a nursing home not three blocks from our campus. He is a serious man, always has been, and this demeanor has led many to misinterpret his underlying character. One must cut through the crust to find what tenderness lies beneath, and that is exactly what I did on one warm August afternoon.

* * *

Reagan studied Colonel Sanders for any reaction to his request, but the old man was rocking back and forth, looking straight ahead. "Sir," Reagan said, climbing the five steps and now at porch level, "if I could just have a couple of minutes. This paper is very important and . . ."

The man slowly turned his head, and Reagan studied his eyes. The intensity in their stare was fear-provoking, but the sadness behind them offered a welcoming solace. Reagan had taken two more steps toward him when he saw the man's hand loosen its grip from the arm of the chair and offer a reluctant invitation.

Sitting side by side, the two gazed at each other for a moment before Reagan finally broke the ice. "Mrs. Tindale tells me you were in the armed forces. She said you fought overseas and that you have received several medals."

* * *

William Moore was born on a steamy-hot Independence Day, July 4th, 1898, in Brooklyn, New York. His father was the son of Irish immigrants, and his mother was a fiery redheaded country gal from Little Rock, Arkansas. They were a poor but proud family, with William's father walking the street beat in some of the toughest neighborhoods patrolled by New York's finest. His mom operated a maid service and took on sewing projects that would keep her busy, late into the night. Two years younger than him is William's sister, Claire, now his only living relative.

William Moore never got married, never fathered children, never owned a house or a car, and never had a pet. Despite it all, he is not bothered by the things that he doesn't have. He just appreciates the things that he does. At the age of seventy-five, William Moore has accomplished more in his lifetime and contributed more to our country, and our society, than most men could ever dream of.

* * *

"Young man . . . Reagan, I think you said your name is. Interesting name. You are a hard worker, not like the last couple of deadbeats we've had around here, and I admire that. Hard work is the key to stability and happiness. When things seem to be falling apart around you, you can take pride in your willingness to put in a hard day's work. You also treat Mrs. Tindale with kindness and respect, and you have good manners. All of these traits will serve you well in life and open many doors for you that would have otherwise been off limits.

"For these reasons, I will answer your questions. I will help you with this important paper of yours, but in return, before you leave, I will have a favor to ask of you. Now, what is this paper about, and how can I help?"

* * *

On December 7th, 1941, Japan bombed Pearl Harbor. On December 8th, 1941, William Moore, at the age of 43, reenlisted in the United States Army. He was assigned to the Signal Corp and would soon find himself commanding a troop of soldiers, most of them less than half his age, as they stormed Omaha Beach on D-Day. William Moore was at this point serving his country in this, his second world war.

Twenty-seven years earlier, a sixteen-year-old high school dropout and all-around troublemaker had been marched into the Army Recruiting Office in central Manhattan. No words were spoken between father and son, but when they were finished, there were two signatures on the required document. One attested to the fact that William was a willing volunteer, and the other was vouching that he was old enough to be there. At the time, neither declaration had been sincere.

The recruiting officer who signed off on the document had a hunch, but his not challenging either falsehood would usher in one of the bravest fighters, strongest leaders, and, ultimately, highest decorated soldiers the army would ever know. Before his service was over, William Moore would achieve the rank of Lieutenant Colonel and would be awarded the Military Cross, the Distinguished Service Cross, a Purple Heart, and the Medal of Honor.

* * *

After Reagan and William Moore had spent an hour together, William Moore excused himself. When he returned to the porch, he was carrying a wooden cigar box and a scrapbook. They spent the next hour flipping through the book, which contained military communications, newspaper articles, and letters, including one from President Harry Truman, and looking at the medals and other mementos in the box. William Moore, now with a proud smile on his face and an evil giggle to accompany some of his tales, was obviously having a good time sharing his stories. It occurred to Reagan that maybe William Moore wasn't a crabby old man after all, as Mrs. Tindale had described him. Maybe he was just lonely. And possibly the reason he doesn't talk much about his past was because nobody ever asked him about it.

Reagan reached into his pocket, pulled out his watch, and saw that it was 5:00 PM. In an hour, dinner would be served for the residents of the nursing home. He had taken ten pages of notes and felt adrenaline rushing through his veins. He was ready to get to the library, in front of a typewriter, and write his report. But there was one thing he needed to do before he left.

"Lieutenant Moore, I know you will need to be heading in for dinner soon, and you mentioned that there is something that I can do for you to repay you for your kindness." As the lieutenant stared into Reagan's eyes, Reagan made a promise to himself that he would visit with this man every chance he got. He would make every effort to do justice to this hero's story in his paper, and maybe he would include the tales of his accomplishments in a book he hoped to write one day.

"Reagan, I know this might sound a little odd, but I've always wanted to write a poem. I have some ideas in my head, but I need someone to bounce them off of and to help me get them down on paper. If you wouldn't mind, I would be most appreciative. And, by the way, my friends call me Willy."

* * *

The Twilight
By William Tyler Moore
The twilight ushers in a sorrow born from one's misgivings.
Darkness approaches, blurring the sparkle of life's hopes and dreams.
Fear not the waning sun, for its departure will bring, finally bring, an awakening.
An awakening that bares the soul, rests the spirit, and sets the mind at ease.
An ease that you will feel, suddenly feel, finally feel, and feel from now on.
A peace will cover you like a thick blanket on a cold winter's day.
Cherish it. Coddle it. Sit alone on the front porch with it, for it is you:
A long-awaited introduction to you, and everything about you.
Open your eyes. Embrace the light. Enjoy the renewal,
Never forgetting the ever-darkening abyss that somehow exposed the truth.
As dreams fade, the sky clears, welcoming a new knowledge.
A knowledge that with it brings new focus, new hopes, a new vision.
An ending. A beginning.
That together will protect you from and keep you safe in
The Twilight.

* * *

Reagan's face was still bright red when he returned to his seat. His paper had received a standing ovation from the class, and Marty had shouted, "Way to go!" along with his high five.

Jackson was shaking his head and, as he took the cookie Reagan handed him, said teasingly, "I can't believe you and this colonel guy wrote a poem."

Beverly McNamara was waiting outside of the classroom, and as she approached him, Reagan noticed that she had tears in her eyes.

"Reagan, that was a beautiful story. It touched me. Is there someplace we can talk, privately, I mean . . . just the two of us?"

Two hours later, the sign on the door to his dorm room once again read "Open For Business," and the wrappings from two of Reagan's bottom-drawer collection had been disposed of.

Reagan was lying on his bed. His hands were behind his head, and he was staring up at the ceiling when his smiling roommate walked through the door.

Reagan had somehow conquered the freshman curse, but he wasn't feeling liberated. He was in a funk—a mood that one day he would come to understand, and when he did, it would reset his priorities and change his life forever.

CHAPTER TEN

Stephen Crain sat at the picnic table located in the far corner of the courtyard. He had seen them come out of their apartment. He had been at the Tanglewood Apartment Community for over an hour watching them. Watching the mother push her five-year-old son on a swing. Watching as the young boy slid down the slide and crawled on the monkey bars. Watching as they played together on the seesaw.

He knew who they were because the family's last name was on the mailbox, the mailbox that Crain had discovered next to the office, near the front of the complex. Under their name was their apartment number, #316. When he'd driven to the back of the complex looking for apartment #316, he'd spotted it. He'd spotted the tall skinny man's motorcycle in the parking lot.

He knew that the tall skinny man wasn't home. The tall skinny man was at work at the Gainesville Police Department. He knew this because he had called the number and had heard Sergeant Gary Glaser answer the phone. There had been no conversation.

Stephen Crain was here today to deliver a message, and he had every intention of doing so. He had all the proof he would need to convince her, convince the tall skinny man's wife that her husband was cheating on her. Ruin his life. Return the humiliation that the tall skinny man had so viciously inflicted on him.

Stephen Crain thought back to that night, how he had been slapped around, thrown to the ground, and laughed at. How Polaroid pictures had been taken of him as he was lying there, naked and erect. How he was made to agree that no rent would be due for six months, or else.

Stephen Crain watched again as the mother played with her son, kicking the ball now, back and forth, getting very near to where he was sitting.

She was a particularly attractive woman, with a slender body and large, very large, breasts. She had on a cotton dress, and with the sun shining in the distance; he could see that she was wearing nothing underneath it. Stephen Crain was getting extremely excited.

They were moving ever so close, kicking the ball back and forth, back and forth. He watched as the mother kicked the ball once more. She kicked it too hard this time, and it got past the little boy. It kept rolling and rolling, finally coming to rest under the picnic table where Stephen Crain was sitting.

"Hey, mister, do you want to play kickball with me and my mommy?"

Stephen Crain studied the little boy and then looked over at the smiling woman walking his way. "I would love to if it's okay with your mom."

Stephen Crain looked deep into the mother's eyes as the little boy pleaded, "Can we, Mommy? It would be fun. Two against one."

The mother was looking over at the man at the picnic table. He seemed harmless, maybe even a little bit lonely, and Carly Glaser certainly knew what it was like to be lonely.

"Sure we can, honey. Two on one is always fun."

Stephen Crain stood as she approached him to introduce herself. He noticed something that surprised him in her gaze. Tenderness, maybe, but it was more than that. She didn't appear disgusted by his appearance. Her smile even offered a dash of flirtation. Women didn't normally look at him that way.

"My name is Carly Glaser. This is Gary."

"You can call me Junior," the boy said. "That's my nickname. Come on, let's play."

Stephen Crain didn't give them his full name, and he didn't deliver his message. Suddenly, he had another plan.

* * *

Dear Diary,

I only have a few minutes before heading to work, but I haven't written to you in a couple of weeks and wanted to fill you in on some crazy things happening in my life.

I've told you recently about my new attitude. Well, I still have it, and it is wonderful. It's not that I don't still miss Ronnie, I always will, but I can't control the fact that he's gone. The only thing I do have control over is myself, and I might even be losing control of that.

Last Friday, I met Gary in the shopping center parking lot off of University Avenue. It was the middle of the day, and there were people all around. He pulled up next to the Ray in his patrol car and told me to hop in. He was in his uniform, and I was wearing a short dress and nothing else. He was more aggressive than ever. It was so incredibly sexy. I can't stop thinking about it.

Speaking of Gary, I can't decide if I love the guy or hate him. You know, not real love . . . just love. He pissed me off two weeks ago. He was being an ass at our Frisbee ball game and got into a fight with that cute Reagan guy. I've told you about Reagan. Poor kid's got the hots for me so bad it hurts to watch. Gary gave him a big black eye. I felt so sorry for Reagan that I called him the next day and invited him over to the trailer. I will tell you about that visit some other time.

Then, just when I'm about to call it quits with Gary, he comes to my rescue again. Turns out, that worm of a landlord of mine has been spying on me, and we even think he has been coming into my trailer and going through my stuff. Yuck! Gary set a trap for him and caught the slime watching me and beating off in the trailer next door. Gary kicked his ass. I think he might have even pissed on the guy. I don't expect to see that scum around here for a while.

So, I was trying to find a way to thank Gary . . . in addition to the parking lot fun, I mean. I invited him over for dinner this Thursday, and he agreed to skip out on his drinking buddies early that night. I think he will like what I have planned for dessert. I invited Terri Spencer to join us.

Yikes, I'm late. Got to go!

C

* * *

"I can't believe you didn't fuck her. Really, Reagan, I am beginning to wonder about you. I'm starting to think that you're missing Danny Miller, that old roommate of yours, if you know what I mean."

"Jesus Christ, Jake, shut the hell up. Someone's gonna hear you. I wish I had never told you about it."

Reagan pulled back the curtain from his shower stall and looked under the toilet doors, making sure that no one else was in the bathroom with them.

Jake Johnson was the acknowledged clown of Murphree E. Everything was a joke to him, but even when someone found themself the brunt of Jake's weird sense of humor, they couldn't help but enjoy Jake's goofy demeanor.

Jake was tall and lanky and always had a smile on his face. He had been born and raised in Nashville, Tennessee, but he had somehow escaped the allure of Vanderbilt University and the University of Tennessee and had made his way south to the University of Florida.

Jake's fun-loving attitude had made him instantly popular with the residents of the Murphree complex, both boys and girls, and Reagan often wondered how Jake's three-box supply was holding up.

"I mean, the girl did everything but wear a white shirt with a giant fat black arrow pointing down to where she wanted you to go."

With no one else in the bathroom as the two of them finished their showers, Reagan decided to let Jake talk himself out. Better to let him vent now, rather than later when someone else might hear him.

"So, let me get this straight. She calls you on Sunday morning all worried about your black eye . . . rrrright!

"By the way, she has a very sexy voice. The next time she calls and I answer the phone, I'm gonna invite myself over to her little love nest.

"Anyway, she insists that you come over to her place that afternoon so that she can take a look at your boo-boo and play nursemaid. I'm guessing that the only eye she wanted to nurse was the one in your pants.

"So you get there, and she's wearing nothing but a t-shirt. This beautiful blonde invites you into her trailer, and she doesn't even mention your black eye. She lights up a joint, which, Reagan, I'm sure you just pretended to inhale, and you both had a couple of beers.

"After a while, she says she's a little sleepy and asks you if you want to take a nap. She goes over and lies down on her bed, moving to one side so that there is plenty of room for you to crawl in next to her. But do you follow her lead? Nooooo! You hit the panic button, get up, say good-bye, and haul ass back to campus. Holy shit, dude, I'm honestly starting to wonder about you."

"It wasn't like that, Jake." Reagan was toweling off and moving toward the sink to shave. "She's more like a friend. I mean, more like a big sister. And she has absolutely no interest in me. Besides, I think she might just be a virgin."

Jake had finished up his shower and was standing naked behind Reagan, who was lathering shaving cream on his face. Reagan glanced in the mirror and saw Jake's exaggerated smirk.

The lanky kid from Tennessee had absolutely no muscle on his chicken-bone body. His carrot-colored curly hair, which matted him from head to toe, looked like an orange Brillo pad against his cotton-white skin. Other than the one attribute that Reagan wished he hadn't noticed in the mirror, Jake had no redeeming physical appeal whatsoever.

Reagan realized at that moment that it was Jake's fun-loving and outgoing personality that more than made up for his lack of desirability, a trait that Reagan wished he himself had more of.

"A virgin? Have you lost your mind? You told me yourself that she had been living with a fly-boy for several months. Those types don't just invite hot babes to move in with them to play cards and tiddlywinks. Reagan, you've got your head so far up your ass that you're gonna cut your colon with that razor of yours."

Reagan secured his towel, opened the bathroom door, and headed toward his room, where his roommate was still passed out, recovering from a late-night date. He had decided that defending himself to Jake was a waste of time for a couple of reasons, not the least of which was that Jake's assessment was dead on. He was pretty sure that Charley wasn't a virgin, and he also knew that he could have had her right there, in her trailer, in the middle of the day.

But he did consider her a friend, and how would that change if they had sex? On the other hand, she was the most beautiful girl he had ever laid his eyes on. Would he be kicking himself for the rest of his life for his panic attack and quick exit? What was she thinking about him now? Would she ever give him a second chance? Whatever happened to getting just a kiss on the first date?

As Reagan quietly got dressed, he decided to wipe the entire incident from his mind. With midterms not too far around the corner, he was looking forward to spending his afternoon with Molly Turner, hitting the books in her dorm's study hall.

Reagan was also excited about what the two of them had planned for afterward. Molly had been bragging about her family's famous lasagna recipe. She told him that her mom was a second-generation immigrant from Sicily, where their family had owned restaurants for several generations.

It had gotten close to begging, but Reagan had finally convinced Molly to prove it, and she was preparing the dish for them to enjoy that evening after they finished studying. *A home-cooked meal. Wow!* Molly had asked Reagan to bring the wine and a large appetite.

They ate in the kitchen on the top floor of Graham Hall. Molly had placed a red-and-white-checkered cloth on the table, and on top of it, two candles were burning. Molly's dorm room was next to the kitchen, and with her door open, they could hear the soft Italian music that was coming from her record player.

Sure, he considered Charley a friend, but Molly was a true friend. They had gotten close in just a few weeks, and Reagan really enjoyed spending time with her. With their platonic relationship agreed to, and with the understanding that Molly already had a steady boyfriend, any of the normal boy/girl pressures were out the window.

There would be no debate at the table that night. No one would storm out of the room crying. The conversation quietly lingered as they slowly finished the second bottle of red wine. The meal had been unbelievably delicious.

Reagan was in deep thought as he made his was back to his dorm room on that warm starlit night. *What a fabulous evening. Maybe the best one I've ever had.*

* * *

It was the third tall boy of Old Milwaukee that really loosened her up. They had played two-on-one kickball for about an hour before Junior, having won every game, got bored and wanted to go inside to watch the afternoon cartoons. Carly Glaser asked Stephen to wait a minute. After getting her son settled in, she came back out of the apartment with two beers in her hand and a question in her eyes. The answer was yes, he would love a beer, and they sat down at the picnic table and popped the tops in unison. Stephen Crain wasn't sure what was going on, but he was not about to do anything to ruin the moment or let anything get in the way of his plan.

His plan was coming together quickly, and one day soon, it would all happen. He couldn't imagine a more humiliating moment, the tall skinny man walking through the door, home from work early for a change. The little boy would be gone, off visiting a friend. The tall skinny man would call her name, looking past the empty living room and kitchen to the cracked bedroom door, sounds of sexual satisfaction filling the room. At that moment, that fabulous moment, the tall skinny man's rage would become uncontrollable.

When he burst through the door, the tall skinny man would see his wife on top, sweat pouring from her face, passion and pleasure in her eyes, finishing up what had been hours of lovemaking, hours spent with him, Stephen Crain, in their bed. The tall skinny man would lunge toward him, not expecting the surprise, the rifle, Stephen's uncle's rifle, loaded and ready. He would use it if he had to, kill the man who had disgraced him. Kill her, too, if he needed to. He wouldn't get caught. He never got caught.

Yes, it was the third tall boy that really loosened her up. Up to that point, their conversation had been mostly casual and introductory. He had not had to talk much. The poor woman was starving for adult attention. He had explained that he was the owner of the Shady Oaks Mobile Home Community. She knew exactly where it was and had read about his aunt and uncle's tragic accident. She reached across and put her hand on his as she offered her condolences, their first touch. Stephen Crain was glad that his excitement was hidden under the table.

After returning with their third beer, she started to talk about her life with Sergeant Gary Glaser. The couple had met at a fundraiser, which the Gainesville Police Department held annually for their women's auxiliary. That year it had been held at the posh University Club.

Her father, the chief of police, had actually been the one who introduced her to the newly hired police officer with "unlimited potential." Gary Glaser was a charmer, for sure, and after their fourth glass of champagne, he asked Carly if she would like to see the magnificent view of the city from the roof of the Seagle Building that housed the University Club.

Gary had been correct. The view was unbelievable. He lit a joint, and they sat on a stoop to watch the sunset. "It was so romantic, and I don't know what came over me, but I did everything he asked of me, demanded of me, actually. It wasn't like that, though. I have to admit I enjoyed it, all of it, all two hours of it. He hasn't done that to me in such a long time."

Yes, it was the third tall boy that really loosened her up.

Four months later, with her father standing sternly beside her, Carly would become Mrs. Gary Glaser in front of the Justice of the Peace. Several months after that, Gary Junior was born. "My pride and joy, the only thing that keeps me going in this world. If it wasn't for that little boy, I would divorce the bastard. I don't care what Daddy says. Would you like another beer?"

As she got up and went inside, Stephen Crain sat in shock. His knees were trembling from excitement. This was all too easy. Nothing in his life had ever been this easy. If it wasn't for the kid inside, he would take her. Take her right now, in that bed, the bed where the tall skinny man slept. *But the kid is here, and I need take advantage of this moment now!*

Stephen Crain, deep in thought, pretended to listen but barely heard the words coming out of Carly's mouth while they sat there for another hour, sipping their beer. He was jolted back into the moment when he felt her foot, under the table, rubbing against his foot, then his calf, and then between his thighs. *I have to make my move now!*

"Would you like to come over to the Shady Oaks sometime? I can show you around the big house, and we can drink a couple of beers. I have some great pot, homegrown right here in Gainesville."

Carly paused for a moment, appearing to regain her sober composure. She was looking his way, but not at him. It was more like she was looking through him. Looking for something, anything. Stephen Crain was terrified. Had he gone too far too fast?

"I would love to."

Stephen looked again into her eyes, such sad eyes, now staring back at him, looking longingly at him. "How does Thursday work? Around seven? That's Gary's night out with the boys. I can get a sitter for Junior."

* * *

The approaching thunderstorm had darkened the afternoon sky. The pressure-drawn winds whipped through the trees, causing their limbs to snap back and forth in a violent dance. The temperature had suddenly dropped from its normal mid-nineties to low enough that there was actually a slight chill in the air. This chill, along with the chill running through his veins, caused one of the two men to reach into the back of the official-looking vehicle and retrieve his jacket.

They paused for a moment outside of the house, facing each other and rehearsing their spiel for the third time that day. Each was trying to gain strength and composure from the other's presence. It didn't work. It never worked. No matter how many times they performed this task, it didn't get any easier. They had agreed earlier in the day that it was actually getting harder, almost unbearable.

They covered the entire state of Florida. In recent years when things had been hot and heavy, there had been five teams just like theirs. Now they were the only ones left. With each walk toward a home, with each knock on a door, with each look in the eyes of the mother or father at the moment of dread, they would lose another part of their souls, their hearts, their spirits, gone forever.

Rita Mae had been in her kitchen singing and cooking all day. The annual revival at her church, the First Baptist Church of Gainesville, would start the following morning, and from the look of her bulging icebox, the participants were going to be well fed. She had not slept well the night before. She had awakened suddenly at three in the morning and had not been able to get back to sleep. Over coffee, she convinced herself that it was just an old-lady thing, and besides, it would be good to get an early start on her chores.

Heidi barked, but only twice. The two men had climbed the rickety stairs in unison, and the man wearing the jacket knocked on the screen door, which rattled. Hearing the ruckus, the happy cook turned toward the door only to see Heidi cowering back in her corner. Rita Mae's gaze rested on the men standing in her doorway. Time froze. It couldn't be. There had to be some sort of mistake.

Her ladle fell out of her hands and onto the floor. She quickly followed it, down on her knees, praying, sobbing.

The facts surrounding Tyrone Miller's death dribbled into the community over the next two weeks. At first, all they were told was the he had died in a non-combat-related incident. Then it was reported that there had been some sort of fight in a bar. Somebody said that they had heard that Tyrone had been ganged up on.

Once all of the details of Tyrone's murder finally reached Rita Mae, her family of friends, and their surrounding neighborhood, the small town of Gainesville, Florida, would become an internationally monitored hotspot.

CHAPTER ELEVEN

*T*he sun pierced the southeastern skyline, illuminating Paynes Prairie, a 21,000-acre marshland just south of Gainesville, at precisely 5:53 AM on Saturday, September 15, 1973. To the occupants of this vast swamp-bowl, this day would be like any other: the search for food, the effort not to become food, the pursuit of a mate in an attempt to satisfy the inborn yearning to participate in the reproductive process, just another day in the swamp.

At some levels in the evolutionary chain, certain species will take comfort in the bond created by the close association with their own kind. They might even be willing to protect these companions, to a degree, from outside adversaries wishing them harm.

There of course could be an occasional frolic or other playful moment between members of the clan. Maybe a fight would break out, brought on by the selection of, or challenging the longevity of, the pack's leader. But, for the most part, in this marshy bowl, things move slowly, change is almost undetectable.

But even the serenity and predictability of this swamp, along with that of thousands and thousands of swamps just like it, can be thrown into chaos, unsettled by outside forces or unforeseen occurrences. A fire, too much or not enough rain, a disruption caused by elements surrounding its boundaries, the introduction of unharmonious species to its delicate ecosystem, all of these factors and many more unwelcome outside pressures can upset the gentle balance of the swamp's everyday life.

Paynes Prairie itself had a history of radical change brought on by factors the swamp had no control over and could never fully recover from: encroachment from all sides, storm-water and waste-water runoff, and the introduction of exotic species.

In the late 1880s, the swamp's drainage became so blocked that for fifteen years it flooded and became Alachua Lake. Steamboats operating daily as shuttles carried tourists and other travelers across the lake, to and from their destinations.

And then, because of an occurrence brought on by an unanticipated phenomenon, the prairie had suddenly reappeared, sending the steamboats back to the Mississippi River from where they had originally arrived.

But it wasn't a drought or evaporation facilitated by the summer sun that had resulted in the lake's demise. No one dug a ditch or a canal and intentionally drained it.

It was the sinkholes that opened up underneath its bottom and sucked its water into the Florida aquifer, draining the lake and taking with it many of the species that had woken up, hours earlier, to a beautiful sunrise, believing that that day would be just like any other day.

On this particular Saturday, September 15, 1973, in the swamp-bowl called Gainesville, Florida, not unlike many other swamp-bowls just like it across the nation, change was no longer occurring slowly. This day would not be like any other day, and tomorrow would be altogether different. The pressures from unforeseen occurrences had this particular ecosystem in a tailspin, and those who had piloted the plane in the past were no longer trusted. For the younger generation, the ground had just been sucked out from under their feet, and they were all scattering, in a million different directions, trying to find their own place to land.

* * *

On-campus orgy parties had suddenly become commonplace, and if one was well connected, he or she, especially she, could find oneself invited to at least one of these lurid gatherings almost every night of the week. Some blatant party throwers had even started advertising them on the bulletin boards that were scattered throughout the university's dormitory complexes.

Reagan, books in hand, on his way to the plaza, was reading one of these ads between sips from a water fountain:

Strip and Dip
Friday Night
Thomas Hall E - Top Floor
BYOB & P

The most popular complex for these parties had been Senior Towers. It had the most generous co-ed visitation hours, and in the Towers, even these limitations were rarely enforced.

Jackson, who was trying out for the university's track team, had received a personal invitation to one of these parties from a senior member of the team's female 4x400-meter relay squad. The theme of that party had been "blind love," and every guest had received a mask at the door before stepping inside.

Reagan gulped down one more sip of water and while continuing on his way, thought back to the recap of this party that Jackson had given to a spellbound group of his buddies over a beer the previous evening.

"So, first off, I couldn't decide what to wear. I mean it sounds crazy, but what do you wear to a party where you know you're not going to be wearing anything? Do you know what I mean?

"I get off the elevator on the top floor, and I hate elevators, they scare the pants off of me. That, of course, would help me with what happens next. I'm greeted at the door by two of the hottest girls on campus, and they are in the buff. I mean nothing on except those funny-looking masks with eye-holes, you know, like the Lone Ranger wears.

"First, they take my clothes off. By the way, I wore jeans and a t-shirt. Then they fold them for me and put them in a row on the floor in the hall-way. They put a mask on me and hand me a flashcard with the number twenty-three written in blue ink. One of the girls whispers in my ear that if I can find the matching card inside with twenty-three written in pink, I will win some sort of prize.

"So, picture this: Here I am, walking into this crowded room with nothing but a six-pack of beer to cover my . . . well, you know. Then, as I turn the corner toward the kitchen, this girl, who I'm sure I've never seen before, comes running over, smiling from ear to ear, and bouncing up and down with excitement. She is gorgeous, and she is carrying the matching card. She starts kissing me and rubbing all over me. It was pretty wild, I gotta tell you, but that's when things started going downhill.

"First, someone grabbed the six-pack from my hand and told me that they were going to put it in the cooler. I never saw it again. Then, Lilly, at least that's what she said her name was, and I were trying to find a place to . . . well, you know.

"We went into all four bedrooms, the living room, and we even walked out onto the balcony. It was wall-to-wall naked people. You couldn't help but rub up against them, men and women. And no one seemed to care, but it was starting to creep me out. It was dark with just a few candles lit, and the whole place reeked of pot and incense. There was white powder on the table and pills of all sorts in a bowl. There was some crazy-looking guy in the corner, and he was really starting to freak out.

"So, anyway, Lilly and I couldn't even find a place to sit down. People were going at it two, three, four at a time. I mean, I saw one bed where there were at least ten people rolling around on top of each other.

"I excused myself for a second to go find my beer, and when I came back, Lilly had found a spot on the couch. The problem was that when I looked over at her, I could see that she was sitting there making out with two other guys. That was all I needed to see. I couldn't get out of there fast enough, back to the dorm, into the shower. I think I will stick to one-on-one from now on, if you know what I mean."

Walking along, Reagan shook his head at the memory of Jackson's tale. He paused at the corner to let a few cars go by, including a Gainesville Police Department cruiser, a rare sighting on campus, before crossing the street and taking the shortcut behind the Chemistry Building. He wasn't exactly sure how many of the rules his parents had laid out would be broken, or how many items on his own list would be compromised, but he had already decided not to participate in any of the campus's orgy parties.

But a date or two now and then would be nice. He reminded himself, *Reagan, to get a date, one has to actually ask a girl out—something you haven't exactly done yet.*

Reagan was still kicking himself at that thought when he looked up and saw Terri Spencer, Ye, and Yang sitting in the center of the Plaza. Ye spotted Reagan at the same moment and came running across the lawn, turning cartwheels, and jumping up and down with delight. She stopped three feet in front of him and, now with a serious look on her face, said, "Mister Reagan, thank you for coming to help us with our mathematics."

* * *

Like most colleges and universities throughout the country, athletics had become a significant part of everyday life at the University of Florida. Proper fitness levels and healthy eating habits were increasingly popular, brought on not only by government-sponsored national advertising campaigns but also by this generation's desire to look and feel its best. Taking care of oneself was something their parents hadn't done, so it must be the right thing to do.

Jogging had turned into a favorite pastime, and books about it were filling the bookstore shelves. Jim Fixx would soon become every jogger's hero, and on any given day in Gainesville, one might spot Frank Shorter running the streets, training for his next marathon.

Intramural sports competition was very popular, with teams being organized in the dorms, fraternities, and sorority houses. Football, basketball, handball, racquetball, soccer, tennis, volleyball, swimming, track, you name it, and it was happening all around campus.

Another favorite pastime, of course, was following the university's varsity sports programs, especially the football team. Florida was an up-and-coming member of the up-and-coming Southeastern Conference. The school's football players were idolized on campus, and, as would be expected, they were always the first to get dates with the prettiest girls. One such fellow was Anthony "the Moose" Mosul. The sound of his bellowing voice coming from the distance stopped Reagan and Ye in their tracks as they were crossing the plaza lawn.

"Yo! Yo! Everybody listen up. Who's the fastest beer drinker this side of the Mississippi? I think it's Ray-guns Davis. Come one, come all, to see this man in action."

Reagan turned to see the Moose in full stride, heading their way. He was flanked by three of his teammates, and they were all wearing their varsity jerseys. The Moose wore #74. He was the team's starting right offensive guard, and he was a mountain of a man with a heart of gold.

Reagan had described Anthony Mosul to his father when he had called home a couple of days earlier. "Dad, the guy is as big as a house. He must outweigh me by over a hundred pounds, but he is a gentle giant, the nicest guy you would ever want to meet.

"He must have some sort of switch he turns on and off. I walked over and watched the Gators practice the other day, and Anthony was knocking guys around like they were sticks. When he wasn't in the scrimmage, he'd pace back and forth on the sideline, looking like a madman with steam coming out of his ears.

"On one play, he missed his block, and the coach sent him off to run a lap, you know, as punishment. On his way back around, he took on a two-man practice dummy all by himself. He drove the thing from one side of the field to the other and then sent it tumbling, flipping it completely upside down. It took four trainers to get the thing turned upright again. I'm telling you the guy has a switch of some sort.

"Lately, he has really taken me under his wing. He is always at the Hog, playing pinball. If I do pledge Sigma Chi, I'm thinking about asking Anthony if he will be my big brother."

Signing off, Reagan had continued; "Anyway, Dad, I've got to go. Say hi to Mom and Sis for me, and, no, I don't need any supplies yet." His dad hadn't been able to completely hide the disappointment in his voice while saying good-bye to his son.

By the time the Moose and his entourage reached them, Reagan and Ye had been joined by Terri and Yang. Introductions were made, and the Moose, whose theatrics were unparalleled, went into a descriptive recap of the now famous beer-guzzling contest and the night the Sigs had dethroned the Delts.

"So, I walked into the Hog just in time to see the flag drop, and there's my little buddy here, in my seat, the anchor seat."

Under normal circumstances, Reagan might have been offended by being called someone's little buddy. The truth was, however, that he was the Moose's little buddy, so he was in no way bothered by the distinction.

"Some asshole cop held me up for over an hour, or I would have been there myself. But if I had been there, we might not have ever discovered the champ here. Anyway, it's about to end in a tie when his number is called, and Reagan here lets the chump across from him get halfway through his pitcher. Then with a smile wider than the Grand Canyon, he exhales and slams one back like I've never seen before.

"Sent the Delts home with their tails between their legs. The good news is that most of their girls stayed at the Hog with us, and did we have a party? How about it, Reagan? I bet you got a few phone numbers that night!"

While the Moose continued his tale, Reagan looked around at his study partners for the day. Yang had stopped two steps behind them with a terrified look on his face. Terri, who was obviously smitten with all of them, was trying to get noticed by at least one of the players, and when she finally locked in on the Moose, she gave him one of her best *please ask me out* looks.

Ye was standing there, belly button-high to Anthony and staring straight up at him. She hadn't moved an inch since the introductions were made, and she appeared to be in complete shock. She looked as if she had rounded a corner and stumbled onto an alien army sent to destroy the universe.

*   *   *

This was the second Saturday in a row that their Frisbee ball game had been rained out. Terri, who had taken on the role of the group's coordinator, had called Reagan early that morning to let him know the game had been canceled again. Her second call to him that day came later in the afternoon when the weather had cleared up.

On that second call she had explained that Ye and Yang were doing very well with their English assignments but were having fits with math, a subject that Terri was herself having trouble with. Reagan didn't think twice about volunteering to help, and it wasn't even the memory of Terri's vice-grip clamp on his balls that had persuaded him. He liked Ye and Yang very much, and the more he got to know Terri, the more he admired her, especially her willingness to tutor their Chinese friends.

* * *

Terri Spencer, an only child, had been born into a wealthy Gainesville family and had grown up in a big house on NW 22nd Street, just a few blocks from Florida's campus. Her dad, an outdoorsman and a good-ol'-boy building contractor, had always wanted a son. He dreamed of taking his boy fishing and hunting. He couldn't wait to have a partner to play golf and racquetball with. And, of course, as the little fella got older, he would have a buddy to drink beer with. They would watch sports together. He would have someone to confide in, talk guy stuff with, and share father-and-son secrets with.

Terri's dad had to admit, however, that he was a little jealous of his older brother, who, after five boys, had finally fathered a little girl. The newest member of that family would quickly become his brother's "little charmer" and the apple in his brother's eye.

Terri's dad couldn't have been happier when his turn finally arrived. Terri Lynn Spencer was brought home from the hospital on May 19, 1953. Her mother came home two days later following a post-delivery procedure. It seemed like the bond that was formed in those two days between Terri and her father would last them a lifetime. In time, she would fulfill each of her father's dreams. She would become both his "son" and the apple of his eye.

Terri was a tomboy from day one. Her nickname, "the Bruiser," which was given to her while she was still in diapers, stuck with her all through her high school days. She lettered in four varsity sports and received scholarship offers nationwide, but Terri was a Gator, and she wasn't going any place else.

When their place-kicker went down with an injury in her senior year of high school, the men's head football coach had snuck her, uniform and all, onto the field, where she had kicked the winning field goal, a forty-two-yarder with five seconds left, to win the regionals. Terri Spencer wasn't afraid of anyone or anything, and she protected her turf.

From an early age, her relationship with her dad had been more of a friendship than the type of bond one would typically expect between a father and his daughter. He never kept secrets from her, but she would always keep his secrets to herself. Her dad was a free spirit and lived life to its fullest.

She was told of the affairs he was having while he was having them, and knowing her mother's prudish nature, Terri didn't necessarily disapprove of her father's emotionless indiscretions. She was always welcomed along on men-only camping trips, gambling junkets, and even some of their boys' nights out.

Her dad told her all about his business dealings, even if they were shady, like the time he had paid cash for a travel trailer and then had given it to a man from the county in exchange for favorable permit approvals.

For his part, Terri's father always showered her with anything and everything she could possibly want. Only the best for his little bruiser: clothes, sports equipment, and vacations, and he even built her a big screened-in swimming pool in the backyard when she asked for it. In his eyes, nothing was too good for his best friend, and Terri genuinely appreciated her dad's generosity.

Dad's latest surprise had been a canary-yellow Pontiac GTO. Reagan was sitting in the shotgun seat, admiring the car's sporty interior, when Terri, nuzzled proudly behind the wheel, fired her up. Ye and Yang were in the backseat giggling and tickling each other. Following their three-hour study session, the friends were on their way to the Hog for a beer and then off to Terri's "favorite spot in the world" to watch the sunset.

* * *

With the hottest part of the day behind them, the sunset brought with it a gradual hush, slowly blanketing the inhabitants of the Paynes Prairie swamp-bowl. Some of the swamp's inhabitants had survived the day, some of them had not. The nighttime and its welcomed darkness would allow the survivors time to regroup and rest up for what would be another day—another day just like every other day in the swamp.

To the four friends who had walked along the railroad tracks and then hiked a trail to the prairie's boundary, the next few minutes would be breathtaking and, for at least one of them, remembered forever.

As they stood there taking in as much beauty as their eyes could absorb, they were unaware that the marsh's splendor concealed a turmoil stirring within its belly. Nothing on the surface even suggested the turbulent activities underneath. One must be in the mix to truly understand what is going on around them, but to get into the mix, one must be willing to dive into the bowl.

The four stood there hand-in-hand until the sun was completely gone, and its aftermath faded into darkness. The moon was soon fully up, and stars filled the sky. The swamp was still and silent. Reagan turned to Ye as she offered a prayer, spoken with perfection.

"It is just beautiful, Mister Reagan, isn't it? Don't you hope that it will always be just this beautiful?"

CHAPTER TWELVE

*I*t was Wednesday afternoon, and Reagan was lying on his bed in his dorm room, trying to build up the courage to do it.

He hadn't seen Jackson for two days and didn't expect to see him anytime soon. The mysterious note that his roommate had left for him simply read, "Reagan, I'll be at my dad's for a couple of days. Bad things are about to happen. Do not come into our neighborhood! If Heidi shows up, call me, and I'll come and get her. I'll explain everything the next time I see you. Please watch after my things for me while I'm gone." Reagan had tried to call Jackson at his father's home three times since reading the note, but there had been no answer.

With Jackson gone for a while, Reagan had the room all to himself, and he was determined to get a date for the coming weekend. He'd gone through his list of phone numbers and had made six calls. With sorority pledge retreats in full swing, all of the girls he had phoned were tied up one way or another. They all seemed genuinely glad to hear from him, but he still didn't have a date. Then it hit him. *Sherri Miles works at the Rat on Wednesdays.*

Since standing her up, as she had so harshly put it, Reagan had made an effort to get back into her good graces each time he'd been back to the Rat. First, he simply delivered a note apologizing and explaining that a friend in need had dropped by unexpectedly. That went nowhere. Next, he brought Sherri a vase full of wildflowers that Sally Tindale had helped him pick and arrange. That effort had been awarded with a closed-mouth grin and an icy thank-you.

When the box of chocolate-covered cherries he had handed her the previous Friday night resulted in a *stop trying so hard* look, Reagan was about to throw in the towel. Shortly there after, however, when Sherri delivered a pitcher of beer to his table, Reagan, from the corner of his eye, detected a brief reappearance of that killer smile and sparky attitude.

The truth was, despite his previous blunder, Sherri thought his attempts at reconciliation had been quite cute. She still wanted to go out with him, and she had already decided to accept his apology. Nonetheless, she was not going to give in easily. She was going to make him work extra hard for it this time.

But Reagan didn't know any of this, and an hour later, he still lying in his room trying to build up the courage to do it.

* * *

Jamal Spikes had posted lookouts at the outer boundary of each of the eight roads leading into his neighborhood, and his instructions had been very clear. There would be no violence until after the memorial service this coming Saturday. In the meantime, outsiders would be discouraged from entering the area, even if they were just passing through. For the time being, Jamal only wanted to know who was in the 'hood and what they were doing there.

His guards, who were all wearing blue jeans, sunglasses, and leather jackets, were riding bicycles and carrying baseball bats. They quickly got the attention of not only the passersby but also the police chief, who had subsequently ordered twenty-four-hour patrols of the neighborhood. Sergeant Gary Glaser had been put in charge of the operation and was instructed to report any unrest, night or day, to the chief personally. Things were at a boiling point, and the article that had run in the *Gainesville Sun* that same day hadn't helped matters.

Local hero dies in a barroom brawl
Three arrested and released

United States Army Sergeant Tyrone Devon Miller, a Gainesville native and local high school sports hero, was pronounced dead early Monday morning, September 17th, in Heidelberg, Germany. The details of Sergeant Miller's death are still under investigation by the Navy's internal affairs unit; however, the Sun has learned, through a reliable Heidelberg affiliate, that he died as the result of injuries suffered in a barroom brawl.

According to eyewitnesses, Sergeant Miller had been dancing and shooting pool with an off-duty female bartender when three United States Navy pilots entered the bar. The pilots, along with the female bartender, are white. Sergeant Miller was black. A verbal and then physical altercation broke out, with the fight reportedly spilling

out onto the street before Sergeant Miller was finally overpowered and, subsequently, suffered life-ending injuries.

The three Navy pilots were arrested but have since been released. The Sun has been unable to determine if the three men will be facing any further charges related to this incident. Our attempts to contact the Navy spokesman assigned to this investigation have been unsuccessful.

A local Gainesville military source told the Sun that bar fights, similar to the one ending Sergeant Miller's life, have become all too commonplace with our nation's troops overseas. He noted that very few of these altercations result in significant disciplinary action because it is oftentimes impossible to assign blame or gather evidence that will hold up in a court-martial proceeding.

Sergeant Miller, who was twenty-four years old at the time of his death, is best remembered locally for his achievements on the grid-iron. As Gainesville High School's starting fullback in the late 1960s, he holds that school's rushing records for total yardage and points scored. He will also be remembered for his work with local youth groups. Sergeant Miller briefly attended the University of Florida before enlisting in the Army.

Sergeant Miller is survived by his mother, Rita Mae Miller, of Gainesville. Memorial services will be held at the First Baptist Church of Gainesville this coming Saturday at 6:00 PM. The service will be open to the public.

* * *

Carly Glaser's best friend, and the only friend she confided in, was Maria Sanchez. Maria, a full-figured Cuban-born emergency room nurse, worked the day shift at Alachua General Hospital. She was not at all ashamed of her body and delighted in showing off her ample curves. She would always wear tight, revealing dresses and loved it when men would stop what they were doing and watch her saunter by.

Maria, who was in her mid-thirties, lived in a second-floor apartment at the opposite side of the Tanglewood complex from the Glasers. She had never been married and didn't seem interested, at least as far as Carly could tell, in getting tied down to any one man. Maria was outgoing, fun-loving, and appeared, on the surface, anyway, to be enjoying life to its fullest.

The girlfriends had never really discussed the details of their love lives until a couple of days earlier, when after too many beers, Maria let it slip out that she was seeing a married man.

Obviously embarrassed by her disclosure, she quickly tried to back-track, explaining that this man's visits were sporadic and that he would come over for one reason, and one reason only. "I'm not trying to steal him from his wife. He just gives me what I need. Afterward, we drink a beer, and then he leaves. There's really nothing more to it than that. I know I should call it off before I get us both in trouble and somebody gets hurt, but I just can't. I like things just the way they are."

Carly had gone to her friend's house on this day to ask Maria if she would watch Junior the next day, Thursday, for a couple of hours. Carly had no intention of telling Maria the truth about where she was going, or what she planned on doing once she got there, but, once again, after a couple of beers, their conversation loosened up, and this time it was Carly who let her guard down.

Although Maria did agree to babysit, she didn't like what she was hearing. Carly told her that she and Gary hadn't had sex in over a year. She went on to say that they very seldom talked, unless it was about Junior, or "the damn police department." "All Gary does, on the rare occasion that he is at home, is drink beer, smoke cigarettes, and watch sports on the TV."

The revelation, however, that concerned Maria the most was when Carly told her that she suspected Gary was cheating. "He always stays out late, comes home drunk, and smells of . . . well, you know, sex!"

Carly went on to say that the man she was going to see the following day, although not at all attractive, at least paid attention to her. "He even told me how pretty I am. Those are words I haven't heard in such a long time."

Maria was beside herself. She wasn't sure exactly what she should do. She didn't like seeing her best friend suffer like this. She didn't want to see Carly make a huge mistake and do something that she would regret forever. And she certainly didn't want to see this whole mess come between Carly and Gary, causing them to divorce, a move that would almost certainly result in Gary's moving out of the apartment complex. After that, Maria reasoned, he would be in the complex only on rare occasions to visit his son, making certain other things so inconvenient.

Maria needed to come up with a way to fix this, not only to help her best friend and possibly save the marriage, but also because Maria liked things just the way they were.

* * *

The sea breezes from the Gulf of Mexico and the Atlantic Ocean were converging over Gainesville, bringing about nightfall earlier than expected and promising a powerful thunderstorm. Under Jamal Spikes' mandate, the neighborhood north of University Avenue and east of NW 13th Street was quiet, maybe even too quiet. That was not the case in other neighborhoods throughout the city.

In an otherwise orderly neighborhood east of Williston Road, there had been reports of gunfire, and the fire department had responded to three fires within a six-hour period. The causes of the blazes had been reported as suspicious, and one of them had destroyed an entire wing of the local elementary school.

The police department had been monitoring large gatherings of black youths in the downtown area, and two carjackings had been reported in the commercial district just east of the interstate. The chief had ordered "all hands on deck," which meant that even if they were off-duty, his entire staff needed to be reachable and ready to respond immediately to a call.

With Tyrone Miller's memorial service still three days away, there was even talk of asking the governor to deploy the National Guard unit stationed in nearby Jacksonville.

Well-known members of the community, both white and black, including politicians, religious leaders, and law enforcement officials, were urging the citizens of Gainesville to remain calm and peaceful. Not one of them believed for a second that their words would be effective, and everyone was bracing for the worst.

On campus, at the University of Florida, very few undergraduates, including Reagan Davis, had read the morning paper. There was no talk of Tyrone Miller's death, and virtually no one knew of the surrounding unrest. As far as these students could tell, it was just another day of studying, socializing, athletics, and, of course, getting ready for their next party. To them, the neighborhood just northeast of campus, and its problems, was a million miles away.

It was for this reason that the sight of a young man carrying two suitcases, wearing a book bag, and hurriedly leaving Murphree E in the pouring rain was a surprise to Reagan. It stopped Reagan in his tracks, and the shock of it caused him to delay his questions for a second or two. He was hoping first to develop his own theory. The circumstance had Reagan wishing and hoping that what he was watching wasn't really happening. Just as his roommate was about to scurry around the corner and out of sight, Reagan called out. "Jackson, is that you? Can we talk a minute? Hey, my friend, what's your hurry?"

* * *

Just a couple of hours earlier, Reagan had finally gotten up the nerve to go to the Rat to confront Sherri Miles one more time. He would simply march in, order a beer, and wait until the right opportunity presented itself to ask her out. No apologies this time, no flowers or candy, just a simple question: "Would you like to go out with me this Saturday night? We could grab some dinner and go to a movie, anything you want." Reagan had rehearsed his lines over and over again and was finally ready to do it.

The Rat was packed for a Wednesday night. Several intramural teams had decided to hit the closest watering hole to throw a few back after their games had been rained out.

Reagan found a table in the corner, sat down, and went unnoticed by the waitress for a few minutes, an oversight that he did not mind one bit.

Sherri Miles was indeed working that evening. She was very busy taking orders, delivering pitchers, and dishing out that killer smile.

Reagan watched her in action, and as he did, he felt his courage slipping away by the minute. *God, she is beautiful. Look at those long legs, that incredible hair, and, wow, what a body. I'm kidding myself if I think she is going to go out with me after what happened. She could have any guy in this place. Just look at all of them staring at her, watching her every move.*

On her next trip his way, Sherri caught sight of Reagan sitting at the table, pretending to read a book. She headed back to the bar and returned in a couple of minutes with a pitcher on her tray and a disbelieving look on her face. "That will be three bucks. I would normally let you run a tab, but, unfortunately, you have a reputation of skipping out of this place unnoticed."

Reagan decided to ignore the sassiness. "Hey, Sherri. How are you tonight? Wow, the place is packed. Are you the only waitress on the floor?"

Sherri looked around the room, making sure that none of her customers had immediate needs. She then pulled up a seat, turned it around, and straddled it backward. She was inches from Reagan and had a schoolteacher's serious look on her face. "Okay, Reagan, here's the deal: I'm gonna give you a second chance, but no screw-ups this time. Do you hear me?"

Thankfully, Reagan was able to swallow the second word of his unplanned "yes, ma'am" response.

"I'll bring you my address and phone number before you leave here tonight. Pick me up at seven thirty sharp, Saturday night, in that fancy car you told me about. We'll go to dinner and then to Big Daddy's for a couple of drinks and a few dances. You do know how to dance, don't you? Then if you behave yourself and resist the urge to bolt, we can go back to my place for a nightcap. And Reagan, I love Italian food. It puts me in the mood, if you know what I mean."

That look was back in Sherri Miles's eyes, and Reagan almost fell out of his seat as he watched her walk away.

Reagan hardly noticed the pouring rain as he walked back to his room. If there were puddles on the sidewalk, they weren't affecting him. He was walking ten feet off of the ground. He could hardly believe what had just happened.

And then, just before reaching his dorm, he saw his roommate. Jackson was carrying his suitcases and backpack, hurrying away into the darkness. Reagan thought his eyes were fooling him. Maybe this was all some sort of a dream. As it turned out, it was a nightmare that he was about to wake up in the middle of.

"Jackson, please wait up. Where are you going? What in the world is going on?" Reagan caught up to his roommate in the tunnel where Jackson had stopped and put down his suitcases.

"Hey, Reagan. I'm glad I ran into you. I came back to get my things. I left you a note, but I really wanted to talk to you privately." Jackson, who wasn't making eye contact, was looking around nervously, making sure that no one was watching them. "This awful thing with Tyrone, it's turned the whole world upside down. It's just not safe for us . . . I mean, for me to . . ."

"Are you talking about Tyrone Miller, Rita Mae's son? What happened to him?"

"Jesus Christ, Reagan. Are you living in a cave? He was killed, jumped in a bar in Germany by three white guys who were pissed off because he was dancing with a white girl. It's got this entire town turned upside down. It's not safe for anyone to be on the streets. It's certainly not safe for me to be living with a—"

"With a white boy? Is that what this is all about, Jackson? I didn't know you felt that way. I thought we were friends."

"Reagan, I don't expect you to get it. The way you were raised, you have no idea how much pinned-up hatred there is. There are people who would hurt me, maybe even kill me, just because you and I are friends. My father certainly isn't safe as long as I'm living with you."

"Oh, my God! Rita Mae! She's lost her son. She's got to be devastated. I've got to go see her. I've got to go see her right now!"

"Reagan, you're just not getting it. You can't go see her now. You might not ever get to go see her again. You would put your life, and hers, in danger. Do you want that? Now, I've got to go. I'm sorry about all of this, but it's bigger than just you and me and our friendship. It's just the way things are."

"Well then, things need to change. It's not the way things should be, not now, and certainly not in the future." Reagan watched his roommate's eyes as Jackson once again scanned the area for onlookers.

"Reagan, I agree with you. But this thing, as you call it, it started a long time ago, and it isn't going to end until—"

"Until people like you and I do something about it. Jackson, can't you see, as long as we're running away from it, they win. We need to stop running, and be a part of the solution. We can't let them go on winning."

Reagan noticed the tears in his friend's eyes just before Jackson turned around, picked up his bags, and ran into the rainy night.

CHAPTER THIRTEEN

*I*t became readily apparent that there would be nothing ordinary about this particular Thursday. Everything that could go wrong probably would. Time felt as if it was standing still. On the other hand, things that no one seemed to have control over were moving full speed ahead. There was just a feeling of restlessness, and everyone appeared to be on edge. It might have been better if everybody had just stayed home and in bed for the day.

The sensational lightning that accompanied the all-night rain lit up the night, achieving the ironic outcome of calming things down. Several transformers around town and in the vicinity of the university had been struck by the lightning, leaving a good portion of the campus, including the Murphree complex, without electricity.

That morning, Reagan had been jarred awake by the bright rays from the sun shining through the window next to his desk. On the desk sat his electric alarm clock, and through his squinting eyes, he noticed that the clock read 3:24 AM. Looking across the room, Reagan noted that Jackson's bed had not been slept in and was made up military style. This second observation caused Reagan to roll back over and pull the sheets up over his head while he pondered the discrepancy between the sunshine and the time on the clock.

Without looking, Reagan reached over and felt around for the gold watch that he always kept on the nightstand next to his bed while he slept.

Crap! It's 7:45 AM. I've got fifteen minutes to shower and get to pre-calc. There's a test today. I promised Molly that I'd get there a half hour early to do some last-minute review. Now I'll be lucky to get to class before the bell rings.

It wasn't until Reagan was wrapped in a towel and rushing down the hall toward the bathroom that he noticed that the lights were out. *It's dark in here. What the hell! How am I supposed to take a shower and shave? What in the world is going on around here? I'm not even awake yet!*

Reagan reached Peabody Hall a couple of minutes late. He had managed to shower, but there had not been enough light in the bathroom to

109

shave. He had thrown on his jeans and t-shirt, but he had been unable to locate a clean pair of socks, so he put his sneakers on without them. Everyone on campus seemed to be moving in slow motion, and Reagan found it odd that his mad dash to class caused a number of his fellow students to point fingers and snicker in his direction.

It was not until he reached Peabody Hall and saw the sign on the door that he realized what was going on. He was dripping sweat from every pore on his body, and as he looked around to see if anyone was watching him, he felt his face turning bright red with embarrassment.

All classes canceled today due to the electrical outage.

"Hey, Reagan, looks like you might need to buy a wind-up alarm clock. And, by the way, your t-shirt is on backward and your zipper is down. To think, I was relying on you to help me study this morning."

Molly was sitting on the picnic bench, not ten feet from the door where Reagan was standing. She had just finished a conversation with two girls who were also in their pre-calculus class. One of the girls was a very cute brunette whom Reagan had had his eye on, but any hopes along those lines were suddenly dashed as he watched the girls walking away, looking back at him, and giggling.

Reagan's heart was pounding from his mad dash as his eyes darted downward, hoping that Molly had been kidding. She had not. After quickly correcting the problem and deciding to ignore the t-shirt issue for the time being, he strolled toward the bench, trying to regain his composure.

"Hey, Molly. Wow, with a friend like you, who needs enemies?"

Molly glanced over her shoulder at the girls as they rounded the corner and out of sight.

"Oh, I'm sorry, Reagan. I didn't mean to embarrass you. I should have known you had a crush on her. She is really pretty. Anyway, I happen to know that she's dating a senior, so I wouldn't waste my time if I were you. Listen, I hear the student union has electricity. Do you want to walk over and grab something to eat? I'm starving after watching your full sprint across the lawn."

On their walk to breakfast, Reagan was finally able to calm down and come to grips with what was happening around him while Molly spoke. "So, have you got any big plans for the weekend? I'm probably heading to Tallahassee to watch a football game unless you want to get together and study or something." Molly's tone was soft and inviting.

Reagan glanced her way but detected nothing else out of the ordinary. "As a matter of fact, I have a date for Saturday night. It's with that girl from the Ratheskellar that I told you about. We're going to dinner, and then to Big Daddy's to listen to some music and dance."

"You finally got up the nerve to ask her out? Reagan, I'm proud of you. Now that you've broken the ice, I know you're gonna get a lot more dates. You know, you're not a bad-looking guy. There are a lot of girls who would love to go out with you."

Reagan looked over once more at her emotionless expression before grabbing her hand and squeezing it twice. "Thanks, Molly, that was a very nice thing to say. I appreciate it."

Their hands lingered together for a minute as they walked the rest of the way in silence.

* * *

That morning, Sergeant Gary Glaser had assembled his task force in the back room of the Village Inn Pancake House on NW 13th Street. With only three exceptions, all of the sixteen men sitting at the table giving the sergeant their full attention were his regular drinking buddies. Two of the outsiders, sitting wide-eyed and to the sergeant's right, were new to the force, having just received their badges. Sitting next to them was the only black cop in the bunch, Melvin Peters.

Melvin Peters, a mountain of a man, had been with the Gainesville Police Department for eighteen years. During that time, he had also achieved the rank of sergeant. Big Bear, as he was often called, had risen within the department much slower than most. That especially included Gary Glaser, who, everybody agreed, was on the fast track to becoming a lieutenant. The fact that Melvin Peters and Gary Glaser were both sergeants was the only distinction the two of them had in common.

Sergeant Melvin Peters was a deeply religious man, and although genuinely loyal to the GPD, he always put his faith, family, and friends ahead of his professional duties. He was not a fan of the "golden boy" and didn't mind voicing his opinion on the matter. Melvin had publicly confronted Gary Glaser on several occasions regarding his locker room antics, foul language, and general disrespect for virtually everyone and everything. Melvin Peters particularly despised Gary Glaser's nonstop bragging about his sexual conquests.

Melvin Peters had been summoned to this gathering early that morning and was not at all happy with this particular assignment. As the meeting was called to order, this fact became increasingly obvious.

"Okay, gentlemen. Listen up! For the time being, you are under my supervision. You will report to me, and only to me, on matters associated with this mission. Operation Hotbox, as we will refer to it, is under my complete control, and I have been given the authority to call the shots . . . all of the shots.

"Our mission is simple. We will operate under a zero-tolerance policy. Anyone even suspected of disturbing the peace, or assembling with the intent to riot, will be cuffed and booked. We will get these troublemakers off of our streets before innocent people are placed in harm's way.

"Our assigned area is from University Avenue on the south, up to NW 8th Avenue on the north. NW 13th Street is our western boundary, and we will cover all the way east to Main Street.

"Overtime pay has been approved by the captain, and we will patrol the neighborhood in twelve-hour shifts, four cars per shift, two cops per car. I will be in the rover car and available twenty-four/seven. Everyone on this side of the table, including the two rookies and Peters, will work the night shift, seven 'til seven.

"Our first assignment, and I want this accomplished by daylight tomorrow, is to get those leather-jacketed thugs off the street and back into their homes. If they're not happy with that, we've got a nice cot and a warm meal waiting for them downtown.

"Now, let me make this very clear. I don't give a rat's ass what happened a thousand miles from here over in Germany. All I care about is keeping our streets quiet and safe. The kind of crap that's been going on over on the east side of town had better not happen in our 'hood, and definitely not on my watch. Does anybody have any questions? Good! I want everyone wearing their vests. Dismissed."

Melvin Peters took the last bite of his doughnut, grabbed his hat, and, along with his new partner, Officer Daniels, one of the rookies, headed toward the door. Before walking out of the restaurant, Peters looked back at Gary Glaser, who was sitting at the table, surrounded by his cronies. By the way his "new supervisor" was carrying on, it was obvious that Glaser was very proud of himself.

Melvin Peters thought back to the briefing. *What was it exactly that he said? Oh yeah, I remember.* "*You will report to me, and only to me, on matters associated with this mission.*" *Perfect!*

* * *

To say that Carly Glaser was a nervous wreck would be an understatement. She had never done anything like this before and had spent the past couple of days planning out every detail in her head.

She knew that Gary would be working extended hours for the next week or so and wouldn't be home until around 7:00 PM to shower and change clothes before his night out with the boys. Typically, he would spend a few minutes tossing the ball with Junior before putting him down to bed. Taking this all into account, she had asked Maria to first make sure that Gary's motorcycle was gone from the parking lot and then to come over at 8:00 PM.

Carly had already decided on what she was going to wear, and it was hanging front and center in her closet. It was a short, bright red dress that would be accented with dark-tinted pantyhose, a garter belt, and a pair of black high heels. This same outfit at one time, had been Gary's favorite. Back then, he would always tell her how incredibly sexy she looked in it. The last time she had worn it for him, he hadn't even seemed to notice.

Carly hadn't given Maria all of the details of her date, including exactly where she was going, or her new friend's name. She did, however, want to leave contact information, so she wrote down Stephen's name, address, and phone number on a piece of paper. She folded the note, put it in an envelope, sealed it, and, on the front of the envelope, wrote, **Open in case of an emergency only**!

Trying to think of everything, Carly had been worried that if someone took her parking spot while she was out, Gary might notice that her car had been moved and might question her about it. He was a cop, after all. To alleviate this concern, Maria had suggested moving her car into Carly's parking spot and then swapping back again when the evening was over.

Carly packed an extra pair of underwear, breath mints, and some spare makeup in her purse. She had bought two bottles of red wine using her own stash of money, and they were hidden under the front seat of her car. She would wear her favorite perfume but would remember to wash it off in the shower when she got home.

On boys' night out, Gary never made it home before one in the morning, but to play it safe, Carly told Maria to expect her back by midnight. That would give her and Stephen four hours to do whatever it was they were going to do, and Carly had spent hours thinking about that.

With everything in place, Carly's nervousness was transforming into anticipation. She felt like a teenage girl again, all excited about breaking the rules and sneaking out into the night. She would be going to a place and doing things that only she and one other person knew about. If for only a few hours, she would be free again, calling her own shots with no one to judge or belittle her.

As she watched her husband burst through the door, scoop up their son, head to the kitchen for a beer, and then back out the door without even acknowledging her, she knew she was doing the right thing.

She was so excited about the next few hours that her legs were starting to tremble and her heart was thumping in her chest. She sat there on the couch, drinking her own beer and smiling. She was confident that she had the whole affair planned out perfectly. She had thought of everything. Nothing could go wrong.

*   *   *

Charley had asked Terri to come over early that evening to help her cook dinner, so at 8:00 PM, the yellow Pontiac GTO was already parked alongside the white Stingray, right outside of the fourth trailer on the right.

When Charley answered the door, her guest handed her an overflowing grocery sack, a bag of pot, and an unexpected gift that was wrapped in bright blue paper and tied together with a yellow ribbon.

With her hands full, Charley received a passionate kiss and a smack on the butt before the two of them went inside. Gary wasn't expected until after ten, but the girls had plenty of things to talk about, including the events of the previous evening. They quickly unpacked the groceries, opened a bottle of wine, lit a joint, and slid into the matching pink nightshirts that had been in the gift box.

The day before, Charley had worked her first night shift at Pleasure Palace. She was only filling in for one of the girls who had been called out of town, but nonetheless, having been chosen from the group of dayshifters had been quite an honor. She had made four times her usual amount in tips and had also created quite a stir amongst the joint's regular patrons.

The most noteworthy part of the evening came when Terri Spencer, having been told by Charley about the temporary promotion, had walked through the door, paid her cover, and sat down on a chair, stage-side, with a wad of tip dollars in her hand.

Bubba McGraw was not accustomed to having single females enter his establishment, especially unaccompanied. There was, of course, no rule prohibiting this, and unless the female turned out to be a jealous wife or girlfriend, her being at the bar usually resulted in additional entertainment for his regulars. Terri's visit that night had proven to be exactly that and much more.

Bubba had been standing outside, smoking a cigarette and jawing with two of his most affluent clients, when the yellow GTO pulled into the parking lot and right up to the front door.

"Mind if I leave it parked here?"

The three men watched with admiration as the driver slid out of the car and strutted straight toward them. She wasn't wearing much in the way of clothing, but what she was wearing made them want to see "more." She had a hot little body and a confident smile, and she obviously was not in any way intimidated by her surroundings.

"Will one of you gentlemen get the door for me and point me in the right direction? I'm here to see the new superstar I understand you have dancing tonight. I think she goes by the name Tiffany."

Bubba opened the door, collected Terri's two dollars, and pointed her toward the stage. "She's up next. Grab a seat up front for the best view."

Terri settled into the last remaining seat and immediately had several wannabe sponsors offering to buy her a drink. The next song started, and "Tiffany" came on stage to a big round of applause. Noticing her buddy sitting front and center, Charley flashed Terri a big smile and started slowing stripping out of her outfit. When she was down to only her G-string, she started wiggling her finger seductively, daring Terri up onto the stage.

Seconds into the routine, Terri was already standing, facing the Pleasure Palace's soon-to-be most popular nightshift dancer, and handing out dollar tips. With each tip came a kiss. Each kiss became more passionate than the previous, and the patrons loved everything about it. Dollar bills were pouring onto the floor from every direction, and the crowd started chanting, "Up on stage! Up on stage!"

The girls were into their second bottle of wine and still giggling about the night before when they decided it was time to start cooking. Gary would be there before they knew it, and they wanted everything to be ready for him. Having discussed their plans in detail, they were pretty sure he would be happy with what they had in store for him.

* * *

At precisely 8:20 PM, as had been agreed upon, Sergeant Gary Glaser, sitting at his desk at GPD headquarters, picked up the phone and dialed his house. With the all-hands-on-deck order in place, he was sure that he would be the only one in the squad room at the time, and therefore, his conversation would not be overheard. He had even given the room a good walkaround before placing the call. The conversation that was about to take place needed to be private.

Boys' night out had been canceled for obvious reasons, but his wife didn't need to know that, especially after what he had been told. This scenario had been exactly what he had been hoping for. Finally, he had found a way to gain his freedom without losing his job and his reputation. She would be blamed for it all. He would play the jilted husband who understandably couldn't be expected to forgive his cheating wife. Nothing could be more perfect. Now he just needed the details. He had to catch her in the act. Then he could bring the whole thing out into the open and gain the freedom he so desperately longed for.

The phone rang only once.

The voice at the other end of the line was a quivering whisper. "Gary, you can never tell her that I was the one. You have to promise me. You didn't hear any of this from me, okay?"

"Stop worrying. I've told you I have a lot of sources. I would have probably found out about this anyway. Now tell me, where did she say she was going? Who is this guy? I want to thank him personally. Give him a medal or something."

"She didn't tell me who he is or where they are going. I asked her like you wanted me to, but she wouldn't say anything."

"For Christ's sake, Maria, how am I supposed to catch her if I don't know where she is?"

"Why don't you try one of your sources, Gary?" The sarcastic voice was on the verge of tears, and Gary was afraid that he was about to lose her cooperation.

"Maria Sanchez, get a hold of yourself. This is perfect for us. Carly will never know you were involved, and now you and I will get to spend more time together, a lot more time. Wouldn't you like that?"

"Gary, you know I would love that. Do you promise? What if you forget all about me? What if I never get to see you again?"

"That's ridiculous, Maria. Think about it. We're in this together. I need you as much as you need me. Now concentrate. She must have said something that will help me."

There was a long silence on the other end of the line, and Gary started to lose his patience. He was having trouble containing his temper.

"Gary, I told you she didn't say anything, but . . ."

"But what, Maria? Please!"

"She didn't say anything . . . But she did leave a note."

CHAPTER FOURTEEN

*M*elvin Peters slid into the passenger side of the patrol car, glanced over at his new partner, and said a prayer under his breath. He had just spent a half hour, over burgers and milkshakes, getting to know Darren Daniels and laying out some ground rules. The kid was nice enough, seemed very intelligent and enthusiastic, but man, was he wet behind the ears. And this was not exactly the ideal assignment on which to be breaking in a rookie. For everyone's sake, Melvin would need all the help he could get . . . *Amen!*

Peters had explained that they were going to make a couple of stops in the neighborhood and that afterward, he needed to drop back by the precinct. The sergeant had left his bulletproof vest in his locker and wanted to retrieve it for two reasons. First, he was trying to set a good example for his protégé, and second, he didn't want to suffer the consequences of going against the direct orders of his new supervisor.

Daniels took a left off of University Avenue onto NW 10th Street. At the sergeant's direction, he pulled the car over and stopped a couple of feet away from one of the leather-coated lookouts. The young man was sitting on a curb beside his bicycle, smoking a cigarette, and trying his best to ignore them. Sergeant Peters rolled down his window and studied the boy for a long minute before clearing his voice loudly enough to get the young man's attention.

"Well, if it ain't the Big Bear, slummin' the hood," the boy said. "Not used to seein' ya ridin' shotgun. Who's the new boy? He even old enough to be drivin'? He sure ain't be shavin' yet. With him coverin' for ya, ya best have eyes in the back of yo head."

"I don't got time for your bullshit today, Slim. Even if I did, I've never heard an intelligent word come out of your mouth. And look at how you're dressed. Don't you look like a damn fool, hanging out on a street corner wearing a leather jacket in ninety-degree heat?

"Now stand up and listen to me. I need to see my nephew. You got any clue to his whereabouts, or is that sort of thing too high up on the food chain for you?"

"Well, no sir, Officer, I ain't seen Jamal all day. I has no ideas where he be."

"Don't you be sass-mouthing me, Slim. I'll haul you in right now and put you in a cell with somebody a lot tougher than you are.

"Now, I need to talk to Jamal. I'm not here to arrest him. I just need to spend a couple of minutes with him. So you get on that bike of yours and go tell him that I'll be at his house in a half hour. Do you hear me? If he ain't there when I get there, I'll be back to find you. And when I do, we will all take a ride downtown, and I'll let my partner here see about finding you a daddy."

Their next stop was at Rita Mae's home, where Daniels was instructed to wait in the car. Melvin Peters had been by Rita Mae's house to pay his respects the day before, but there had been a line outside of the door and all the way to the street. On this day, there were just three people sitting on the porch stoop and several more hovering inside.

When Rita Mae saw Melvin Peters walk through the front door and remove his hat, the tears she'd thought she'd run out of came streaming back. She was too weak to stand, so Melvin walked across the room, knelt down in front of her, took hold of her hands, and looked straight into her bloodshot eyes.

"Rita Mae, I am so sorry. You know how much I loved Tyrone. He was like a son to me. He brought out the good in everyone. We are all going to miss him terribly. And all of us will be here for you. You know I will. You can call me any time of the day or night, and I'll be right over."

For the longest time, Rita Mae sat there, her whole body shaking, looking into Melvin's weeping eyes before finally saying, "Bear, you knows he looked up to ya. You wuz his hero. From ever since he wuz a little boy, he wanted to be juz like his uncle Bear. I juz can't believe he's gone."

She was staring through him, and Melvin could tell that there was something else she wanted to say, so he waited.

"Bear, this thing . . . it be bad enough all by itself. I don't want nothin' else bad comin' of it. Tyrone wouldna wanted that himself."

"I know, Rita Mae. And we're gonna do everything we can to keep things calm and safe. But there's a lot of built-up tension out there. I'm afraid things might get ugly for a while. We'll get it all straightened out, though, and back to normal as soon as we can." Melvin looked deep into Rita Mae's eyes again. He was glad that his words didn't appear to be registering with her, as he realized at that moment that things would never be back to normal in Rita Mae's life.

The grieving mother was squeezing Melvin's hands with all of her strength. She looked over at the open bible on the table by her lamp. She looked over at Heidi, who was curled up in the corner, having not moved a muscle all day. She looked at the pictures of Tyrone on the table. And then with the glare of a lost soul, she looked back into Melvin's eyes. "Lord, help us all. It juz don't seem right. None of it seem right."

After spending a minute with the other visitors, and before walking out of the door, a broken-hearted Melvin Peters looked back once more. Rita Mae was bent over with her head in her hands, sobbing and struggling with her words. "Bear, don't ya let nothing happen to ya. I juz couldn't stand it."

Jamal Spikes was indeed waiting in front of his home when the patrol car pulled up, and Daniels was once again told to wait in the car.

"Hey, Jamal. Thanks for being here," Melvin said. "How's your mama?"

"She's fine. Mean as ever. Ya wants ta come in and say hey?"

"No, I can't right now, but you tell her I came by, hear me? Now, what I came to say is that you got to pull your boys off the street. We're starting around-the-clock patrols of the neighborhood tonight, and we have orders to give them one warning and then haul them in and lock them up. They're gonna be gone one way or another, and they'd be much better off at home than in a jail cell downtown with everything else that's going on."

"Uncle Melvin, whoever give them orders be a fool talkin'. Ya know as well as me that my boys be the only reason there ain't been no problem in the 'hood. With 'em gone, this whole place get open up to trouble. It's gonna be like a bomb been goin' off. This is crazy shit yo talkin' now. Crazy shit."

* * *

Gary Glaser was sitting stunned at his desk when the phone he had just hung up started ringing.

How could this be happening? His wife was whoring around with possibly the only man in the city that he couldn't confront. Stephen Crain had him by the balls. The scum knew all about his affair with Charley, and he wouldn't be shy about spilling the juicy details. *How in the world did that little worm manage to talk Carly into coming over to his house, anyway? How desperate is she? How did they even meet?*

Instantly, none of that mattered. He needed to get to the Shady Oaks and put a stop to whatever was going to happen. If he was lucky, Carly would already be gone, having come to her senses. If not, he would chase her out of the house before Crain had a chance to say anything. He would send her home and deal with her later. Then he would handle Mr. Crain, once and for all.

As he gathered his leather jacket, sunglasses, and pistol, he studied the phone, which was on its sixth ring. He should get it. It might be Maria calling back with more information. Maybe Carly had already come home. He could put this whole thing off and go enjoy whatever Charley and Terri had planned for the evening.

"Hello, Sergeant Glaser speaking."

"Hey, Gary, it's the captain. I just tried calling your house, but the line was busy. Anyway, I'm glad I caught you at the precinct. I should have known you'd be working tonight. Always at it, that's how you're gonna make lieutenant. Listen, the mayor has just called for a press conference at eleven o'clock tonight. He wants to make the late news. He asked that I be there along with my task force leaders. That, of course, includes you."

The captain continued, "I'd like to ride the neighborhoods to see what we're dealing with firsthand before having to answer questions from those damn reporters. Grab my squad-car keys out of my desk and pick me up at the house in fifteen minutes. I need to walk the dog, but I'll be ready to go when you get here. In the meantime, I'll call Carly and tell her to tune in to the newscast."

"Chief . . . " Completely caught off guard, Gary stuttered for a few seconds before finally saying, "No, that won't be necessary. I've got to call Carly anyway. I'll see you in fifteen minutes."

Out of options, Gary studied the phone number that Maria had given him. He had written it down on a pad of paper next to his phone, along with Stephen Crain's name and address. His only shot at this point was to call Crain and talk to him, man to man. Maybe the worm had some decency hidden deep inside that Gary could reason with.

He rehearsed his insincere words out loud: "Crain, this is Sergeant Glaser. I understand that you have a visitor this evening that shouldn't be there. She needs to leave your house immediately and be home with our boy within fifteen minutes. If you keep your trap shut, and you know what I'm talking about, then you and I can come to an agreement, call it a truce if you want to. If not . . . Let's just put it this way, Crain: You'll be better off on my side in this matter. Do you understand me? Do we have a deal?"

Glaser picked up the phone and dialed the number. It rang ten times before he hung it up. If either of the occupants of the king-size waterbed heard the phone ringing on their end of the line, neither of them had said a word.

Gary Glaser grabbed the keys from his boss's office and stormed out of the building. If he hadn't been in such a hurry, he might have noticed the big man standing in the shadows of the hallway that led to the locker room. And he might have remembered to take the note by his phone along with him.

* * *

It started off as a peaceful protest in front of the Naval Recruiting Office, which was located downtown at the corner of Main Street and University Avenue. At first, there were only five participants carrying signs and chanting, "Justice for Tyrone . . . Justice for Tyrone."

Several passing cars honked in support, and a couple of others slowed down, shouting out obscenities with racial overtones.

Word got out, and the crowd quickly grew in number. Before long, they were more than one hundred strong.

A local news station dispatched a camera crew and its top reporter to the scene. By the time the crew arrived and was set up in the adjacent parking lot, the assembly had grown exponentially and was spilling out onto the street, blocking traffic in all directions.

An unexpected early-season cold front had passed quickly by, leaving behind a brisk northwesterly wind along with cooler and drier air. Someone got the idea to build a bonfire smack-dab in the middle of the city's busiest intersection using lumber from a nearby construction site.

The downtown liquor store was packed with protesters stocking up for what would turn out to be a long night. The first of these patrons had paid cash and carried their bottles out in paper sacks. It wasn't long, however, until the multitudes from the street had overrun the store. Before the owner was able to get everyone out and secure the locks, his shelves had been stripped bare and his cash register cleaned out.

It all happened so quickly. Cars were backed up in all directions, and their occupants were becoming increasingly impatient. Horns were honking, and tempers were flaring with shouting matches breaking out between the mostly white commuters and the black protesters.

Someone threw a brick, which rocketed into the skull of an elderly black man who had been part of the original gathering. After that, all hell broke loose, setting off what would prove to be the most violent and chaotic two days in Gainesville's history.

* * *

The frantic call blasted loud and clear from the CB radio inside of the captain's squad car. "This is Sergeant Peters for Sergeant Glaser. Come in, Sergeant. We have a Level 4, 10-1 Emergency. The situation is out of control. There is at least one fatality, three overturned vehicles, and at last count, six businesses are on fire. We are awaiting your instructions. Come in, Sergeant. What's your 20?"

Gary Glaser's 20 was pulling into the Shady Oaks Mobile Home Community. He was staring at his wife's car parked under an oak tree directly in front of Stephen Crain's house. The fact that she was really there, inside with that scum, had just hit him. His head was spinning. He felt like he was having some sort of a bad dream. He knew that any minute, he was going to throw up.

He had made the split-second decision to drive to Shady Oaks and spend a couple of minutes dealing with Crain. By his calculation, this would cause him to be about twenty minutes late picking up the chief. He reasoned that this was an excusable amount of time that could easily be explained away if the need arose.

Trying to regain his composure, Gary Glaser was looking to his left, where he saw Terri's yellow GTO parked next to Charley's Stingray, when the radio once again interrupted his thoughts. This time it was the captain calling from his scanner, and he didn't sound happy.

"Sergeant Glaser, this is the captain! Where the hell are you? You were supposed to be here ten minutes ago. You had better be right around the corner or—" Luckily, the captain released the call button before Gary, and every other cop in a squad car that night, could be a witness to the rest of his threat.

Glaser was cussing under his breath as he turned the car around. He exited Shady Oaks onto SW 34th Street and was soon doing close to one hundred miles an hour with his lights flashing and the siren blaring. He took a deep breath and picked up the microphone. "Chief, I encountered an unexpected delay, but I am on my way. Ten minutes max. Over."

* * *

They hadn't talked long. When Carly had walked in, Stephen Crain was having trouble believing his eyes. She was here. She was really here, and she looked beautiful. He told her so and then watched her eyes as his compliment seemed to melt her apprehension.

He opened the wine and poured each of them a generous glass. They sat on the couch together and talked, but they didn't talk long.

Carly mentioned that she had only a couple of hours and told Stephen that his home was very lovely, so nicely decorated. They finished their wine, and Stephen asked her if she would like a tour. She did, and they started and ended the tour in the master bedroom.

It was dark in the master bedroom, so Stephen asked Carly if he could light a candle before she removed her clothes. He wanted to watch her. That sounded like a good idea to her, so Carly lit the candle herself. She slowly stepped out of her high heels and removed her pantyhose. She lifted her dress up over her head, leaving her black bra and garter belt on as she slid into the king-size waterbed.

Stephen had undressed and was waiting for her there, in the waterbed. She came to him and assumed the dominant position, pinning his hands back, but not before he had reached behind her, undoing the clasp of her bra. Her breasts were big, and they were perfect, and at this moment they were all his. If his plan worked out, and he knew it would, they would soon be his forever. She would soon be his forever.

She reached down, and he was ready. She was ready. She closed her eyes and moved ever so slowly. She was remembering now how this felt. Her body shuddered with her first. There would be many more.

When it was time for her to leave, she got up, took her clothes into the bathroom, and got dressed. She did want another glass of wine, but there wasn't time. They had used up all of their time.

Stephen told her once more how beautiful she looked, and she kissed him on the lips. Then she kissed him again.

Before she left, he handed her an envelope. He told her that she might find the information in the envelope interesting and informative. He said that maybe one day it might even be helpful, that he sure hoped so. She kissed him again on the lips and walked out into the darkness.

When Carly was gone, Stephen Crain quietly slipped out of his house. He tiptoed through the leaves and across the drive. The lights were on in the fourth trailer on the right, and he would soon be in the trailer next door, watching. He lit a candle, took his pants back off, fired up a joint, and made sure the petroleum jelly was close by.

The entertainment for the evening was two women. They were completely naked and going at each other like animals in heat. He would watch as long as he wanted. He would watch whenever he wanted.

Gary Glaser was no longer his problem. He had handled Gary Glaser and would handle him again if he needed to. Gary Glaser was no match for him, and soon, he would have everything Gary Glaser had lost. Have them all to himself. Whenever he wanted them. However he wanted them.

He was getting close, and as he watched the women's passion peaking, he remembered his own conquests during his visits to the fourth trailer on the right. He had been there many times, and he would be there again. He would go there again soon. He would go there to collect the rent, and he would not be accepting cash.

CHAPTER FIFTEEN

*I*t was not until Jacksonville's National Guard unit arrived at 3:00 AM on Friday that things finally started to calm down. The GPD had done their best to contain and disperse the crowds, but about the time they would think they were making progress, another altercation or emergency would be reported.

So far, twenty-five people had been transported to Alachua General Hospital, and two of them had died. The elderly black gentleman's injuries had caused excessive bleeding, and the paramedics had been unable to stabilize him during transport. The other fatality was an eight-year-old white girl, whose family lived a quarter of a mile from the violence. She had been struck in the head by an errant bullet while she was been riding her bicycle on the patio in their backyard.

The fire department had called in backup units from all surrounding counties and the City of Ocala, but they still had their hands full. An entire block in downtown was ablaze, and the whipping winds were blowing embers as far as two blocks away. There was a report that a policeman had been shot in the chest and had been driven to the hospital by his partner.

The mayor's press conference had not turned out as he had hoped. Instead of being able to report that the situation was stabilizing, he had to admit that the city was in shambles, and he couldn't commit to a timeframe when Gainesville might return to normal.

He declared a dusk-to-dawn curfew and pleaded with the citizens to settle down and return to their homes. One problem with his plea was that those who were not in their homes were not watching the press conference. The second problem was that even if they had been, it wouldn't have mattered.

The entire city council, the police chief, and several of his officers had accompanied the mayor to the press conference and stood before the cameras. Several religious leaders stepped up to the microphone and offered prayers of love and reconciliation. One black bishop reminded the viewership that "the dream" did not contain violence or promote hatred. The entire entourage, and particularly one sergeant, looked shocked and devastated. There were tears in the mayor's eyes as he concluded his message with a prayer for peace.

The National Guard came with 200 troops. They were dressed in riot gear and carried heavy weaponry along with an ample supply of tear gas and pepper spray. They approached the uprising from the south and east, forcing many of the rioters into the neighborhood northwest of downtown. A second flank secured the western boundary along NW 13th Street. Sergeant Glaser's men had been assigned to the north perimeter, patrolling NW 8th Avenue.

At 4:53 AM on Friday, September 14, 1973, the announcement officially came across the spectrum of law enforcement radios: The rioters were contained, encased and surrounded in a one-square-mile neighborhood being called the Hotbox. Orders were to stand off unless engaged. Arrests would begin at daylight. No one was permitted in or allowed out of the Hotbox.

* * *

Earlier that evening, Maria Sanchez had just turned off the TV in the Glasers' house when her pager went off. The entire evening newscast had been dedicated to the riot, and she had watched in horror at the size and volatility of the angry crowd. She had listened carefully to the mayor's statements and had seen Gary standing behind him. She had no idea what to expect when Carly walked through the door.

She called the hospital and was told that all emergency room personnel were to report to work. Policemen had been instructed that medical professionals were exempt from the mayor's curfew. She was to make sure that she had her badge with her just in case she was pulled over. In anticipation of heading out, Maria was gathering her things and had just stuffed the opened envelope, along with its contents, into her purse, when she heard Carly unlocking the door with her key.

"Oh, hi there, Maria. I thought you might be asleep on the couch, so I let myself in. Are you okay? You look upset."

Maria studied Carly's eyes for a few seconds before responding. If Gary had confronted his wife that evening, there was no sign of it in her expression or demeanor.

"I'm fine, Carly. I just . . . I mean . . . Have you heard what's going on downtown? Did you happen to catch the evening newscast?"

126

"Now, Maria, I think you might know the answer to that question. I didn't go over to my new friend's house to watch TV." Carly's face turned bright red. The unplanned admission had left her lips before her brain had engaged. She was feeling blissful and wanted to tell someone about her evening, but that conversation would have to wait. "Anyway, what's going on downtown that has you so on edge?"

Before Maria had a chance to answer the question, the phone rang.

"Who could that be at this hour? Gary never calls here on his boys' night out. I hope my mom and dad are okay. Excuse me a minute, Maria, while I get this."

Maria looked over at the phone. Her heart was racing, and she felt the need to leave. She glanced around to make sure that she had all of her things and started walking toward the door, but Carly's stern look and sky-ward-pointing index finger stopped her in her tracks.

"Hello? . . . Well, hello, Gary, what are you doing calling . . . Of course I'm at home. Where else would I be? . . . At the office? I thought . . . Junior's just fine. He's sound asleep."

Maria nodded her head in affirmation.

"No, I haven't been watching the TV. I've been reading my . . . Okay, but call me when your meeting's over and tell me what's going on."

Carly hung up the phone and turned back toward her friend. "That's odd. Gary's at the precinct. His night out was canceled for some reason. Why was he surprised that I was home? Anyway, Maria, you have got to tell me what is going on."

Maria looked over at her friend. How could she have betrayed her like this? Sure, Carly was cheating, but Gary was cheating, too, and Maria knew it wasn't just with her. Gary had even admitted as much to her early on in their relationship. But Maria didn't care. She would welcome him, however and whenever he had time for her. Even standing there at that very minute, she wanted him. She wanted him so badly that it hurt.

Maria suddenly realized that she'd done nothing but make a bigger mess out of the whole thing, and she knew that her actions could one day come back to haunt her. But there was nothing she could do about it now, and she needed to get to work. She looked again at Carly. She owed her friend an explanation, but for the time being, she would have to stick to the events of the evening.

She would tell Carly about the riots. She would tell her about the press conference and how Gary had been standing behind the mayor. She would tell her about the fatalities, the fires, and the curfew.

She would not tell Carly about the conversation she had had with Gary. She would not tell her about opening the envelope. She would not tell her that Gary somehow already knew a man named Stephen Crain. She would not admit that she had fallen in love with Carly's husband. And she would not remind her friend that they needed to swap back their parking spaces.

Carly gave Maria a big hug at the door. "I can't tell you how much I appreciate everything. You're the best friend ever. Please be careful on your way to work. From what you've just told me, it's very dangerous out there."

After Maria had left, Carly slipped out of her clothes and took a long hot shower. She put the unopened envelope that Stephen had given her in the drawer with her underwear. She would read that some other time. She didn't want anything to change the mood she was in at the moment.

After kissing Junior on the head and tucking the covers around his shoulders, she climbed into bed herself and fell fast asleep.

Sometime in the middle of the night, Gary had come home, showered, and changed clothes, but she had been sleeping so soundly that she hadn't heard him. He had left a note on the dining room table. He would be working around the clock until this mess was cleared up.

She put the note down after reading it, and then it suddenly hit her. *The envelope! The emergency note with Stephen's address and phone number! Where's the envelope? Oh, my God!*

* * *

Jackson seemed genuinely confused at the sight of twenty men standing in his front yard, carrying tree branches and chanting, "Uncle Tom . . . Uncle Tom." He was glad that his father, who was in the house sleeping, wasn't outside to witness this.

At first, Jackson was certain that this visit was meant to be some sort of scare tactic or warning. It was only when they approached him, formed a circle around him, pushed him to the ground, and start punching and kicking him that he finally realized his plight and started to put up a struggle.

It was 5:00 AM on Friday morning, and most of the rioters had dispersed, somehow slipping into the night and back to their homes. The remaining throng, however, was drunk and angrier than ever. They were outraged at having been pinned into the neighborhood like dogs in a cage and were looking for someone or something to take their frustrations out on. They were in a black neighborhood, and it made no sense to be causing damage here.

But then someone had mentioned it, said something about a black boy whose house was just down the street, something about how his college

128

roommate and his best friend was a white boy, something about how they hung out together, went for runs together, and played sports together.

They were drunk, and they were angry. They had been looking for someone or something to take their frustrations out on, and they had just found it.

Jamal Spikes saw them as they passed his house and knew where they were heading and why. The man leading the way was Terrance Tyler, a professional boxer who had just gotten out of prison, having served time for armed robbery and aggravated assault. Terrance Tyler was a bad man, and Jamal Spikes knew it. Jamal needed to get word to his uncle, and he needed to do it fast.

Jamal reached the corner of NW 10th Street and NW 8th Avenue in less than two minutes. When he approached the flashing lights and attempted to cross the street, he was taken down by three police officers, clubbed in the back, and cuffed. He was then lifted off of the ground and slammed into the side of a patrol car. One of the officers used his riot stick to smack Jamal on the back of his legs, bringing him to his knees.

"God damn it, you motherfuckers! Stop it! I need to see my uncle. I need to see Bear. I need to see him now before somebody else gets killed."

Monroe Jackson Sr. was aroused from his sleep by the ruckus that was taking place outside of his bedroom window. He pushed hard against the bed, steadied himself with the night table, and slowly lifted his fragile body to a standing position next to the window. He pulled open the shades, wondering what could be going on at this time of the night. He saw what was going on, and he wasn't about to let this happen again.

Sirens were blaring, and red lights were flashing in the distance when the old man reached the front porch, rifle in hand. He quickly had Terrance Tyler in his sights and his trembling finger on the trigger.

"You take your hands off of that boy! Do you hear me, Terrance? You back away, or I will blow your fucking head off! Don't you doubt me!"

As the police car reached the scene, two officers jumped out and ran toward the crowd, guns loaded and ready.

Terrance Tyler was hovering over Jackson. He had his arm cocked and was ready to throw another punch. He looked first at the old man on the porch, then behind him at the approaching cops, and finally at his gang that was still chanting, watching him, and egging him on. Surely he had time for one more punch.

* * *

129

"So, Sergeant Peters, this is your second trip to our emergency room in one day and as I understand it, the second time your partner here, Daniels, had to put you over his shoulder, deposit you in the back seat of your patrol car, and drive you over here. You're lucky that your partner is a weightlifter, and you're damn smart to have been wearing your vest. It saved your life both times."

The emergency room nurse had just finished hooking up the IV and taking her patient's vitals. He would be okay, but this time he was on orders to stay at the hospital until the doctors had given him a thorough examination.

Earlier that evening, Sergeant Peters had tried to break up a confrontation between a knife-wielding rioter and his pistol-toting adversary. The bullet had caught Peters in the center of the chest, knocking him to the ground and cracking a rib.

Despite the nurse's theatrical recounting of the events, Daniels on that occasion had merely assisted his partner to the patrol car and, at the chief's insistence, had driven him to the hospital to be checked out. After thirty minutes, an impatient Sergeant Peters had checked himself out and returned to his duties.

The nurse's description of Daniel's heroics during the latest incident was, however, quite accurate.

Monroe Jackson Sr., as it turned out, was not the best marksman. That was a good thing for one Terrance Tyler, who was now incarcerated in the city's jailhouse, but not such a good thing for Sergeant Peters.

This time, the bullet made contact just below the sergeant's collarbone, causing internal bleeding and resulting in the big man losing consciousness. After calling for backup, dispersing the mob, and cuffing both Terrance Tyler and Monroe Jackson Sr., Daniels deadlifted his partner off of the ground. He then carried Peters to the patrol car, checked him for a heartbeat, and drove him to the hospital.

"Nurse, could you come over here for a minute?"

Melvin Peters was wincing and trying unsuccessfully to push himself up into a seated position. "I want to thank you. I mean, not just for me, but for everything you are doing. I know it's been crazy around here, and . . . anyway, thank you. Please tell me your name. Whatever you have me on is blurring my vision, and I can't read your name tag."

"Well, Officer, thank you. Those are very kind words. We don't get that sort of appreciation in the emergency room very often. Sanchez. My name is Sanchez."

"Maria Sanchez?"

"Yes. How did you know that?"

Melvin Peters studied the nurse as she continued writing something on her clipboard. He suddenly felt sorry for her and wanted to do something, anything, to return her kindness.

"Never mind that, but, Nurse Sanchez, I do have a favor to ask of you. Would you hold my hand and pray with me? Sometimes just a little prayer can offer us salvation and point us in the right direction. Trust me, I know for a fact, it works."

CHAPTER SIXTEEN

*T*he cold front that had moved through a day earlier had reversed its course and come back as a warm front. As if looking for a target, the low-pressure system driving the front stalled out directly over the city, bringing with it hot, muggy air along with a torrential downpour.

The mayor declared the weather system a gift from God, and at his department heads' meeting that Friday morning, he stated the obvious: "This type of day will not be particularly conducive to outdoor public gatherings of any sort. Let it rain, Lord. Let it rain. If we can just get through the service tomorrow evening, things should start to calm down."

What the mayor didn't know was that there was a large contingency within his town whose aspiration was in direct conflict with his optimistic prognosis. This particular group, whose members were now being referred to as the Hotbox Gang, had their own plan, and the word was spreading.

Following the previous evening's shooting incident, the Hotbox Gang had managed to scatter in a dozen directions and had successfully slipped through the border patrols. As previously contrived, they had reassembled in an isolated wooded area about a mile south of downtown. Even with Terrance Tyler, their leader, under lock and key, the gang did a pretty good job coming up with ideas of their own.

As daylight struggled to emerge through the dark black clouds, the group reached a consensus.

The memorial service was to take place at 6:00 PM the following day. Afterward, the attendees were scheduled to march five blocks east along University Avenue to a city park just outside of downtown. A tree would be planted in remembrance of Tyrone, and the chairman of the city council, an elderly black statesman, would preside over the occasion, where he would proclaim, "This day is and will forever be remembered as Tyrone Devon Miller Day. God bless our fallen hero. May he rest in peace."

Just north of where this ceremony would be held was a section of town often referred to as the Duck Pond, a prestigious white neighborhood.

The Hotbox Gang's plan was simple. After the dedication, they would scatter. Then they would reassemble an hour later, curfew or not, in the Duck Pond area. There would be fifty of them at least. If the National Guard and the police department wanted to trap them inside of that neighborhood, so be it. The Hotbox Gang would have plenty of things to keep themselves occupied.

* * *

Power had been restored to all parts of the city, including the university's campus, and despite wishes to the contrary, classes were back in session. As the students of Marty Schemer's political science class sloshed through the door and removed their rain gear, they were greeted by an unusual sight.

Their graduate assistant was sitting at his desk in front of the room with a single piece of paper in his hands and duct tape across his mouth. When all of the class members, with one exception, had arrived and taken their seats, Marty stood up and cleared his throat from under the tape. He glanced up at the class and then looked back down at the paper, which he was now holding as if it were coated in poison. He cleared his throat once more and then started to read, tape still over his mouth.

A moment later, a voice from the back of the room chimed in, "Marty, we can't understand a word you're saying with that tape over your mouth."

Marty stopped reading, put down the paper, and pointed his right index finger toward the ceiling. With his eyes shining as if a light bulb had just gone off, he headed over to the blackboard and wrote the words, "You can't hear what I'm saying. Why is that?"

He then turned back to the class and with his hand gestures asked for an answer to his question.

"Because you have tape on your mouth?" someone suggested.

Marty shook his head and lowered his eyebrows.

"Because you have a cold and you don't want us to catch it?"

Marty shook his head again, and his frown became even more pronounced.

"Because you decided to give us all an A on the midterm and you didn't know how to break the news to us?" That response got a laugh and then an ovation from the class. It even had Marty smiling under the tape, but he was still shaking his head.

There were several more unsuccessful attempts, and Marty, growing more frustrated by the minute, was tapping his head, signaling the class to use their brains.

Reagan, who had yet to venture a theory, looked over at Marty's desk, and saw that the piece of paper Marty had been reading from was a memo written on the university's letterhead. That's when it hit him. Marty Schemer had been censored, and he was not happy about it.

"Because you're not supposed to talk about what you really want to talk about today?"

Marty looked over at Reagan and raised his clenched fist in affirmation. He then moved directly in front of Reagan's seat and started curling his fingers toward himself, urging Reagan to continue.

"Because what you wanted to talk about is a sensitive subject, and the administration, your bosses, don't think we can handle it? They think it might stir things up? Cause us to protest just like we did about the war? Voice our opinions? Exercise our rights? Do something that they haven't been able to do, begin to solve the problem, really solve it?"

Marty was frozen in place, looking down proudly at his protégé and friend. And then, with a nod of his head and an open-eyed stare, he gestured to Reagan to come to a conclusion.

"They told you that you couldn't talk about the riots that are going on downtown or the situation that caused them. So, since you can't talk about it, you want us to spend the rest of the class talking about it amongst ourselves."

Marty gave Reagan one final nod. He then walked back over to his desk drawer and took out a manila envelope. The envelope contained newspaper clippings, a copy of the administration's memo, and a note outlining the class's assignment that would be due on Monday. The note simply read, "Tell me in one hundred words or less what you think."

Marty Schemer then turned around and walked out of the class without looking back.

* * *

Gary Glaser was still in full uniform when he walked through the door. His shift was over, and he was worn out. The past thirty-six hours of his life had been the longest and most exhausting he could remember. All in all, so far, there had been two fatalities, twenty-seven arrests, thirty-nine people hospitalized, and an estimated two million dollars in property damage. Just keeping up with all of the paperwork was a twelve-person job, and he and his team were frazzled.

He removed his gun belt and threw it on the kitchen table, walked over to the bed, untied his shoes, slid out of them, and then let himself fall facedown onto the pillow. He hadn't had time to come to grips with the events taking place in his personal life, and he wasn't in the mood to confront them right now. He was just too damn tired.

"Hey, Gary. Wow, you look beat."

There was no response.

"Can I get you anything?"

"A beer. I would love a cold beer."

"Sure, not a problem. I'll be right back."

While she walked over to the refrigerator, Gary rolled over and took off his shirt. He slid out of his pants and socks and lay back down, this time on his back, with the pillows propped up behind his head.

She saw that he was lying there in just his underwear and t-shirt, but she didn't say anything about it and tried not to be too obvious with her glances. "Here you go."

"Thanks."

Gary studied her for a minute as she stood above him. He watched closely as she slowly savored the first sip of her own beer. She was really quite beautiful, he thought. Had he been taking her for granted now that their relationship was merely a matter of convenience?

Perhaps it was time for him to rethink things, make a change in his life, and reevaluate this relationship. *It's not every day that a girl like this walks into your life.* It would be a real shame if somehow he let her slip away. Maybe their relationship could be a lot more than it had turned out to be. But he would have to change. She was not going to accept his running around. Could it be time for him to finally settle down? Or maybe this was all senseless conjecture. He was, after all, totally exhausted. "Come over here and lay down next to me . . . please."

"Are you sure, Gary? You look so tired, and it's . . ." She looked at her watch but didn't finish her thought.

"Come over here!"

Cuddled up next to him, she put her head down on his chest and wrapped her arm around his waist. He couldn't see the expression on her face or read the reflection in her eyes. She lay there for a minute not saying a word, looking down at his handsome body and his increasingly impressive package.

"So, what did you wind up doing last night?" he asked.

"Oh, you know, the regular. I just sat around here reading my book and knitting."

Gary chuckled. "Now I know that's not the truth."

"Well, okay, I'll fess up. But remember, you weren't around, and a girl does have certain needs."

"So, you managed somehow to take care of those needs without me?"

"Yeah, but it wasn't the first time, and I hate to tell you it won't be the last."

"It wasn't the first time? But I thought . . ."

"You don't think you know everything about me, do you?"

"Well, I guess not. Not after what you just confessed. But I do appreciate your honesty, and I suppose I can forgive you this time. I'm not Mr. Perfect myself, as I'm sure you've figured out."

"I know you're not, but after what I did, I couldn't blame you for being mad." She was still looking down at him. *Damn, he was impressive! Last night had been fun, real fun, but nothing could ever replace the likes of Gary.*

If he felt up to it, she would do it. She could never say no, not to him. She knew she didn't love him, not like the love she remembered, but she did love the thought of him, and she'd been thinking about this moment ever since their last time together. *And why is he being so sweet and understanding?* They hadn't talked like this in so long, and it was tugging at her heartstrings.

"Do you think you could ever give it up? I mean, be with just one guy? Fall in love again and be faithful to just him?"

"I don't know, Gary. You know how bad I've been hurt. I'm not sure I could go through that again. Can you understand that? And, by the way, last night was a lot of fun. You wouldn't expect me to give that up, would you?" She tickled his stomach, trying to lighten the mood. "And tell me why you're asking me about all of this anyway, Gary. I'm pretty sure that you have already made up your mind about your direction in life."

"You never know. People can change." He stretched his neck to look into her eyes and saw where they were focused.

"Take them off. I know you want to."

"Take what off? I don't know what you're talking about."

"Don't you lie to me again, or I will be mad at you! After what you did last night without me, I should turn you over my knee! Now take them off!"

When they were finished, she laid curled up next to him as he slept. He was so strong, so confident. She felt totally safe when she was with him. Despite it all, she was happy that they had met, and she hoped things would turn out . . . turn out for the best . . . for everyone involved.

She looked over at the clock. She would let him sleep for an hour, and then she would wake him up. There was plenty of food in the refrigerator. She would make him a snack and a cup of coffee. They would enjoy some more small talk, and then he would leave.

For now, she would just hold him close and listen to his heartbeat. There was nothing perfect about this man or their relationship, but she knew that it was what it was and that they would always share a special bond no matter what happened. She looked down at the ring on his finger and closed her eyes. Soon he would need to go. He would need to go because he had somewhere else he needed to be.

* * *

At 4:30 AM, three young men dressed in white robes with hoods, carrying unlit candles, and smoking cigars left the house and headed his way.

They were on their way to find Reagan Davis.

There was no one else on the street at that time of night. It was pitch dark along their walk with the exception of an occasional streetlight penetrating a thick fog that had settled in.

More than fifty men had been at the meeting that evening, and the decision had been unanimous. Now it was up to these three, and these three alone, to deliver the message, and this particular message, without a doubt, would change Reagan Davis's life forever.

* * *

Earlier that day, following their teacher's exodus, Marty Schemer's political science class had worked itself into a frenzy. After reading the articles about Tyrone Miller and his senseless death, they felt as if they needed to do something. They admitted to themselves that whatever they did would most likely turn out to be a waste of time, but doing nothing was totally unacceptable. But what could they possibly do? What could twenty-five kids going to school in Gainesville, Florida, do about an unjust murder that had taken place on the other side of the globe?

Beverly McNamara stood up in the back of the room and instantly had everyone's attention. "I'm the incoming vice president of the student body. Our offices are on the third floor of the Reitz Union. Usually, at this time of day, there's no one in the place. There is a phone bank. We have thirty phones in all, along with phone books for almost every city in the country. I mean hundreds of them, including Washington, DC.

"The university covers the cost of all long-distance phone calls. If each of us can make ten phone calls an hour and we stay there until five o'clock . . . Well, I'm not very good at math, but maybe we can stir things up. Maybe we can let the right people know what's really going on in our corner of the world and what we expect them to do about it."

With that said, the entire class gathered up their things, put their rain gear back on, and headed to Reitz Union to man the phones.

On the walk over, Reagan and Beverly worked on the script that would be used for every phone call. The message was simple: Tyrone Miller's death was a tragedy. The fact that no one was being held accountable for it in any way was unacceptable and unforgivable. This was a young man who had gone off to serve his country and, because of the color of his skin, would never come home.

The violence that was taking place on the streets of Gainesville was wrong, but what was also wrong, and what would certainly lead to even bigger problems, was the government sweeping this whole matter under the rug. Something needed to be done about this, and it needed to be done immediately.

By 5:00 PM, they had made close to one thousand calls. They had called every listing they could find in the phone books under United States Navy. They had called the offices of local politicians. They had called the governors' offices in all fifty states. They had dialed the phone numbers of congressmen, senators, mayors, county commissioners, and city councilmen.

Mostly, they had spoken to aides or secretaries, but on several occasions, they had actually been put through to the real deal. When this happened, Beverly McNamara would step in and take over as the group's spokesperson.

They were done for the day, and they were worn out, but they were proud of themselves. They had just agreed to continue their efforts the following week and were packing up to leave when two things happened. Marty Schemer walked through the door wearing no duct tape, and then one of the phones rang.

"Hello, this is Reagan Davis. May I help you?"

"Yes, Mr. Davis, this is Lawton Chiles, Senator Lawton Chiles. I'm calling to speak with a Beverly McNamara. Does she happen to be there with you?"

Reagan's face lost its color, and his frantic pointing at the phone had everyone's undivided attention. "It's Senator Chiles. Beverly, he's asking to speak with you."

Without a hint of hesitation, Beverly walked over and grabbed the phone from Reagan, who was white as a sheet. "Hello, Senator. Thank you so much for calling. I have my entire team here. Do you mind if I put you on the speaker? . . . Okay, here we go."

"Miss McNamara, how are you today? And hello to your team. I just wanted to let you all know a couple of things. First, my office has been receiving phone calls from all around the country. Young people like you all are speaking out, and rightfully so. I also want you to know that your concerns are not being ignored.

"We have been looking into this matter for several days now, and although I'm not at liberty to disclose specific details, you should keep your eyes on the news for certain upcoming developments. I think you will be pleased with what you discover."

When the phone call ended, everyone stared in silence at Beverly. Then, slowly, all eyes drifted over to Marty Schemer, who was still standing in the doorway, not believing what he had just heard.

Marty bought the first round of pitchers at the Ratheskellar, and then the second, and then the third.

Finally, at 10:00 PM, Reagan excused himself to the handful of his classmates who were still sitting at a table listening to Marty pontificate. He went to say good-bye to Sherri Miles, and after reconfirming their plans for the following evening, he headed back to his room. He had an early morning the next day with a lot to do, and he wanted to get a good night's sleep. He also had a big decision to make and needed to be clearheaded when he made it.

* * *

The pounding on the door startled him. Reagan thought for sure that he must have been dreaming.

Bam! Bam! Bam!

No, he was not dreaming. The alarm clock read 4:55 AM. It was pitch black outside. His heart was pounding. "Reagan Davis, open this door!"

When he opened the door, standing there in front of him were what looked like the three wise men. They were all wearing hoods, holding burning candles, and chanting under their breaths. Reagan looked closer. He thought he recognized them, especially the one in the middle. It was Moose. *What in the world was Anthony Mosul doing here at this hour?*

"Hey, little buddy. We have some good news for you. You're gonna be a Sigma Chi!"

CHAPTER SEVENTEEN

*W*ith his big date scheduled for that night as well as something else that might take up his time earlier in the evening, Reagan had made a deal with Hiram. In exchange for getting Saturday night off, he had agreed to be at the Hog at 10:00 AM Saturday morning.

Hiram, as a matter of routine, would give his place a good hosing off, as he referred to it, once a month. This much-needed undertaking included carting all of the tables and chairs out of the restaurant and into the parking lot, where they would be washed down with a cleaning solution. While they were drying in the sun, the inside of the Hog would be thoroughly scrubbed down. The walls, the bar, the kitchen, and the bathrooms; everything would be hosed off.

Until recently, Hiram had enlisted the talents of three Hungarian sisters to assist him with this task. Last month, however, the youngest had rebuffed his advances for the first time. Subsequently, Hiram had not yielded his characteristically generous tip, and all three of them had walked off the job. Hiram had chuckled to Reagan three days earlier on the phone, "I guess she just got tired of being hosed off."

As Reagan was pulling the orange bullet into the parking lot, he was surprised to see Lou Rollins and Karen Stein waiting at the front door. As he would soon find out, Karen had volunteered for this duty as a way of redeeming herself for an unexcused absence one week earlier. She had volunteered Lou as punishment for his confessed indiscretions committed while attending a bachelor party earlier in the week.

Karen, obviously still fuming, wouldn't elaborate on this touchy subject, but later that morning, with her out of earshot, Lou would. "We all wound up at the Pleasure Palace. Reagan, if you haven't been there, you have no idea what you're missing. The girls are red hot, especially the one they call Tiffany. Anyway, at closing time, we talked a couple of the dancers into coming back to the hotel room we had rented for the night.

"In no time flat, we were all swimming naked in the pool. We made such a ruckus that the night manager almost kicked us out of the place. Unfortunately, I drank too much and passed out on the couch before the fun really got started. Karen doesn't believe that part, but it's true . . . damn it.

"When I got back to Murphree the next morning, Karen was waiting out front, and she wasn't very happy. Anyway, that's why I'm here. That, and the fact that Hiram has promised me free beer for the rest of the month.

"By the way, I heard about what happened to Jackson. Have you talked to him?" Lou suddenly had a look of concern on his face.

"I have, Lou. I called his dad's house yesterday. Jackson's fine, just some bumps and bruises, nothing broken . . . physically, that is. His dad has been released from jail, and it doesn't look like any charges will be filed against him. Unless, that is, they can find a way to charge him for being the worst shot in the world.

"Anyway, Lou, I'm worried about Jackson. He didn't sound like himself. He seemed very detached. He would only talk for a couple of minutes. I hope to run into him this evening at the—"

"Reagan, you're not thinking about going to the service, are you? Because if you are, I think you are making a huge mistake. It's very dangerous downtown right now. Please tell me that you'll think about this long and hard—"

At that moment, Hiram and Karen came out of the restaurant and into the parking lot, carrying a pitcher of beer along with four glasses. Their arrival disrupted the conversation, but Lou was still giving Reagan the evil eye as the four of them toasted to a job well done.

The Hog was spotless. Lou, it seemed, was out of the doghouse. Hiram had been so pleased with their labors that he handed each of them a twenty-dollar bill, and Reagan was still struggling with his dilemma.

* * *

Lou had not been the first person that particular morning to advise Reagan concerning this matter.

After the unexpected middle-of-the-night visit by the Moose and his entourage, there was no way Reagan was going to be able to get back to sleep. He kept looking at the pledge pin he had been given and thinking about the things he had been told.

It was a high honor to have been selected as a pledge, and with the prestige of becoming a brother, his future dating opportunities were unlimited. He knew that there were a lot of great fraternities on campus, but

Sigma Chi had been his favorite by far. There was only one problem: Mom and Dad would need to get on board and agree to the extra expense.

Reagan knew their Saturday routine. They would wake up at 7:00 AM and spend their first half hour in the living room sipping coffee, talking, and reading the morning paper. His dad would be the first one into the shower while Mom would go into the kitchen to start cooking breakfast.

That's when he called home. He needed to talk to his mom first. *As soon as she hears the excitement in my voice, she'll find a way to make this happen!*

His plan worked. At least he thought it did. Her parting words were, "I'm sure we can work something out, sweetheart. I'll talk it over with your father and we'll— Oh, here he is now. He wants to say hi!"

"Hello, son. Well, aren't you up bright and early this morning? Headed to the library, I hope?"

They caught up for a few minutes, and Reagan thought it was wonderful to hear his dad in such a great mood. Before they hung up, however, a stern fatherly warning had been issued.

"Now, son, you've got to promise me something. Stay away from all of that rioting up there. I read in the paper this morning that those Navy boys have been rearrested, but that won't calm things down overnight. You do remember our agreement, don't you? Don't go near it. It's nothing that concerns you. Do you hear me loud and clear?"

"I promise, Dad. And, by the way, I could use some more of those . . . well, you know . . . "

Even after taking his plans for that evening into consideration, Reagan's bottom dresser drawer supplies were still nearly intact. In asking for them, however, he hoped not only to change the subject but also to renew the bond that he and his dad had forged regarding the subject.

"Well, son, I will take care of that . . . that thing . . . you just mentioned right away. And whatever it was you and your mom were discussing, well, we'll work that out too. Good-bye, son. Love you. Study hard!"

* * *

After finishing up at the Hog, Reagan's next stop that morning was the nursing home, where he was sure Sally Tindale would have a list of chores waiting for him. When he looked up at the porch, he saw Sally sitting alongside Lieutenant Moore, and for a split second, he thought he caught a glimpse of them holding hands. *Now, wouldn't that be something else!?*

After Reagan said hello to both of them, Sally scurried inside to make some iced tea and Reagan walked around to the shed to retrieve the lawn mower. With all of the recent rainfall, he had not been able to mow in quite a while, and the grass was up past his ankles. He cranked up the mower and started his laps, and before he knew it, his mind was a million miles away.

* * *

The only real hero Reagan had ever known, with the exception of the lieutenant, had been one of his sister's many boyfriends, Chad Johnson. Chad lived next door to their house in Miami Springs, and for the longest time, he'd had a crush on Alice. Alice, in turn, had been very fond of Chad, but she had never been a one-guy girl, and thus Chad's watchdog proximity concerned her. Nonetheless, Chad had received plenty of Alice's attention when she felt like giving it to him.

Reagan always enjoyed playing the annoying little brother, and when Chad came over to visit, he would join them on the front porch and pretty much refuse to leave. Chad would eventually find something to bribe his nemesis with, and Reagan would reluctantly go into the house to get out of their hair, but not out of earshot. Reagan's bedroom was adjacent to the front porch, and with the window cracked, he could hear everything they were saying.

As time went on, Chad took a genuine liking to Reagan. When Alice wasn't in the mood, the two guys would toss the football around, play cards, or go for a swim in the backyard pool.

Chad was a bigger-than-life charmer, standing well over six feet tall, with a muscular body and a rugged face. He was a natural storyteller, had a gregarious laugh, a barreling baritone voice, and a smile that lit up the room. He had never had a little brother, and over time, he adopted Reagan to fill that position.

One day from his room, Reagan heard Chad tell Alice that he had been drafted and that he needed to report for duty in three days. Then the two of them went for a walk and were gone for a couple of hours. When they returned, Reagan heard Chad ask Alice, "Hey, how about saying goodbye to the little guy for me. I'm not sure I can handle that."

Reagan didn't know at the time what a draft was, or what reporting for duty meant. He was shocked to hear that there was something that Chad Johnson couldn't handle, and he didn't want to even think about his "big brother" going away.

Six months later, Reagan would begin to understand these things and the consequences that came along with them.

Chad returned to Miami Springs after serving five months in Vietnam and one month lying on his stomach in the VA hospital. When he made his first return visit to the Davises' front porch, he was still unable to sit down.

As a result, he stood on the first step for over an hour, leaning against his crutches.

It had been a nighttime mission, and they had been ambushed. Against his sergeant's orders, Chad, hearing a cry for help, had turned around and run back toward the swamp. Upon reaching his mark, he had bent over and deadlifted the wounded soldier over his shoulder. With just a few feet to go before reaching the safety of the tree line, machine gun fire rang out, and Chad had been shot several times in his buttocks.

Reagan, sitting and listening on the porch, was amazed not only by his hero's bravery but also by how he told this incredible story so lightheartedly.

"Yeah, you could've figured I'd go over there and come back with nothing but lead in my ass."

The war had not changed him. If anything, this bigger-than-life-man had grown in stature.

Two months later, he was gone again, and seven months after that, he was back on the porch. This time he was in a wheelchair, with casts on both legs.

"There's a reason that they tell you not to jump out of a helicopter at twenty feet. But you know me, not much between the ears. I guess I will need to be more careful from now on. I don't want to come back in a box."

This time, Chad Johnson had saved the lives of three of his fellow soldiers but had shattered bones in both of his legs in the process. Chad was now eligible for a medical discharge. He could return to civilian life. He did not have to go back to the war, but he did anyway.

It was two years before Reagan saw Chad again, and when he did, he would hardly recognize his "big brother." On a lawn chair in the front yard of the house next door sat a broken man. He was half his previous size, with graying hair and shaking hands. He had spent the past eight months in the mental health ward of the VA hospital. He hadn't been wounded this time—not physically, anyway. This time it wasn't something he had done that caused his suffering; it was something he hadn't done.

Chad's "little brother" sat beside him on the lawn every day for the next two months. Reagan would talk. Chad would not.

The night before he did the unthinkable, Chad walked over to the porch and sat on the chair just outside of Reagan's window. "Reagan, can you hear me?"

"Yes, Chad, I can hear you."

"Then listen carefully. Don't ever turn your back on your friends. Don't ever walk away when they need you. Fight fear with everything inside of you, because if you don't, there will be nothing inside of you left."

* * *

"Reagan! Reagan! You've mowed over the same patch of grass four times. Are you paying attention?"

Reagan reached down and killed the motor on the lawn mower. "Sorry, Lieutenant Moore, I mean Willy. I guess I was just daydreaming. Hey, do you have a few minutes? There's something I need to run by you."

* * *

Reagan had never been inside of a Baptist church, and he had never been to a black person's funeral.

As a matter of fact, he had been to only one funeral in his life, and it had been the funeral of his grandfather. That particular service had been held at the Grace Lutheran Church in Miami Springs, and it had been presided over by Pastor Wright, a kind and loving soul. Thinking back, Reagan remembered that the entire service had lasted less than an hour.

The service for Tyrone Miller was to be at 6:00 PM. Reagan's date with Sherri Miles was at 7:30 PM. It was about a ten-minute drive to her place from the church. He had brought a change of clothes, and as he had done numerous times in the past, he would change in his car, out of his suit and into his favorite jeans and collared shirt.

This time, Sally Tindale had personally selected a dozen red roses from her garden. She had cut them, arranged them alongside white baby's breath flowers, and then wrapped them in pink tissue paper with a bright red bow.

The orange bullet was sparkling clean, and Reagan had his favorite Doobie Brothers tape ready to pop into the cassette player. He had purchased a bottle of red wine that actually had a cork. He had planned for everything. Everything, that is, except for what happens inside of a Baptist church during a black person's funeral.

Reagan had purposely gotten to the church a few minutes late. As he had hoped, everyone was already inside when he arrived. His plan was to slip inside the door unnoticed and sit in a back row. He would keep an eye on his gold watch and, if need be, could leave quietly without disturbing anyone.

He slowly opened the door and was stepping inside when he first heard the wailing sounds filling the completely packed church. Everybody was standing, crying, hugging, and praying out loud. The minister was at the altar with his hands raised toward the heavens, preaching, and the choir was behind him, singing a gospel song and dancing about.

Reagan quickly noticed that he was the only white person in attendance, and suddenly, he started to feel as if he had made a huge mistake.

145

As he turned to leave, the church door slipped out of his hands. It made a crashing sound as it slammed shut. A rippling silence swept through the room, and all eyes slowly drifted toward the back of the church. Everyone was looking at Reagan, including Jamal Spikes and two of his men. They were not only looking at Reagan but were heading his way, and they didn't look happy to see him.

Just as they reached him and started shoving him toward the door, Reagan heard her voice. "Back away from that boy." Rita Mae Miller had left her seat in the first pew and, with the assistance of her cane, was standing, facing the back of the church.

All eyes shifted her way as she hobbled slowly toward Reagan.

Jamal Spikes and his accomplices peeled away, giving Reagan some breathing room.

In the center of the church, Rita Mae paused. She did a sweeping assessment of the congregation and then thumped her cane against the side of a pew, calming the intensifying buzz.

"Y'all hear me and hear me good. That young man be a guest of mine here today, and I want yuz to be payin' him the same respects that yuz be payin' me. Reagan, yuz come down here and sit beside me, ya hear?"

Reagan took a deep breath, swallowed hard, and then brushed by Jamal Spikes on his way to Rita Mae.

"Now, my son, Tyrone, he'd been a lot like this boy here. Polite, respectful, kindhearted, he knowed his manners, and hows to behave in front of folks. These two mighta been friends iffin' my young 'un had lived long enough. And the reason he ain't livin' is cuzza alls the hate out there . . . and in here. Yuz hear me? As the Lord be my witness, that needs to be stoppin' right here, right now! If Tyrone's life is ta mean a thing, his passin' can't be 'membered with sticks and guns. God help us if we all can't finds a way to lives together in peace!"

When Reagan reached Rita Mae, she looked deeply into his eyes, and with tears in her own eyes, she said, "Thank yuz for comin', young man. Yuz be a brave soul, and I'd be honored with yuz bein' my family today. I lost my boy, and ain't nothin' ever gonna be bringin' him back, but I believes the Lord sent yuz here to be with me today cuzza he knowed what it be like to be losin' a son."

As they approached the front of the church, Reagan saw Jackson in the third row, several seats in from the aisle. Their eyes locked, and time seemed to stand still. Jackson slowly made his way to the aisle, and the two of them were soon standing face to face. A handshake folded into a hug. "Reagan, I think you're right. As long as we're running away from it, they win. Give me a few days to make sure that my dad's alright, and I'll be moving back in."

* * *

Reagan sat on the second stoop of the inside stairwell of Building G. He was at the Pointe West Apartments, just outside of Unit 121, and he was still in his suit. He had the roses in one hand and the bottle of wine in the other. It was going on 9:00 PM.

After the service ended, he helped Rita Mae to the waiting limousine and then rushed back to his car. He stopped at the nearest phone booth to call Sherri. There had been no answer. When he got to her place, he knocked several times on her door. There was no answer.

As he was standing to leave, he heard the phone ringing inside of her apartment. He heard her answer. She was home. He decided not to knock again.

He left the roses by her door and walked outside. He was getting into his car when he suddenly heard a voice behind him.

"Reagan, don't ask me how, but I've just heard what you did today. Listen, we don't have to go anywhere tonight. If we get hungry, we'll order a pizza. Bring that bottle of wine with you, and let's go inside. You have had quite a day!"

CHAPTER EIGHTEEN

*J*ackson was leaning against the light pole marking the spot at the top of the hill on 34th Street. His arms were folded across his shirtless chest as he looked down the hill with an expression of disbelief.

"As far as I'm concerned, you are all pretty slow, but that right there might be the slowest white man I've ever laid my eyes on."

Reagan, who was still suffering the remnants of a massive hangover brought on by certain indiscretions two nights earlier, looked over at his roommate and smiled. It was sure great to have his running buddy and good friend back. Living alone for a couple of weeks had had its advantages, but there was just something about Jackson being around that amplified Reagan's entire college experience.

"Yeah, Jackson, I can't argue with you there. I'm not sure he's going to make it. What do you think, Terri? Should we trot back down there and give him a hand?"

Terri Spencer had not been able to turn down the invitation to join them on their pre-Frisbee ball game warm-up run. There was no way she was going to miss out on this. Nothing could keep her from being a witness to and enjoying every minute of the prize Jackson had won in his political science class.

The distinction had been handed out for the top grade on the midterm exam. The reward? "One day spent with your graduate assistant doing anything, within reason, the winner wants to do." Both Jackson and Beverly McNamara had posted perfect scores. Beverly had acquiesced, handing Jackson the honor.

Terri had recently completed a political science class during the summer session with Marty Schemer as the instructor, and she couldn't imagine it—she couldn't imagine Marty playing Frisbee ball, let alone running the three miles it would take to get to the game.

"Oh no, Reagan, he signed up for this gig. I think we should let him enjoy every second of it. By the way, I'm not sure you would make it back up the hill yourself. How much did you have to drink Thursday night, anyway? You still look like hell."

Two weeks had come and gone since Tyrone Miller's funeral. Following the news that the three Navy pilots were being held on manslaughter charges, a turn of events that Marty's political science class was taking full credit for with tongue in cheek, the town of Gainesville had quieted. There had been no more riots or rallies. All neighborhoods had returned to normal. It was as if the black community had gone through the stages of denial and anger and was now in a state of mourning.

The National Guard had disengaged the Sunday morning following the service. The curfew had been lifted that same day. The Hotbox Squad had been disbanded, and the police department was back to its regular schedules. The mayor was breathing a major sigh of relief and could refocus on his reelection campaign.

The police chief had handed out several commendations. Both Melvin Peters and Darren Daniels received the Mayor's Gold Star Award for bravery above and beyond the call of duty. Gary Glaser had been summoned in front of the city council, where he received a plaque of appreciation. Each council member left his or her perch, coming down to shake the sergeant's hand, congratulate him, and thank him for his outstanding leadership. Rumors within the department were that his promotion was only weeks away.

The UF campus had also mellowed in advance of midterm exams. Very few parties had been posted on the billboards, the Ratheskellar had been nearly empty all week, and the libraries had been full. Everyone on campus was on edge.

This was it. Bad test scores at this point would not end a college career, but they would be a good indication of one's ability to cut it. Students, especially freshmen, were very subdued, studious, and extremely nervous, to say the least.

Reagan's last midterm had been Thursday afternoon. Coincidentally, Thursday had also been Jackson's last test and, on top of that, his eighteenth birthday. If there had ever been a reason to party, this was it. And party they had. Reagan still remembered only parts of the evening, and every memory that popped back into his head was more painful and embarrassing than the one before it.

It had been Reagan's idea to start the evening at Big Daddy's Lounge. Thursday night was ladies' night, which meant that all ladies drank for free, and, as Reagan had described it during his birthday party recruiting sweep

149

through the dorm, "When ladies drink for free, they will eventually become anything but ladylike."

Jake Johnson was the first to order a round of shots. Reagan had never had a shot but took an instant liking to them. They were sweet and delicious, like candy. *There couldn't possibly be much alcohol in them.*

Reagan couldn't remember the girl's name, and how was he to have known that her boyfriend was the lead singer in the band? He did remember, however, that she was spilling out of a loose-fitting white halter-top, that she was a good dancer, and that she was a really good kisser. He seemed to recall going out into the parking lot with her, where they had puffed on a cigarette. *Yuck!*

Then, after a couple more shots, and a couple more dances, the band took a break and all hell broke loose. Reagan's recollection was fuzzy, but he did remember Jackson running interference for him as he sprinted toward the exit. Only now was he beginning to remember bits and pieces of what had been going through his mind during the chase.

Where did I park the car? Shit! There it is. Get in quick. Lock the doors. Hit the gas. Damn, that was a close call!

I shouldn't be driving. I've had too much to drink. I'll pull into that parking lot and go into that bar to call a taxi. What is the name of this place, anyway? The Pleasure Palace. Hey, isn't that the name of the place Lou was telling me about?

* * *

Dear Diary,

Wow! It's been a crazy couple of weeks. First off, Gary and I broke up. Well, I'm not sure you would actually call it breaking up. He's up for a big promotion at work. He seems to think that they are watching his every move, and he doesn't want to do anything that could hurt his chances. I guess he's afraid that we might get caught. I've never known Gary to be afraid of anything, but he wants this promotion so bad, and I want it for him. He deserves it.

I had to work Thursday night, but he came by in the afternoon to talk. He said everything would be back to normal soon. He said he might even have a big surprise for me after this is all over. Lord knows what that could be. Anyway, we said goodbye for over two hours. He was unbelievable. I thought the trailer was going to flip over. I'm gonna miss that!

My really big news is that my dad called me this week. Well, the nurse actually called and talked to me for ten minutes before Dad came on the line. He is in the VA Hospital in Jacksonville. He admitted himself into the drug and alcohol rehab center. Six weeks now without a drink. He sounded so good. Just like the dad I remembered as a little girl before Mom died.

After I said goodbye to him, the nurse got back on the phone and told me that I could come to see him in three weeks. She also whispered that he could use a little spending money and explained that he was too embarrassed to ask for it. Other than that, she said he was doing great and that she was certain he had turned the corner. I was so happy that I cried for over an hour after we hung up and was late for work.

My best customer at the Palace, Robert, I've told you about him, has been very good to me lately. I guess that's because I have been very good to him, very good! Anyway, I had saved up over five hundred dollars, so I drove to the Western Union and wired it to my dad. I still have plenty left for groceries and gas, and I have another date with Robert next week.

Oh yeah, the funniest thing happened Thursday night. Reagan Davis, my Frisbee ball buddy, came in, actually stumbled in, to the Palace. He didn't know that I worked there, and he almost fell over when he saw me up on the stage.

He said that he was too drunk to drive, but he sat front and center drinking beer for over three hours. I had to keep him from nodding off a couple of times. I asked him twice, but he didn't want me to call him a taxi.

After we closed, Bubba helped me get him into the Ray. Reagan was completely out of it and couldn't remember where his dorm was. I didn't know what else to do, so I brought him home to the trailer. I'm not sure what he was thinking, but the next thing I knew, he was taking off his clothes and climbing into my bed. I would have let him do me. He is pretty cute. Anyway, he tried twice to put a rubber on but . . . well, you know.

He was so drunk I doubt if he remembers a thing. I'm gonna see him tomorrow at the game. That should be quite interesting. There is somebody at my door. Got to go.

C

* * *

"Charlotte Summerland! It's Stephen Crain, your landlord. We need to talk, and we need to talk now!"

* * *

Marty Schemer had finally made it up the hill and was bent over, gasping for air. Jackson and Terri had long since given up on him. They had placed a last-one-there bet and were in an all-out sprint toward the field.

"Jesus Christ, Reagan!" Marty was finally regaining his composure. "So, you do this every week? Please don't tell me how we're getting home after the game. I'm sure I don't want to know. I need to walk for a little while. Now tell me more about this Charley girl. We got interrupted earlier. Sounds to me like after what happened Thursday night, you might have yourself a new girlfriend. You know, not just an appetizer. This one could be the main course."

"First off, Marty, you can't say a word. Promise?"

"Promise."

"Well, to start with, she's gorgeous. You'll see for yourself in a couple of minutes. I would never have guessed that she was a stripper, but when I walked into the Pleasure Palace two nights ago, there she was, up on the stage. She had nothing on but a G-string, and her body is unbelievable.

"She was all over me between dances, and she insisted that I wait for her to get off work. Then she drives me to her place. She lives in a trailer in the Shady Oaks Mobile Home Community. We just passed it.

"I think we smoked a joint and split a beer, and then she tells me to strip down and climb into her bed. I know we did it at least twice. I wish I could remember that part a little better.

"When I woke up, she was cooking me breakfast. She drove me back to get my car, and the whole time, she acted as if nothing had happened. It's going to be a little awkward seeing her this morning."

"Awkward? Reagan, the only thing that could be awkward is if you two go on pretending that nothing happened. You need to thank her, tell her how much you enjoyed yourself, and ask her out on a date. Sounds to me like you've hit the jackpot. If she is as good-looking as you are telling me, you need to seal the deal. Trust me, man. I know women. What you do in the next few minutes will decide whether you ever get invited back into that trailer."

When they reached the field, Reagan pointed to his right. "This is where we play, and that right there is Charley. What do you think?"

"Holy shit, Reagan! I mean, holy shit!"

* * *

"What can I do for you, Mr. Crain? What's that in your hand?"

"It is an eviction notice, Miss Summerland. As you can see, it has been signed by the Clerk of the Circuit Court. You have three days in which to vacate the trailer and leave the Shady Oaks for good. You have been constantly behind on your rent. And by the way, you don't even have a valid lease. That was in your old boyfriend's name. Anyway, you're out of here. Do you hear me?"

As Stephen Crain turned and marched toward his house, a smile came across his face. He listened carefully for her footsteps behind him. He knew she would follow him. He knew she would beg him to let her stay. She would do anything. He had her trapped like an animal in a cage. And, boy, did he have plans for his prisoner.

"But, Mr. Crain, I thought you and Gary had—"

He had been right. They were already halfway to the house, and she was right behind him. He could tell from her voice that she was holding back tears.

"I don't give a damn about your policeman boyfriend. The next time he trespasses in this park, he's likely to get his head shot off. And by the way, if you do call him about this, his chances of getting that promotion I've been reading about in the paper are over. Not only that, I think it's high time that little wifey of his finds out what's going on between the two of you. I think she needs to know what her husband really does on Thursday nights. And by the way, sweetheart, you and your skinny cop aren't the only ones with pictures."

Stephen Crain felt the excitement rushing through his veins. He also felt the pounding in his pants. That was good. He would need that in just a couple of minutes.

No longer would she face the wall with her eyes closed. No longer would she make him wear a rubber. She would do anything and everything he ordered her to do. She would worship him. He would make her beg him for it. From now on, she would be his, and only his. And then one day, he would introduce her to Carly Glaser, and on that day, both women would perform for him and only him. He would take pictures and send them to the tall skinny man, and there would be nothing that the tall skinny man could do to stop him.

"But, Mr. Crain, please! Can I come in? I'm sure we can work something out."

* * *

Marty Schemer might have been a slow runner, but when it came to tossing a Frisbee, his talents were unparalleled. He had a way of floating the disk high into the air and sending it gliding gently back to earth, right into the arms of his receiver. Unofficially, the game ended with Marty, Terri, and Ye winning fifteen to six.

With Gary absent, the experience had been much less competitive. Everyone had been relaxed and carefree. When the game was over, Marty promised to return and be a part of the Frisbee ball gang every chance he got. But he stressed that next time, he would drive his car and skip the three-mile warm-up.

"Hey, Charley, I'll carry the cooler back to your car for you."

Charley had iced down two six-packs of Miller High Life, and the gang sat in the middle of the field until the last can was empty.

Reagan had been looking for a chance to get Charley alone, and this was it. "Thanks, Reagan. That would be very nice of you."

"Charley, about the other night, I wanted—"

"Reagan, there is no need to . . . well, you know. That sort of thing just happens sometimes."

"That might be true, but that sort of thing doesn't happen. I mean, I mean, with such a beautiful . . . You know, it's not like it's never happened, but I try not to make a habit of it. I don't want you to think . . ."

"Reagan, you don't have to explain. And thank you for the compliment. I know it wasn't me, and I'm glad that you don't make a habit of it. It's just that after a few drinks, sometimes things like that just happen or don't happen. I'm sure if we were to ever . . . But don't feel like you have to—"

"Charley, you don't understand. What I am trying to tell you is that it was you, and I would love for it to happen again. Just like the other night."

"Just like the other night, Reagan? I find that a bit odd."

"And, Charley, no one else needs to know, if that would make you feel better."

"Reagan, I would never tell anybody, if that's what you're worried about."

"Why would I be worried about that? If it were up to me, I would let everyone know. I'm proud of it."

"Preppy, you are one strange dude, and I do think you just got off the bus from Mars. Anyway, let's get together again real soon. I would enjoy that."

Charley kissed Reagan on the cheek, took the cooler from him, and placed it on the passenger seat. Out of his line of sight, she smirked and rolled her eyes. She waved good-bye to the gang, hopped in her car, and fired up the engine. She couldn't remember a more uncomfortable conversation, and she had had several uncomfortable conversations lately.

Reagan stood for a minute and watched the Stingray disappear around the corner.

"Well? How did you do? Do you have a date?" Marty had hurried across the field, dying to know the outcome of the discussion between Reagan and Charley.

"Wow, Marty. I know it's hard to believe, but I think she likes me. I mean, I think she really likes me!"

CHAPTER NINETEEN

Monday was chores day at the Sally Tindale Nursing Home, and nothing, at least on the surface, seemed out of the ordinary on this particular Monday. Every resident, despite his or her physical or mental capacity, was given at least one assignment. Among other things, there was dusting to do and windows to clean, and, of course, someone had to tackle the pile of towels and sheets on the floor in the laundry room. "Well," as Sally put it, "this whole place could use a little sprucing up, and it is, after all, chores day."

The lieutenant, being the only man in the house, would take on any heavy lifting or mechanical jobs that needed doing: changing light bulbs, replacing air-conditioner filters, and moving the furniture around on the porch so Sally could mop. No job was too big or too small for the lieutenant, and he loved helping out.

But, on this day, it was the lieutenant who needed help. The home's water heater was on the fritz. Its heating element needed to be replaced. None of the ladies were strong enough to help him move the huge tank away from the wall in the utility room. He had tried moving it on his own with no success.

Reagan had just finished his shower and was toweling off when a naked Jake Johnson came rushing into the bathroom.

"Jesus, Jake, why are you always running around with no clothes on, and how is it that you don't trip over that thing?"

"Never mind that, Reagan. There's a Lieutenant Moore on the phone. He says he needs to talk to you. He sounds pretty serious. You're not in trouble, Reagan, are you? You didn't go off the deep end and join the army after that C you got on the humanities midterm, did you?"

"No, of course not, Jake. And Christ, will you please put some pants on. The lieutenant lives at the nursing home where I cut the grass. He's become a good friend. I visit with him a couple times a week. He tells

155

incredible stories, and I take notes. He's also a great guy to bounce things off of. Now, I have got to get out of here. You're creeping me out!"

On the phone, Reagan willingly agreed to head straight to the house after his pre-calculus class and help out with the water heater project. Standing there at the front gate a while later, he was reading, for the third time, the note that Molly had handed him after their class that morning.

Thinking back, he realized she had acted a little strange. She hadn't sat next to him, and she wouldn't make eye contact with him from across the room. After class, she had walked over to him and given him the note. He noticed tears in her eyes as she'd walked away. He'd heard her say, "Reagan, please try to understand." He'd watched her until she was out of sight, and she hadn't looked back. This just wasn't making sense, and no matter how many times he read the thing, he still couldn't figure out what was going on.

"Hey there, Reagan. Thanks for coming over this morning to lend the old man a hand. He's back there in the utility room. I'm afraid he's gonna bust a gut. What's that you're reading there? It looks important." Sally Tindale was up on the porch watering the plants, sporting a curious expression and staring down at the note in Reagan's hand.

As Reagan climbed the stairs, he responded, "Oh, it's nothing, Mrs. Tindale, just a note from my study partner, Molly Turner. I think I've mentioned her to you. I just don't know what I've done wrong that's made her mad."

Sally gently took the note from Reagan's hand and read it softly out loud.

Dear Reagan,

I can't tell you how much I have enjoyed your friendship these past few weeks. You are a very special boy and a great study partner. I have loved our talks, and I feel as if I've gotten to know who you really are. You should be very proud of who you are, inside and out.

I'm afraid that I won't be able to continue our relationship. Please don't be mad at me. One day I will try to explain. Until then, please respect my decision.

Yours Truly,

Molly

Sally folded the note and handed it back to Reagan. "So, you think it's something bad you've done that's caused this Molly Turner girl to write you this note?"

"Yes, Mrs. Tindale, but, I can't begin to—"

"Oh, my poor boy. My poor innocent boy."

* * *

It was standard procedure at the Gainesville Police Department to conduct a thorough vetting and an updated background check on any officer being considered for a promotion. And, of course, a promotion to the level of lieutenant warranted the investigation being completed in a well-documented and highly professional manner. The rank of lieutenant, after all, was second only to that of the chief of police, and at any given time, there were only three lieutenant positions available within the department.

Lieutenant Perry Stalling, who was only weeks from retirement, oversaw the patrolmen. Lieutenant Mack Tucker headed up the investigators. Lieutenant Barry Helton was in the senior position and in charge of all staff matters and departmental administration.

At his level, Helton answered only to the chief. He would therefore be next in line if and when the chief decided to step down. It was common knowledge, however, that because of lingering health concerns, the senior lieutenant had no interest in advancement.

On this Monday afternoon, the chief, his three lieutenants, and the mayor were gathered around a private table at the University Club, sipping whiskey and smoking cigars. The reason for the meeting was to discuss the possible promotion of one Sergeant Gary Glaser. Everyone knew what was at stake here, and some of what was at stake could not be discussed openly for various reasons.

Mack Tucker had spent his entire professional life with one objective and one objective only: He wanted to become the City of Gainesville's Chief of Police. Everyone at the table knew this, but what four of them were inwardly questioning was whether Tucker would actually make a good chief. He was an excellent administrator and the men loved him, but he had a tendency to panic under fire, a trait not suitable for someone in the top-dog position.

This meant that at stake on this day was not just the promotion on the table. They all knew that, realistically, they might also be choosing the department's next chief of police. This was a fact that weighed heavily on each of them. Subsequently, they had all carefully planned their own strategies for the meeting.

Helton and Stalling were fond of Gary Glaser. They admired his leadership capabilities and his outgoing persona. They were also keenly aware of his shortcomings. Within the department, you were either on Gary's team or you weren't. There was no in-between. Those who had chosen not to take part, or those who had for some reason been purposely excluded from Gary's inner circle, felt like outcasts. This occurrence had created a rift within the department, which was not a good thing, especially when close teamwork is often critical in life-and-death situations.

What these two lieutenants also knew, and what could clearly not be discussed at this gathering, involved Gary Glaser's reputation as a bad boy and a ladies' man. Running around on one's wife would not, on its own, nullify a promotion. After all, this was the police department, a fraternal brotherhood like none other. If this indiscretion were unacceptable, it would be hard to staff a shift. But Gary was the chief's son-in-law, for crying out loud. If word got out, there would be hell to pay.

Helton and Stalling had not discussed it, but each had come to the same conclusion. What they were facing was the worst of two evils.

The mayor sat at the head of the table and had only one thing on his mind, being reelected. The chief, who had been his close friend and ally for many years, was extremely popular with the voters, and the mayor valued his continued backing. Therefore, as far as the mayor was concerned, whatever the chief wanted on this day, the chief would get. "Gentlemen, I know the appropriate protocol in situations like this, but as the mayor, I've got to tell you that I'm not in favor of investing valuable staff time investigating an individual who we all know and trust like family. Gary Glaser is a fine young man. Carly is my goddaughter. Junior is like a grandson to me. I just don't see the point in racking up overtime, especially with what we've just been through as a department. Those damn riots ate a huge hole in our budget!"

The five men sat in silence for a long moment. The mayor was carefully studying the eyes in front of him, weighing any potential opposition to his strategy. Perry Stalling and Barry Helton sat without expression, staring at each other. Mack Tucker was squirming in his seat.

The chief, who was admiring the length of the ash on the end of his cigar, was the next to speak. "Well, I appreciate that, Mr. Mayor. You know I do. But we all have to follow certain rules. We've got to cross the t's and dot the i's . . . even if Gary is my daughter's husband. Y'all know that I love him as if he were my own son, but that shouldn't keep us from doing our job. What do you think, Perry? You've been through this a time or two. Any way to get this done without wasting too much time and effort?"

Mack Tucker was staring daggers at Perry Stalling from across the table. Their eyes were still locked when Stalling finally responded, "Well, I've got to agree with the chief. You know the press these days are up our butts. They have access to all of our files, and I'm beginning to think they have someone inside the department tipping them off. We oughta at least go through the motions. Wouldn't you agree, Barry?"

Barry Helton was eyeing Mack Tucker from across the table, giving him a *you're about to owe me big time* look as he responded, "Mr. Mayor . . . Chief . . . I'm afraid I have to agree with Perry. It just wouldn't look right if we completely ignored protocol. That might subject the department to outside criticism, and it could also wind up hurting Gary's reputation, if you know what I mean. Why don't we just put one man on it? A good man! Have him piddle around for a couple of weeks, write up a report for the file, you know . . . blah, blah, blah."

That suggestion brought a broad smile to the mayor's face, and after a moment of eye contact between himself and his chief, he responded, "Excellent thinking, Barry. Do you have any suggestions on who that might be? The good man, I mean."

"Mr. Mayor, with all due respect, I think Mack is in a better position to make that recommendation. Mack, what do you think? Do you have anyone in mind?"

Mack Tucker sat up straight in his seat, trying to maintain his serious expression. He had just been pitched a lob-ball, and he knew it. He scratched his head, looked down at his cigar, and then glanced into the eyes of the other two lieutenants before turning to the mayor and answering. "Melvin Peters, sir. I think Melvin Peters is the right man for the job."

* * *

Maria Sanchez couldn't remember ever being this mad. She still hadn't hung up the phone and was staring in disbelief at its handle. Gary Glaser hadn't even given her the common courtesy of breaking up with her in person. And he had just been over to her apartment two nights earlier, having his way with her. He could have told her then. *He's a fucking coward!*

Sure, he had said that it was just temporary and that things would be back to normal soon. He had even mentioned that he might have a surprise for her the next time they got together, but she knew better. She had been cast aside before. She knew how it felt and what was really going on. He had chosen his promotion over their relationship. Being a lieutenant was more important to him than all of the intimate hours they had spent together.

Even if it means that every night, he will be going home to that cheating wife of his, sleeping next to her after knowing where she's been and what she's done.

Or does he really know? He refused to talk about it the other night. Maybe he thinks I made it all up. I've got to prove to him that Carly is nothing but a slut. Then he will leave her for good and come back to me. And if he doesn't, he can burn in hell. Either way, if I can't have him, nobody can: his wife, his other girlfriends, nobody!

God, Carly, I am so sorry, but I just can't help myself. If I don't get him back, I don't know what I'm gonna do! I never planned on hurting you. Please forgive me.

Never mind that. So, how do I prove it? How do I convince Gary that his wife is a two-timer? The note! Where is that note? The one Carly left for me with her boyfriend's name, phone number, and address.

Maria slammed the phone handle down, stood up from the couch, and walked into her bedroom. She found the note where she had stuffed it in her top dresser drawer and studied it. "Stephen Crain, huh? Well, Mr. Crain, you might just hold the ticket to my happiness."

After walking back into the living room, Maria picked up the phone and dialed his number.

"Hello. This is Crain. Who's this? What do you want?"

* * *

With the water-heater project completed, Reagan and Lieutenant Moore settled into a couple of the rocking chairs on the front porch. The lieutenant had just finished expressing his appreciation for Reagan's help when Sally came through the front door with two glasses of iced tea.

"You gentlemen do good work. I don't remember the water ever being as hot as it is now. Y'all make a good team. And I believe you have a question for this young fella, don't you, old man?"

Reagan sat back and watched the tenderness between them. Each wore a shrewd smile, and Sally had a twinkle in her eyes. Reagan knew that something was up, and he had a pretty good idea what it was.

"Well, Reagan, there is something we need to tell you. I mean something I need to ask you. Sally and I are getting hitched. Right here on the porch next Saturday. I would be honored if you would stand with me . . . I mean as my best man."

Reagan hadn't expected that, and he almost fell out of the chair. Without thinking, he stood and found himself fighting the impulse to salute. He had grown fond of and had developed a deep respect for the lieutenant. And he of course loved Sally. He had hoped that somehow, each of them would find true happiness. The fact that they had found it together was overwhelming and brought tears to his eyes.

"Lieutenant Moore, I mean Willy, it would be my pleasure. I can't imagine a greater privilege. Thank you for asking me."

Sally turned to Reagan and gave him a lingering hug. As she backed away, she said. "And you must bring some friends. And bring a date, Reagan. I insist!" She was patting the note in his top pocket for emphasis.

CHAPTER TWENTY

*G*ary Glaser had two objectives and a simple plan to achieve both of them. His first objective was to make lieutenant. He had confirmed through a very reliable source, Hanna Burgess, the chief's secretary, that if everything went according to plan, his promotion was only weeks away. Hanna had spilled the beans during their after-hours rendezvous in a secluded park on the north side of town.

Gary brought the beer and his talents. Hanna brought the blanket and the information. This wasn't their first time together in this park, and Hanna knew it wouldn't be their last. She was twenty years his senior and not his type, but she had been at the department for thirty-two years, and she had the goods on all of its key players, even the chief and the mayor. Gary needed Hanna on his side to run interference for him and to keep him informed. Hanna needed Gary in a different way, and she enjoyed using her leverage to satisfy that need whenever she felt so inclined.

What Gary learned during a break in the action was that a low-key investigation was to be completed within three weeks. Hanna did not know what team would be handed the assignment, but she promised him that she would try to find out. Hanna assured Gary that once the final report reached the chief's hands and the mayor had been briefed, the announcement would quickly follow.

Even with his promotion looking like a foregone conclusion, Hanna had warned Gary to lie low for a couple of weeks. "Don't get caught with your pants down." They giggled at the irony of that warning coming while his pants were indeed down. "Don't be bragging in the locker room about your sexual conquests. And for God's sake, Gary, try not to piss too many people off, at least until this is all over."

Hanna knew that she was not Gary's only extramarital diversion and that he would never change his brazen behavior, but that didn't matter to her. What did matter was seeing her lover promoted to lieutenant and then eventually to chief. He would occupy the office right across from her desk,

161

where she could keep an eye on him at all times. An added bonus would be their private meetings, during which she would lock his office door and remind him who the boss really was.

Gary knew that all he needed to do was to stay under the radar for a few weeks, not take any unnecessary chances. Get to work early and leave late. Get along with everyone. Don't ruffle any feathers. Kiss up to the chief.

All of these sacrifices were quite doable, and all of them were a part of his simple plan.

Gary's second objective was to be single again. His marriage had been a joke from the start. He had only married Carly because she had let herself get pregnant and because her father had insisted that they "do the right thing." Gary did realize that being the chief's son-in-law had expedited his promotion, but that wasn't the point. He was not cut out for marriage. He wanted his freedom again, his full freedom. But he needed the blame to fall on Carly. He would play the part of the jilted husband. No one would fault him for her indiscretions. If anything, this whole thing might just work to his advantage.

The good news was that his wife was having an affair. If he could only expose that fact to the world, he could get rid of her for good. The scandal might even humiliate her dad to the point of stepping down and leaving the department. Then, with any luck, and with Hanna's help, he would be Chief Glaser within a month or two.

The bad news was that Carly was having an affair with Stephen Crain, of all people. Anyone else would have been perfect, but Crain knew too much, and he wasn't the kind to back down or give in. In a way, Gary admired that about him.

Gary was guessing that Crain was falling for Carly. *He has to be. Surely, the little worm has never had a woman of her caliber anywhere near his house, let alone in his bed. I'm sure Crain would love to pick up the pieces in Carly's life after the divorce.*

Gary's plan was to go over to Crain's house, confront the slimeball. Scare the shit out of him. Threaten him within an inch of his life. And then slowly back down, reason with him, maybe even apologize for humiliating him. Convince Crain that the whole matter was behind them now. Admit that he was no longer in love with Carly. Tell Crain that if he played his cards right, Carly could be his for the taking. Tell him that they had a common goal now but they needed to work together, they needed to trust each other.

And after chumming Crain up, Gary would suggest that they drink a beer together. Maybe smoke a joint. And then cut a deal. Man to man. It would all be as simple as that.

* * *

"Hey, Reagan, any chance I can get you to turn that light out and go to sleep? It's late, man. I've got a biology test first period and time trials at the track in the afternoon. I really need to get some rest!"

"I'm so sorry, Jackson. I'm not sure what's gotten into me. The last couple of nights, I've just been tossing and turning. It's like my head is spinning or something. I might be coming down with a cold."

Jackson sat up in his bed, ran his hand over his face, and looked over at the alarm clock: 2:30 AM. "Reagan, I don't think you're coming down with anything. I think you're just down. Down in the dumps, that is. You haven't been yourself ever since . . . Anyway, whatever it is, you need to come to grips with it."

Reagan looked over at his roommate. They had only been friends for a few weeks, but Jackson had him pegged. They both knew exactly what Reagan's problem was, but neither one of them had a clue what to do about it.

"I think I'll go for a walk, Jackson. I promise I'll be real quiet when I come in. Try to get some sleep. I'm sorry I've kept you awake."

Reagan slipped on his jeans and a t-shirt. He put on his sneakers and grabbed his raincoat out of the closet. It had been sprinkling all evening, and he wasn't in the mood to get soaking wet. The truth was, he didn't know what kind of mood he was in. But Jackson was right. Reagan needed to deal with this sooner rather than later. Maybe a long walk would clear his head and get him back on track.

He grabbed his keys and student ID off of his desk and turned toward the door. He hesitated for a moment and then turned back around. He looked over at the note that Molly had given him two days earlier, which was sitting folded on the desk. He had read it so many times that the paper was starting to tear apart. Reagan picked up the note and slid it into his pocket. Jackson, who was still sitting up in his bed, gave Reagan a nod and a smile before lying back down and pulling the sheet over his head.

Reagan's walk took him past the ROTC building to the track, where he did a lap before strolling past Fraternity Row. It was still sprinkling, and the darkened streets were all but abandoned on this wet, windy night. Reagan found himself deep in thought, but none of his thoughts were making sense.

It had not been his intention to wind up there, but when he regained his composure, he found himself standing in front of Graham Hall, looking up at the top floor. He was focusing on the only room that had a light on.

He sat down on the picnic bench next to the building's entrance and ran his fingers through his hair, brushing away the dampness. *What in the world am I doing here? This is nuts. This empty feeling inside of me is driving me crazy. Come on, Reagan, get a hold of yourself!*

Reagan stood and was turning to leave when he heard a voice behind him.

"Reagan, is that you? What in the world are you doing outside in the rain? You're gonna catch pneumonia." Molly had spotted Reagan through the window of the dorm's lobby. She had been having trouble sleeping, herself, and had come downstairs to study.

Reagan pulled the note from his pocket and extended his arm. "Here, you need to take this back. I don't understand what it's all about, and giving it to me without an explanation was just not fair. If this is about your boyfriend, tell him that we're just friends . . . study partners. He has nothing to worry about. We are friends, aren't we, Molly? Friends don't do this sort of thing to one another. Will you please tell me what in the world I've done wrong?"

Molly walked toward Reagan until they were face to face. She stopped, took the note from his hand, and let it fall to the ground. She looked tenderly at him and then put her hands into his.

"Reagan, I promised myself I wouldn't tell you this, but you're here now, in the rain, making a fool of yourself, so I guess I do owe it to you.

"First off, I don't have a boyfriend in Tallahassee. I never did. I made all that up, and I'm sorry I lied to you. I did want us to be just friends. You're too young . . . I mean, so am I. I didn't want you to think of me like you do all of the other girls on campus, a target, you know. But, now there's this problem. You see, the more I get to know you, the more I—"

Reagan raised his right hand and gently placed his index finger to Molly's lips. With their eyes locked in a moment like none other, time seemed to stand still. They could feel their hearts pounding in unison. Reagan started to speak, but Molly shook her head in protest.

Neither of them had asked for this, but at this moment, there was nothing either of them could do about it, nothing either of them wanted to do about it.

With the raindrops dripping down both of their faces, Reagan leaned forward. He closed his eyes and listened as Molly whispered the words, "Kiss me, Reagan. Please kiss me!"

The next thing Reagan could remember was walking back into his dorm room and seeing that Jackson sound asleep in bed. The skies had cleared, and the full moon's rays were shining through the window next to the desk.

Reagan sat down quietly, pulled out his notebook, turned to his list, and picked up his pencil.

~~7. Don't fall in love.~~

* * *

Stephen Crain wasn't sure what to make of this. Sitting on his couch, and downing beers as fast as he could fetch them, was a big-butted Spanish woman telling him her life's story. He was enjoying watching the assets spilling out of her tight dress, but he couldn't have cared less about her jabber. That was until she mentioned the name Gary Glaser.

Maria Sanchez had called Stephen a day earlier and made the appointment. She had explained that her apartment's lease was up for renewal and that she was considering moving out of the Tanglewood complex. She had heard about Shady Oaks from a friend and was hoping that there was a trailer available for rent. Stephen Crain could tell that her story was bullshit, but out of curiosity, he had agreed to see her.

Hoping that it would prompt her into telling him the real reason she was here, he went into the kitchen to fetch her yet another beer. While delivering it, he decided to get to the point. "So, Miss Sanchez, if that's your real name, you brought up the name Gary Glaser. For reasons I don't care to discuss, I find that to be quite a coincidence. Now, would you like to tell me the true purpose of your visit today, or should I take a guess?"

Maria Sanchez took a swig of beer and studied Stephen Crain for a moment. *What are this weird man's innermost thoughts? What motivates him? Can he ever be trusted?* She knew that she was about to open a door that could never be closed again. What she also knew was that she and Crain had a common interest. If he would only give her the proof she needed to convince Gary that Carly was cheating, the Glasers' marriage would be over. Gary would be hers, all hers. Crain could have Carly if he wanted her. *What in the world does she see in Crain, anyway? He's a real creep!*

Stephen Crain was sipping on a beer of his own and was starting to figure this whole thing out. Maria Sanchez was another one of Glaser's girlfriends. Only this one had Latin blood, and that spelled trouble. She had somehow found out about Carly's recent indiscretion and was here to dig up evidence. She was hoping to get Crain to admit to the affair. She was hoping to come away with some sort of evidence that she could take back to her boyfriend. Crain couldn't wait to turn the tables on his visitor. *This is going to be fun!*

"Go ahead, Mr. Crain. If you guess the real reason I'm here, I will be very impressed. And please call me Maria."

"Very well then, Maria. You are here on a reconnaissance mission. I have something that you need. Your plan was to come over here wearing that short sexy dress and convince me to spill the beans. You want certain evidence that can be used to your advantage. Before I go on, am I hot or cold?"

Maria's open-mouthed stare gave Crain his answer, so he continued. "I might just be willing to work with you under the right circumstances, but you will have to do exactly as I say, or this whole matter will backfire on you. If I do agree to give you what you need, it will be in a sealed envelope. You are not to look at what's inside until you are sharing it with the one you are planning on sharing it with. This will be our covenant, and you know what bad things come from breaking a covenant, don't you now?"

"I do, Mr. Crain. Whatever you say. You're the boss. Now, what do you have for me? A note? Something that was left behind?"

"Oh, what I have for you is much better than that . . . I have pictures."

"She let you take pictures? That's perfect! There will be no doubt. When can I have them?"

"All in due time, Maria. But first, if we are going to be partners, we should get to know each other a little better. Did I mention my waterbed?"

* * *

"Come on in, Big Bear, and close the door behind you. How's your family? Those boys of yours must be growing like weeds."

Lieutenant Mack Tucker was all smiles, and the firm handshake he offered lasted longer than it needed to. This briefing was an important one. The lieutenant needed to get the right message across to Melvin Peters, but he needed to do it in a way that wasn't too obvious.

"They're all just fine, Lieutenant. Thank you for asking. What is it that I can do for you today?"

"Oh, Bear, please call me Mack behind closed doors. We go back a long way, you and me. We have a lot in common. You know what I'm talking about. We put the good Lord and our families first. We take our jobs seriously. We have both devoted our lives to serving the good people of Gainesville, Florida. And because of these things, neither one of us would let anything happen that might weaken this department. You know, making sure that the right people are placed into the right positions, and all.

Keeping the troublemakers out of the top spots. Do you know where I'm going with this?"

"Not exactly, sir."

"Well, I think you do, but then again, I might have gotten ahead of myself. As of now, you're on a special assignment. You will report only to me for the next few weeks. How you handle yourself and what you achieve could determine the future of the Gainesville Police Department for many years to come.

"You have been selected for this assignment by a committee that includes the mayor and the chief. We all have full confidence in your thoroughness and proficiency."

A frowning Melvin Peters knew when someone was blowing smoke up his ass, and he was already having his doubts about this so-called special assignment. "Well, I certainly appreciate the confidence, Lieutenant, but I must ask, what is my mission?"

"You will be conducting the required background check and vetting of Sergeant Gary Glaser, who is being considered for a promotion to the level of lieutenant. Now do you know where I'm going with this?"

"Yes, sir, I do." Melvin Peters, now with a full smile on his face, continued, "I know exactly where we're going with this, Mack!"

CHAPTER TWENTY-ONE

"*D*early beloved, we are gathered together here in the sight of God, and in the face of this company, to join together this man and this woman in holy matrimony . . ."

With this introduction, the minister had the audience's full attention. The setting, the occasion, and the moment would, of course, explain this, but there was something more. There was something about the minister himself: his persona, his warm smile, his knowing eyes, his soothing voice, his slow and deliberate movements. Yes, there was something about this minister that commanded one's full attention.

He was not a tall man, but his mere presence could fill a room. He had collar-length snowy-white hair and piercing dark blue eyes. With an Irish accent, he spoke softly, but his voice easily reached its intended mark. He wore a black robe and held a prayer book evenly with both hands. While delivering his message, his eyes drifted from the bride to the groom and then to those sitting in attendance.

When his eyes met the eyes of one of those in the audience, that person was instantly mesmerized. It was as though he had found his way deep into their thoughts. Listening to his words, it seemed as if he was speaking to them and them alone. When his gaze drifted, that person felt as if he or she had just awakened from a deep dream.

The minister had been a lifelong friend of the bride. He had only recently met her soon-to-be husband, but the two men had developed an instant friendship. In preparation for the event, the minister had spent a number of hours at this house during the past week. He had met all of its occupants. He had also met many of those guests now in attendance as they had dropped by to offer congratulations and to volunteer where needed.

At first, the bride had envisioned a small ceremony to be attended only by the residents of her nursing home along with a few close friends and relatives. The ceremony would have been held on the front porch. A simple, but tasteful, reception would then have taken place in the living room.

But that was before the man from the local newspaper had called asking for an interview. That was before a full-page article including pictures, side stories, and a poem recently written by the groom had been printed. That was before the entire city knew that one of its most cherished citizens was about to marry a national hero. That was before the countless well-wishers had called or come by with presents.

The bride, of course, was delighted by all of the attention and felt obligated to invite each and every one of these visitors to the wedding, an invitation that they had all enthusiastically accepted.

"Marriage is the union of husband and wife in heart, body, and mind. It is intended for their mutual joy, and for the help and comfort given one another in prosperity and adversity."

The minister paused, allowing himself a brief moment to take in and enjoy his surroundings.

It was like something out of a spring poem. Behind him, offering a picturesque backdrop, was a thick hedge of bougainvillea whose purple blooms seemed to have popped to full color that very afternoon. Four towering oak trees provided shade as the moss hanging from their branches danced back and forth, encouraged by the soft warm breeze. The freshly manicured lawn was pocketed with several flower beds, each offering its own variety of magnificent flora.

Directly behind the bride and groom, sitting in white chairs, the one hundred or so guests were all dressed suitably in wedding-day attire. The flower girl and the ring bearer were standing on either side of the bride and groom and rocking back and forth on their feet. A mother in the fourth row stood abruptly and rushed her crying baby out of earshot.

The groom was standing proudly, flanked by his much younger and somewhat nervous best man. The bride, with her daughter by her side, was wearing a smile wider than the bright blue sky.

Sitting together in the back row were seven guests who had been invited by the best man. One of them had just gotten off duty and was still wearing his police uniform. The minister had had the opportunity to meet with, speak to, and assess each of these attendees, and also the best man, before the ceremony.

The Chinese couple was obviously very much in love. They took their studies seriously and were very appreciative of the opportunities they had been allotted. They adored their families and all of their many friends. They had been given the gift of pure happiness, and the minister could sense that this was a treasure that would stay with them forever. He could also sense that this couple would stay together and would one day become man and wife. The minister's spirits had been lifted by his time with them, and he had told them so. What he did not tell them was of a feeling that had come over him—a premonition that they would soon be summoned home to China and that they would never again return to the United States.

"Into this holy estate these two persons present now come to be joined. If any person can show just cause . . ."

The minister had met the best man's roommate two days earlier, when he had come over to the house to help out with some last-minute yard work. It was readily apparent that this was one hardworking lad whose storied background had laid a solid foundation.

There was no question in the minister's mind that this gentle soul would be a success before it was all over. He would graduate at the top of his class and go on to graduate school, maybe even law school, but selfish interests would not inspire this man's life work. He would give of himself to help others. He would become famous, not through self-advancing accomplishments, but because of his tireless pursuit of fairness and equality.

Before heading back to campus, the best man's roommate and the minister had prayed together, hand in hand. The minister privately asked the Lord for the strength this young man would need while grieving the upcoming loss of a very close relative.

"By gathering together all the wishes of happiness and our finest hopes for Lieutenant William Moore and Sally Tindale from all present here, we assure them that our hearts are in tune with theirs."

The minister had approached the pretty blonde who went by Charley and the police officer standing together on the front porch before the ceremony. This brief interlude had left the minister with a bad feeling. Of all of the best man's friends, these two were the only ones who seemed uncomfortable around a man of the cloth. Whatever road they were on was taking them down a path of destruction. And there was something more. The minister had glanced around twice looking for an approaching guest, but there had been no one heading their way. It was just the three of them standing there. Why had the minister sensed the presence of another just before he had felt entirely alone?

"This relationship stands for love, loyalty, honesty, and trust, but most of all for friendship. Before they knew love, they were friends, and it is from this seed of friendship that is their destiny. Do not think that you can direct the course of love, for love, if it finds you worthy, shall direct you."

The most attractive young lady in attendance, as far as the minister was concerned, was the young lady the best man had introduced as his girlfriend. It wasn't just her outward appearance that made her pretty. She drew her beauty from within. She was smart beyond her years. She carried her emotions on her shirtsleeve, and the minister could tell that she was very much in love with her date. This was a love that would last, but it would be rigorously tested. To survive, it would need time, patience, and resilience.

"Marriage is an act of faith and personal commitment as well as a moral and physical union between two people. Marriage has been described as the best and most important relationship that can exist between them."

The minister had married so many couples through the years that he had lost count. Some of them had seemed like perfect fits and some like bookends. It had been his experience that the bookends would often wind up as happy, if not happier, than their counterparts.

The minister had met the last two of the younger crowd just before the ceremony. There was the college professor whose successful career would focus on teaching his students life's real lessons, and the pretty tomboy type who was full of spunk and self-confidence. The minister had interrupted a deep conversation between the two of them and had sensed a budding friendship. Maybe not today, maybe not tomorrow, but these two, he believed, would share something of significance down the road.

"It is the construction of their love and trust into a single growing energy of spiritual life. It is a moral commitment that requires and deserves daily attention. Marriage should be a lifelong consecration of the ideal of loving kindness, backed with the will to make it last.

"Ladies and gentlemen, the bride and the groom will now exchange their vows."

The guests straightened their stances and in unison slid forward a bit in their seats. With the exception of the song of a blue jay that was perched on a nearby birdbath, serenading the event, there was total silence. This was an extraordinary moment. Two very special people were about to declare their everlasting love for one another. No one in attendance had any doubt that these promises would come straight from the heart.

The groom was the first to speak. "My dearest Sally, my travels have taken me to all four corners of the world. I have watched the sunset and the sunrise from a drifting vessel on each of the seven seas. I have met kings and queens, popes and icons, presidents and dictators. I have seen the sorrows brought on by the destructive nature of man's wars. I have observed deep hatred that shames the soul, and acts of love and kindness that melt the heart. I have watched time march on ever so quickly and suffered the loss of so many very close friends. I have been a man of myself and never thought I would be anything else. That is, until I met you.

"For all that I have seen and all that I have done could not have prepared me for the adventure of our union. I stand here before you, a man with a full heart. One who will dedicate his remaining days to your care and happiness. One who will put you and us before all others. I can, only through my actions, begin to repay you for the happiness you have given me. I am yours, full body and soul, from this day forward until death do us part."

Handkerchiefs and tissues were popping out of pockets and purses. There wasn't a dry eye to be found. The blue jay even stopped singing for a moment as if contemplating what he had just heard. The best man, who had helped with the vows, was all smiles. The bride seemed to be drifting back from a faraway place. The minister's eyes paused reassuringly on the groom's before scanning the guests and then resting on the bride, who was the next to speak.

"Sweet William, I am at times perplexed by the twists and turns in life's passage, all along knowing that our journey is chosen not by us, but for us. By the grace of God, I have been blessed all of my life with a loving family, caring and giving friends, and, thankfully, much more happiness than sorrow. I must attest that I had settled into a time of reflection, not one of expectation. But it would seem my destiny is now taking me forward, not backward. And, my love, I am looking forward to every day that I will spend with you by my side.

"The heart's beat, I believe, is like a budding rose. Without nurturing, care, and loving attention, the flower is destined to wither on the vine. My heart today is in full bloom. It has been brought back to bursting splendor by the love you have given me, the friendship we share, and the promise of our future together.

"As you know, you are not my first true love. But your acceptance of my past is one of the things I love the most about you. I have never met another man like you. I'm not sure there has ever been another man like you—your quiet kindness, the unselfish sacrifices you have made, the gentle spirit that is hidden behind that towering strength.

"Before you today, being witnessed by the good Lord, along with our friends and family, stands your devoted companion. I will dedicate my every breath to your happiness. I will care for you when you need care. I will walk with you when you need a friend. I will pray with you when His voice is in your head. I will be yours, full body and soul, from this day forward."

The minister nodded reassuringly at the bride. He took her left hand in his right. He took the groom's right hand in his left. He glanced up at the guests and said, "Let us pray."

* * *

"Reagan, if you want to make love to me, you can."

The ride from Gainesville to Crescent Beach in Marty's Volkswagen bus had taken an hour and a half. They would have made it there faster, but they had stopped twice to stock up on wine and beer and once in a forested area to gather wood for a bonfire. The whole idea had been Charley's.

With the ceremony over and the reception winding down, the Frisbee ball gang had joined the other well-wishers on the front lawn. The final pictures of the day were taken as the guests threw rice at the bride and groom. Everyone cheered and waved as the newlyweds climbed into a horse-drawn carriage heading to an undisclosed destination.

Gary Glaser, saying he had an appointment, had said his good-byes, hopped into his patrol car, and driven away. The minister, standing on the front porch, had watched the remaining youngsters with a curious interest. He wondered if his predictions would be proven true. *They usually are. What must it be like to be in their shoes? Growing up during this tumultuous time, making up their own rules, setting their own boundaries.* The minister looked over at them once more before heading into the house. *How will they come to grips with the mistakes they are bound to make? Will they learn from these mistakes and somehow use this knowledge to make the world a better place? Would they do anything differently if they knew that this evening would be the last time they would all be together?*

On Crescent Beach, the waves were crashing onto the shore. The bright stars filled the sky, and the waning moon was just appearing on the horizon. Marty had brought his guitar, and after lighting a joint and passing it to Terri, he launched into a Jim Croce tune about a roller derby queen. Ye and Yang were singing along at the top of their lungs and getting most of the words right. Reagan lit the fire before reaching into the cooler to retrieve a bottle of ripple. He unscrewed its cap and handed the bottle to Charley. Reagan looked around at the smiles on his friends' faces and knew in his heart that he would never forget this moment.

When Marty took a break to roll another joint, Molly leaned over and whispered something into Reagan's ear. The two of them stood and excused themselves. They walked down the secluded beach hand in hand until they were out of sight. Molly stopped and turned toward Reagan, giving him a long warm kiss and then another.

"Reagan, did you here me? I said if you want to make love to me, you can. It would be my first time, and I can't imagine sharing that with anyone else but you."

It was Reagan's turn to initiate the kiss. When it was over, he put his hands on Molly's shoulders and looked deep into her eyes. He had never known what true love felt like until now. He wanted to make love to her so bad it hurt, but he wanted something else even more.

"Molly, if it's alright with you, I think we should wait."

CHAPTER TWENTY-TWO

*I*n the rear of Marty's Volkswagen van, on their way back to Gainesville from Crescent Beach, Molly whispered, "Reagan, you look sleepy. Why don't you lay your head down in my lap and take a nap?"

Am I dreaming?

Her lap is so comfortable! I can't keep my eyes open. The breeze on my face feels good. Humming noise of the engine. Putter, putter. Right turn. Left turn. What's that smell? Bump. Bump. Bump. Stop. Accelerate. Someone's rubbing my head.

No, Officer, that's not my jeep. I drive a . . . Wait a second! That's Chad's jeep. You can't tow it away. He'll be right back. Chad! Chad! Where did you go?

Why are you arresting me? I wasn't rioting. Who took my clothes? She told me to take my shirt off. I'm naked. I can't go in there.

Right turn. Left turn. Putter, putter. Who's that talking? Two girls kissing and talking. I can't hear you. Please, I need to hear you. No, don't send any more. I have too many. Someone will find them and count them. Mom's standing at the stove. Stirring. Hot sauce. She's making hot sauce. Where's the banana pudding? You can't come in. The door is locked. Please don't come in. Where are my clothes?

Slow motion. I can't move my legs. I'll never get up the hill. Sirens and flashing lights at the top of the hill. Officer Yang, who's in that car? I'm so thirsty. Is there a fountain at the top of the hill? My legs feel like concrete. Yes, Alice is my sister. Does she have the water? I'm so thirsty.

Stop. Accelerate. Two girls talking. Who's Stephen Crain? Bad man. Bad man. Blackmail. Someone's got to stop him. If you don't stop him, I will. Spare key to the trailer? I'll take a spare key to the trailer. Diary? What diary? Talk louder. I can't hear you. Heidi, you have to go home. I can't take you there. I can never go there again. Cookies. So many cookies. What's that smell?

Stay away from the cash register. Don't get caught. Someone's watching us through the window. I can't get caught. My legs are so tired. Lasagna. Molly's lasagna. Why is it so far away? Please hand me my clothes.

Right turn. Left turn. Two girls talking. You missed your period. I missed my period. You missed your period. I missed my period. Who's Stephen Crain? Who's Robert? It's not Gary's baby. Charley, this is Barbara Ann. She knows where to go. She will take you there. Sirens and flashing lights at the top of the hill. Right turn. Left turn. Stop.

Was I dreaming?

* * *

What appeared to be a chance meeting in the doorway of Alachua General Hospital's cafeteria was anything but. And as it turned out, his timing was perfect.

Melvin Peters had spent the past two and a half weeks arduously carrying out his fact-finding mission, and he was getting very frustrated, to say the least. He had arranged for dozens of interviews, rifled through more than one hundred case files, and logged in countless unpaid overtime hours conducting surveillance.

Up to this point, his investigation had uncovered no significant black marks. He had been unable to substantiate any professional impropriety or personal bad behavior that would stand in the way of Gary Glaser's promotion to lieutenant.

Melvin Peters had only three more days before his full report was due, and he was getting desperate.

To say the least, Gary Glaser was good at covering his tracks. If the rumors that had circulated within the department for years were true, Melvin couldn't find any evidence to substantiate them. If the sexual conquests that Gary himself continuously bragged about in the locker room were indeed real, Melvin, at least to this point, had been unable to find any proof that would back them up.

Gary Glaser's cronies were one hundred percent behind him, painting their pal as the perfect cop and a dedicated family man. If his adversaries knew anything, they weren't talking. A couple of them had even admitted to being worried about the repercussions of divulging certain facts. After all, they felt Glaser's promotion was a foregone conclusion, and he was known for his vindictive behavior.

Melvin Peters was sitting at his desk, leafing through his pages of notes, searching for anything. He was hoping to find even the slightest clue, a clue that could lead to a witness, a witness that for whatever reason was willing to come forward with verifiable facts—facts that would yield evidence, evidence that would produce the needed results, results which were being counted on, counted on by Melvin's supervisor, the supervisor who, because of these results, would one day become the department's next police chief.

Melvin Peters closed his notebook and rubbed his eyes. He had been at it for more than ten hours and was ready to call it a day. He opened his desk drawer to retrieve his car keys and sunglasses. He closed the drawer and looked over once more at the notebook. He reluctantly opened it up, flipping to the first page of his notes. He frowned down at the only entry on that page, or any page, for that matter, that had not been crossed out.

He thought back to the night he had overheard the telephone conversation. He remembered reaching the conclusion that Carly Glaser had been somewhere she wasn't supposed to be. He had written down the name Stephen Crain and an address within the Shady Oaks community. He had also written down the name Maria Sanchez.

Melvin Peters then thought back to the night of the riots, the two times he had gone to the hospital. He remembered how kind and caring Nurse Sanchez had been. He remembered the two of them praying together.

At the beginning of this assignment, Melvin Peters had promised himself that he wouldn't involve Nurse Sanchez. Uncovering Maria Sanchez and Gary Glaser's affair would surely cost her job and probably ruin her career altogether. Exposing any evidence that Carly Glaser might also be having an affair was dangerous and could easily backfire.

But Melvin Peters was desperate, and as he sat there contemplating what appeared to be his last hope for a breakthrough, he wondered out loud, "What harm could come from just talking to Nurse Sanchez?"

* * *

"Well, hello, Sergeant Peters. What brings you to our hospital today? I certainly hope you haven't been wounded on the job again."

"Nurse Sanchez, what a pleasant surprise running into you. How is your day going? Please, let me buy you a cup of coffee. I insist!"

The truth was, Maria Sanchez's day was not going well at all. She was fuming. She couldn't remember being this angry or feeling this used.

Over the past couple of weeks, she had tried numerous times to get in touch with Gary Glaser. She had left him messages at work. She had put notes on his car. She had even gone by his apartment, spending time with Carly, hoping Gary would walk through the door. He was ignoring her, and Maria Sanchez did not like being ignored.

Ever since giving in to that slimeball Stephen Crain's quid pro quo, she had carried the sealed envelope he had given her around in her purse. She hadn't opened the envelope until that morning, but now she was frantic. Covenant or not, she'd had to see what kind of pictures Crain really had. If they proved without a doubt that Carly was having an affair, Maria would march them over to the police department that afternoon and hand them to Gary herself. He wouldn't ignore her after that. He would be hers and hers only.

To say the least, the pictures were not what she had been expecting.

Crain had screwed her both literally and figuratively, and her good-for-nothing cheating boyfriend was ignoring her. She hadn't decided exactly what she was going to do about it yet, but it wasn't going to be pretty.

"I would love to join you for a cup of coffee, Sergeant Peters. Tell me, what's going on over at the police department these days? Are things getting back to normal after all of the commotion?"

"Let's sit here. Yes, things are back to normal. To tell you the truth, I'm on a special assignment that is boring me to tears. And please, call me Melvin."

"Okay, Melvin it is. Did you say a special assignment? That sounds fascinating to me. Can you tell me about it, or is it top secret? And by the way, just Maria from now on. Understand? You can drop the nurse part unless you wind up back here again as my patient."

"Very funny. Anyway, I wouldn't usually bore you with mundane police matters, but you did ask. One of my fellow sergeants, Gary Glaser, you probably don't know him, is up for promotion to lieutenant. My assignment is to turn over rocks—you know, make sure that there are no skeletons in his closet that could embarrass the city down the road. This is all just routine stuff. Like I said, pretty boring."

"Not at all, Melvin. It sounds like an important mission to me. We certainly wouldn't want an unworthy candidate being promoted to such a high level within the department, now would we? How's the investigation going, anyway? Any skeletons so far?"

"No, none whatsoever. It looks like it will be clear sailing for Glaser. He's a lucky guy. He's got a beautiful wife, a wonderful son, and now he's about to hold the second highest office within the department. He's got it made for sure. Not much more a man could need in his life than that. Not much room for anything else in his life. Don't you agree with me, Maria?"

Maria's face was turning bright red, and Melvin could tell that he had hit a nerve. He gave things a moment to sink in before going in for the kill.

"Now, there are still three days left before my report is due. There's always a chance that something could turn up. You know, something might even wind up in my inbox, put there anonymously, for example. You just never know about these things, now do you, Maria?"

"No, Melvin, you just never know. Now, I should be getting back to my station. My shift is over in an hour, and I have an errand or two to run after work. Thank you for the coffee, and good luck with your special assignment. I'm guessing things will work out just the way you're hoping they will."

* * *

It was the last Thursday of the month, and the rent was due. Charley, money order in hand, closed and locked the door to her trailer and then headed across the dirt road toward the house. She normally would have mailed the rent to her landlord, and she planned on doing so from now on, but with Gary's promotion just around the corner, and remembering Stephen Crain's threats, she decided to play nice with the worm just this one last time. Not only that, she wanted the pictures Crain had bragged about. If she could get her hands on them and the negatives, this whole thing would be over once and for all.

Charley had been in a good mood all day. She had made an important decision that morning. She had decided to start taking classes at the university again. Before dropping out, she had been a pretty good student. Her favorite class had been journalism, and ever since coming away with the top score on the final, she had dreamed about being a reporter. *What a great way to meet people. I could travel around the world. Maybe even be on the nightly news. It just might be time for me to grow up, decide what I'm going to do with the rest of my life. Time to take control of things instead of letting things take control of me.*

The winter quarter was just weeks away. She planned on sending her application into the registrar's office within the next few days. She could still work at the Palace in the evenings. That would pay for her tuition and cover her bills. Her dad would be so proud to see his little girl receiving a diploma. She had goose bumps just thinking about it.

Knock! Knock! Knock! "Mr. Crain. It's Charlotte Summerland. I have my rent check, and I have something I would like to talk to you about. Can I come in? I'm out of beer, and I sure would like a—"

Stephen Crain unlocked the door and smiled. Not only was his tenant forking over money this month, but he might also receive payment in the more unconventional manner. "Why, of course, Charley, please come in. You know you are always welcome here. Grab a beer or whatever you would like out of the box. I'll roll us a joint. I've got some killer weed. You just have to try it. Make yourself at home. I was just getting out of the shower. Please excuse the robe."

*   *   *

Carly Glaser was not used to having free time on her hands, and she certainly wasn't the type to drop in on someone unannounced, but as she pulled out of her parents' driveway on this particular Thursday evening, she had no place she needed to be. In addition to that rare occurrence, she was also wrestling with a wild hair that was somehow steering her car in the direction of the Shady Oaks community.

Junior had been all excited about spending the night at Grandma and Grandpa's house. Carly knew that her parents would spoil him as usual. It would take her a day or two to settle him back down, but that was okay. Junior was the light of their lives, and they were always excited when he came over to spend time with them.

Carly had known that it wouldn't be five minutes before her dad would have Junior in the backyard tossing the football, and this was something she had been counting on. She needed to spend a few minutes with her mother at the kitchen table talking. If anyone would understand her dilemma, her mom would. And her mom had. The long-overdue conversation had gone much better than Carly had ever dreamed it would. As she was turning left onto SW 34th Street, she was remembering her mother's advice. "Now, honey, don't get me wrong. Getting a divorce is a serious matter. You know no one in our family has ever been divorced. But, having said that, I can't imagine living my life in a loveless relationship. I certainly don't expect you to go on the way things are. These stories you are telling me are very troubling. A man shouldn't treat a woman the way Gary has been treating you.

"But, Carly, you are the only one who can make this decision, and you need to be sure that you are doing the right thing, for Junior's sake, if nothing more. When you're sure, one hundred percent sure, you come back over, and we will sit your dad down and talk to him. I'm warning you, he's not going to be very happy about this at first, but he'll come around. You know he always does. He loves his little girl, and he will always take your side."

As Carly pulled into Shady Oaks, drove up to Stephen Crain's house, got out of her car, and walked toward the door she was thinking two things: *I really need a drink*, and *How is anyone ever one hundred percent sure about anything?*

"Well, Carly, what a pleasant surprise. Please come in. I have someone I would like to introduce you to."

* * *

Marty Schemer was standing at his desk flipping through a textbook and his notes. It was a little more than a week before final exams. Next week was dead week, a week for review and preparation. No new material or tests were allowed during dead week.

Marty closed the textbook and put his notes into his attaché. He had covered all of the required course material for the quarter, and he saw no reason to delve into chapters that would not be included on the class's final exam. The truth was, he was just not in the mood to teach political science today.

"Okay, guys, here's the deal. We can either start our review or we can just sit around and talk. By a show of hands, how many of you would like to start our review?" One hand shot up but was quickly lowered. "Excellent. Now, let's move our tables into a circle. By the way, if you have somewhere else you need to be, please feel free to leave. Class is officially dismissed. This chat is voluntary."

Tables were quickly assembled into a circle. No one left the room.

"Now, what shall we talk about? How about if I start?" He looked around the room expectantly. "So, I live in a house on the south side of town that backs up to the prairie. Every morning, before I get on my bike and peddle over to campus to see your smiling faces, I grab a cup of coffee and take my golden retriever for a walk. Jagger chases birds and rabbits, and I watch the sunrise and think about things. Sometimes I just think about how bad my head hurts and try to remember what all I had to drink the night before." The class broke out in laughter. "This morning, as I watched my dog jump up and down in the tall weeds, it hit me. I mean like a rocket. Like I was just standing there, when I suddenly realized that Jagger is my best friend. You know, like the cliché, but really. I've got to tell you, it totally freaked me out for a minute.

"I mean, it's not like I don't have friends. And, by the way, I consider you all my friends and have really enjoyed teaching this class. But my dog is my best friend . . . really? That's it. I mean . . . I'm just saying.

"Who's next? Zack, what's on your brain?"

As Zack was talking about his shyness around the opposite sex, Jackson leaned over and whispered into Reagan's ear. "Have you decided what to get Molly for her birthday yet?" Reagan shook his head, obviously frustrated. "Well, my friend, you need to get on it. Her birthday is in less than two weeks, and you are going steady. It better be good, whatever you decide. Wait, I have an idea."

A normally quiet girl in the back of the room was just finishing up a three-minute ramble about how much she hated mathematics when Jackson raised his hand and was called on.

"Well, it's like this," he started. "I have this friend whose girlfriend is having a birthday. Now, they have only been dating for a few weeks, but they are in love . . . I mean inseparable." Reagan slid lower in his seat with every word out of Jackson's mouth. "So, the problem is this. He, I mean my friend, doesn't know what to get her for a present. You know, he wants it to be special. Something she will always remember. He doesn't want it to be over the top, something that will scare her away, like jewelry. But he doesn't want it to be too simple, like a box of chocolates. So, if anyone has any advice, for my friend, that is, please pipe in."

When the class dismissal bell finally rang, almost everyone in the class had had something to share. This had been a special group, and they all knew it. Beverly McNamara was commenting on that fact and was the last one to speak. "So, like I was saying, Marty, you're the best. I have gotten so much from this class, and not just things that came out of a book. Thank you! And thank you all for being such wonderful classmates.

"And by the way, Jackson, why don't you tell Reagan to send his girl-friend flowers? Not just any old flowers picked from somebody's garden. Flowers from a florist. Have them delivered to her dorm so that the whole place knows she got them. How about sending one dozen long-stemmed red roses with a note attached? I'm guessing this girl has never gotten red roses, and if I'm right, it will be an experience she will always remember."

CHAPTER TWENTY-THREE

*N*ormally, celebrating one's promotion prior to it being official would seem like a bad idea. If Gary Glaser or his buddies had been even the slightest bit superstitious, Thursday afternoon's gathering at the Red Lion Pub would have been postponed for a week or two. But they weren't, and it wasn't.

The owner brought in six of his top girls to handle the crowd, and these beauties were all dressed to kill. By the time the guest of honor arrived, there were approximately thirty plainclothes off-duty policemen throwing back beers and playing grab-ass.

Gary Glaser was in his element. He loved being the center of attention, and within seconds of walking in, he had a beer in his hand and was working the crowd. Everyone wanted to congratulate the soon-to-be lieutenant, including the waitresses, who were using every opportunity to flirt with him and rub their bodies up against his.

Two of the partiers had been given the assignment of watching the front door. This was an event for insiders only. Nothing that happened here would leave the room.

After Gary had taken the time necessary to shake hands and receive pats on the back from all those in attendance, somebody yelled, "Speech!" Suddenly, the room quieted to a hush.

"Well, I'd like to thank everybody for showing up here today. I really appreciate all of the support you have given me these last few weeks. Everyone here knows that I won't forget who my friends are, and with the exception of a handful of you bozos who I plan on firing . . ."

The crowd burst into laughter, and someone in the back shouted, "How do you think Peters is doing with his investigation, Lieutenant?"

Someone else responded, "He wouldn't know a clue if an elephant shit it on his head." The laughter continued.

"How long until we have to call you Chief?"

Gary held up his hands, quieting the crowd. "Let's not get ahead of ourselves now; one promotion at a time. And as for Peters, don't you worry. He's gonna be just fine at his new assignment, riding the desk!

"Now, I've got something I've gotta do this evening. There's someplace I need to be, so I'm gonna head outta here in a couple of minutes. I want you all to stay and party your asses off. The tab is on me tonight, so drink up!"

With his promotion in the bag, what Gary had to do and where Gary was headed both involved the second part of his plan, becoming a single man again. It was time. It was time to deal with Stephen Crain.

* * *

Melvin Peters wasn't sure when it had arrived or how it had gotten there. He had cleaned out his in-basket that morning. Sometime between his lunch break and when he had looked up later that afternoon, it had appeared, a sealed envelope. On it, the words *For Sergeant Peters' Eyes Only* were written in red ink.

Melvin glanced around at the nearly vacant squad room. No one was looking his way or otherwise paying any attention to him. He reached over, snatched the envelope out of the box, and studied it for a long minute. This could be it. This might just be what he had been waiting for. He took a deep breath and with his right index finger slowly tore open the seal.

The pictures were dark and grainy. There were six of them. Two of them would be the most useful. He did not recognize the blonde, but he could easily make out the face of her lover. He also noticed that the pictures had been taken through the window of what appeared to be a travel trailer. There was a Stingray and a motorcycle in the foreground. Gary Glaser's motorcycle.

Melvin slid the pictures back into the envelope and took a deep breath. This wasn't exactly what he had been hoping for at the beginning of his investigation; however, proving that Gary was having an affair would most likely derail the promotion. *But wait a second.* Melvin pulled the pictures back out of the envelope and studied them. *Damn, no date stamp. These have been developed privately. They could have been taken years ago, maybe even before Gary and Carly got married.* Melvin needed more.

Melvin reached into his desk and pulled out the notes he'd made the night he had overheard the telephone conversation. *Stephen Crain, Shady Oaks Mobile Home Community.* Melvin looked around the room one last time. He grabbed his keys and sunglasses out of his desk drawer. If he was going to get the answers he needed, he knew where he would have to go to find them.

* * *

Stephen Crain had not bothered to change out of his robe and into his clothes. What he was planning would not require clothing.

The two girls were sitting on the couch drinking beer, smoking a joint, and making small talk. He had introduced them by their first names only. If they had figured out that they had certain things in common, it wasn't showing. They were actually getting pretty cozy with each other. He had handed them their second joint along with another beer. *It won't be long now. This is some good weed, laced with something, maybe even MDA.* He walked over to turn the music up louder and then sat down to watch. *This is going to be fun!*

* * *

Melvin Peters took one spin around the Shady Oaks community. It was dark, and with the exception of a few folks who were sitting outside, the place was quiet. Melvin had already spotted the trailer that he'd seen in the pictures. It was the fourth trailer on the right. There were no lights on inside. The Stingray was parked outside of it.

Melvin drove his squad car past the house. He couldn't make out the numbers above the door, but he assumed that it was Stephen Crain's house. Melvin pulled in amongst several large oak trees. He was hidden from sight. He turned off the ignition, pulled out his binoculars, and waited.

After an hour had passed, Melvin started to wonder if he was on a wild goose chase. Unless something went down real soon, this could be a total waste of his time. *Maybe I should knock on the door of the fourth trailer on the right. If the blonde answers, I can show her the pictures and try to get her to talk. Or maybe I should approach Stephen Crain. After all, Crain is fooling around with Glaser's wife. Crain might have some information that could be useful. At any rate, sitting here is getting me nowhere. I need to do something!* He was about to open his car door when he heard it in the distance. It was the sound of a motorcycle, and it was getting closer.

* * *

Gary Glaser had stopped off at the Pleasure Palace. He had hoped Charley would be working. He wanted to tell her how good things were going. He wanted her to know that everything would be back to normal real soon. She hadn't been there, but he had spent a few minutes jawing with

Bubba and had decided to have a couple of beers to prime his pump. He had watched the girls prance across the stage while he rehearsed his plan. *Bad guy then good guy. Soften him up, then make a deal. Come away with just enough proof to confront Carly. Put an end to this whole thing.*

*   *   *

Gary Glaser drove his motorcycle into the entrance of the Shady Oaks community and up the driveway to the main house. He dismounted, removed his helmet, and adjusted the pistol that was wedged between his belt and his backbone. He took one look behind him at Charley's trailer: no lights, no one around, total darkness. Over to his right was a car. He took a closer look. It was Carly's car. *What the fuck?*

Gary walked up to the house and heard the stereo blasting. He tried the doorknob. It was locked. He checked his pistol one more time. He knocked loudly on the door. "Crain, this is Gary Glaser. Open this door now, or I will break it down. This is my last warning."

Inside the house, the two half-naked girls making out on the couch had not heard the ruckus over the music. Stephen Crain, however, had heard it and had gone into his bedroom to retrieve his rifle, his uncle's rifle.

Melvin Peters was sitting stunned in his patrol car. He didn't know exactly what was going down, but he wasn't about to get in the middle of it, at least not yet. He checked the bullets in his gun, tugged at his bulletproof vest, and adjusted the volume on his police radio.

Gary Glaser took three steps back and then charged the door, once, twice. On the third try, the door yielded, and he tumbled into the room doing a summersault onto the floor. When he gained his composure, he looked to his right. "Charley! Carly! What in the hell is going on here?"

He glanced to his left and saw it. "Crain, put that gun away. I'm warning you." Gary's right hand was inching around toward his backside.

The two girls were suddenly sitting up straight on the couch and pulling their clothes together. They had lost any buzz they might have had, and they both looked scared to death.

"Gary, don't shoot him. How do you know Charley? What are you doing here?"

"Never mind that. Now the both of you get up and get the hell out of here now. I mean right now! And Carly, I will deal with you at home when I get there."

Melvin Peters was still in his patrol car when he saw two females running from the house. One of them got in a car, started the engine, and drove past him and out of the community. The second ran into the darkness, in the direction of the fourth trailer on the right.

Bam! Bam! . . . Bam!

"This is Officer Peters. I have gunfire at the main house in the Shady Oaks community. I need backup. Send an ambulance. I'm going in."

* * *

Carly Glaser's hands were still shaking as she unlocked her door and went inside the apartment. She turned on a light, opened a beer, walked into the bedroom, and removed her suitcase from under the bed. She grabbed three shirts and two pairs of pants from their hangers. She quickly folded them and put them in the suitcase. She selected two pairs of shoes and reached for her overnight kit that she kept on the top shelf. She grabbed a pair of pajamas and opened her underwear drawer. She was flipping through her underwear when she saw it.

She had forgotten all about it, the envelope that Stephen Crain had given her the first night she had gone over to see him. She placed her clothing in the suitcase, sat on the bed, and turned on the nightlight. She opened the envelope and studied its contents, one by one. She returned them to the envelope, throwing it into the suitcase before closing the latches. She was now one hundred percent sure.

CHAPTER TWENTY-FOUR

*I*t was Wednesday afternoon of finals week, and Molly had been sitting in the lobby of Graham Hall studying for her last test when she heard, "Oh my God, look at that!" Molly looked over at her roommate, Cheryl. Cheryl had also been studying but now had her mouth wide open and was pointing toward the reception desk. "Have you ever seen anything that beautiful?"

The deliveryman had placed the vase on the table closest to the elevator and walked into the office.

Molly responded, "There must be at least two dozen of them! They're so red and so tall. I didn't know roses grew that tall. Who do you think they're for?"

"I don't know, Molly. Hey, by the way, did I remember to wish you a happy birthday? And did I ever tell you what an awesome boyfriend you have?"

Molly gave Cheryl a passing glance. The birthday girl knew immediately that she had been set up, and her face was turning as red as the roses.

By the time the roommates reached the table, a crowd was forming. Molly opened the envelope and read the note to herself. She then looked up at the large group of girls who had quickly gathered around her.

There was a shout from the crowd: "Read it out loud!"

Molly timidly responded to the request, "Oh, I couldn't do that. It's personal."

"Come on, Molly." Cheryl had taken the lead. "We just have to know what the note says . . . please?"

Molly looked down at the note and read it in silence one more time. She was fighting back tears and knew of only one way to disperse the attention. "Okay, I'll read it out loud." She looked over at Cheryl and gave her a smile. She turned to her audience and cleared her throat. "There is only one thing more beautiful than these roses, and it is the person who is reading this card. With love, Reagan."

When the crowd finally began to dwindle, Cheryl pulled Molly aside. "That was something very special. I feel like I'm in the middle of a romance novel. I know Reagan is working tonight, but when you're done with your final, you need to go surprise him. Jump in his arms, kiss him, I don't know, just do something to thank him. You can borrow my car."

* * *

Hiram Schmidt had spent the past two weeks in the hospital fighting some sort of intestinal infection, and Karen Stein had been put in charge of things at Hoggetowne Pizza and Suds.

Karen had two finals on Thursday morning, so Reagan, who had already finished his last test, volunteered to fill in for her Wednesday night. He was working alongside of Sharon and Pam. It was the first time the three of them had worked together alone.

Karen had warned Reagan about his two coworkers early on, and she had been right. These two girls were boy crazy, they were nuts about Reagan, and they were very competitive. At first, Reagan had enjoyed their attention and had not been shy about flirting right back, but now he had a steady girlfriend, and despite their good looks, or how aggressive they might get, he had to resist.

With it being finals week, the restaurant had been slow all day. When the place emptied out with only a couple hours left before closing time, Pam suggested that they lock up early, do their cleaning, and call it a night.

"Hey, Reagan," Sharon began while sporting a wicked smile, "if you are real good to us and do us a little favor, we'll let you go home. Pam and I will stay here and get the place ready for tomorrow. We know you're anxious to get back to that girlfriend of yours. Why do you have a steady girl, anyway? You're just a freshman. What ever happened to playing the field?"

Truth be known, Reagan was anxious to get out of there. It was Molly's birthday, and he and she had big plans for the evening. He was also dying to hear how the rose delivery had gone. "Real good to me? What exactly does that mean, and what's the favor?"

Sharon finished pouring a pitcher of beer, grabbed three glasses, and headed toward the table that Pam and Reagan were wiping off. "Well, you see, Pam and I have this bet. She insists that she's the better kisser. But I've been told that I am the best kisser in town. We were trying to find a way to resolve this matter, and . . ."

CHAPTER TWENTY-FIVE

*T*erri Spencer used the spare key Charley had given her. Once inside the trailer, she shut the door, locked it, and took a good look around. This was surreal. She felt as if she were in the midst of a bad dream.

* * *

The university was on its quarterly recess, and up to this point, Terri had been enjoying the break. That particular afternoon had been spent with her father, drinking beer and playing pool in his basement. She had just won her third game in a row and was giving him a cocky look while he was racking up the balls for their next game.

"Well, sweetheart, if this college thing doesn't work out for you, you can always make a living as a pool shark."

"Oh, Dad, you're just letting me win. Why don't you switch the channels on the TV and turn up the volume? You might enjoy watching the evening news while I'm kicking your ass again."

Terri's break sent the three-ball into the right corner pocket. "I'm solids."

"We have a camera crew on the scene of a horrific single-car accident at the top of the hill on SW 34th Street just north of Williston Road. There is no report on the condition of the driver, but a police officer told our reporter that the vehicle must have been going in excess of one hundred miles an hour when it struck the light pole. There were no passengers in the car at the time of the accident."

"Jesus, Terri! Come look at this. No one could have survived that. Doesn't your friend Charley drive a white Stingray?"

"Oh my god! Oh my god! I've got to go!"

"Do you want me to go with you, sweetheart?"

"No, Daddy. This is something I've got to do myself."

* * *

Terri moved slowly toward the back of the trailer and into the bedroom. She had come here for one reason. Charley had told her about the diary. Terri didn't want it to get into the wrong hands.

Terri spotted the diary on the nightstand next to the unmade bed. It was open to the last entry. Terri flipped on the lamp, wiped the tears from her eyes, and started to read.

Dear Diary,

My whole world is suddenly falling apart, and I don't know what I'm going to do.

I had a call from my father yesterday. He was back home, and he sounded drunk. He asked me to send him more money. I went to the Western Union this morning and wired him the money I was going to use to pay for my tuition.

I asked him how he was doing. He was crying. All he said was that he misses Mom so badly and that he feels so empty inside. He asked me not to give up on him, and I told him that I loved him. I never took the time to go see him in the hospital. I really should have done that.

My awful landlord, Stephen Crain, shot Gary last week. It's a long story, but Gary is still in the hospital. They don't know if he will ever walk again. That's bad enough, but Crain might not ever be charged in the shooting. He's claiming it was self-defense, and so far, he hasn't been arrested. On top of all that, I think I might be pregnant with Crain's baby. I can't imagine anything worse.

I've been put on probation at work. Someone has been spying on me, and I think I know who it is. Crain must have seen me going into the hotel with Robert, and the bastard ratted me out to Bubba. I'm lucky I wasn't fired, but I'm not feeling real lucky about anything right now. Somebody needs to do something about Stephen Crain. He is a wicked man. He's ruining my life.

I'm sorry to sound so down. It's just that everything has caught up with me all at once, and I don't know who's on my side anymore. I feel like I'm playing the game all by myself, and I'm losing so badly. I could be a better person, a much better person. I just need somebody to help me understand the rules.

I need to get out of here now and go for a ride in my car, Ronnie's car. God, I miss him. I could just . . .

Terri sat for a moment studying the last sentence. She was resisting the urge to finish writing the entry herself. She really didn't want to know how it would have ended.

After a moment, Terri got up and put the diary on the kitchen table next to her car keys. She went back into the bedroom, made up the bed, and arranged the stuffed animals on top of the pillows. Back in the kitchen, she washed the dishes that were in the sink, dried them, and put them away. She picked up her keys and the diary, took one more look around, and walked out the door. She was headed back to see her dad. She needed his friendship now more than ever, and she needed to make a few phone calls.

* * *

Two days later, the Frisbee ball gang held a memorial for Charley. They sat in a circle in the middle of the field. One by one, they took turns digging a small hole about four feet deep.

They had each written a note on the Frisbee and signed it. Terri had even run it by the hospital so Gary could sign it. Ye and Yang placed the Frisbee in the hole, said a prayer in Chinese, and then covered it with dirt.

Reagan glanced over twice at Molly, who had not looked his way. What she had seen through the window at the Hog had not been what she thought it was, but it had been enough, and Reagan wasn't going to press the matter any further.

The friends took turns telling happy stories about Charley, remembering all of the fun times. They cried together, they laughed together, and then they sat for a long time, holding hands in silence.

There was nothing more to say. Ye and Yang were the first to stand and walk away. Jackson soon followed. Marty and Terri, hand in hand, were next. Reagan looked over once more at Molly, stood, and walked in the direction of his car.

He opened the door and was about to climb in when he heard her calling to him: "Reagan, I have something I want to say . . . something I need to tell you." Molly's voice was soft, not angry. Reagan turned and looked into her crying eyes. "I've decided to transfer to another college. I need to be closer to my mom and dad.

"I wanted you to know that I don't blame you. I'm not mad at you. It's not your fault. It's nobody's fault. You weren't ready, and, to be totally honest with you, I wasn't ready either. It's just that sometimes a loving heart welcomes no reason.

"What I wanted to say, Reagan, is good-bye and good luck. I will always remember you. Somewhere deep inside, I will always love you."

CHAPTER TWENTY-SIX

*I*t was a cold and rainy night.

Stephen Crain, sitting alone on the couch in front of his fireplace, had plenty of reasons to celebrate. It had been three months since the shooting incident, and earlier that day, the Gainesville Police Department had announced that the case file had been closed. No charges would be filed. Lieutenant Peters had called him personally that morning with the news.

Crain had heard through the grapevine that the Glasers' divorce would be finalized within the next few weeks. He hadn't heard from her, but he knew Carly would come crawling back to him soon. Before long, she would be all his. Her asshole husband was confined to a wheelchair. He had been demoted for his actions that night and was now working some meaningless desk job within the department.

Yes, if there was ever a night to celebrate, this was it, and Crain was ready. On the table in front of him sat a full bottle of Jack Daniel's, three rolled joints, several magazines, and a jar of petroleum jelly.

* * *

With two hours remaining before sunrise, it was still pitch dark. The moistened leaves would have yielded no sound from the slow, soft, deliberate footsteps. Typically, one would have needed a flashlight to find the way to the house. One would have been smart to wear gloves when opening the unlocked back door.

The police report would state that no unusual footprints had been found. There were no signs of forced entry. Nothing seemed to be out of place. Nothing seemed to be missing.

Tiptoeing quietly through the house, one would have found the kitchen and dining room empty. On the table in the living room was an empty bottle of whiskey and an ashtray holding three roaches. Magazines had been scattered about the stained couch. The last embers from the fire had been flickering, not making a sound.

If one had entered the bedroom, one would have found a snoring man facedown on the waterbed. With the right pocketknife, one would have been able to slice along the seam of the bed, allowing water to drain into its liner. With sufficient hand strength, one would have been able to hold the passed-out man's head down into the water while restraining his kicking legs. It would have only taken a minute for the man's body to become motionless.

The police report would state that one Stephen Crain had been found dead in his waterbed after a night of drinking and taking drugs. A resident of the community had reported a foul odor coming from the house. The coroner had estimated that the badly decomposed body had remained undiscovered for three days. There were no signs of a struggle. The cause of death was drowning. The report would conclude that Stephen Crain's death had been accidental, facilitated by the drugs and alcohol he had consumed.

Before leaving the house, if one had opened the bottom drawer of the nightstand, one would have found an envelope. Within the envelope would have been pictures: private pictures, pictures that needed to be destroyed, pictures that had caused so much damage.

If one had then walked quietly and cautiously under the oak trees to the north end of the community, one would have found a waiting vehicle parked along Archer Road, tucked amongst the trees and out of sight. Once inside, the driver would have offered a hand and a half smile before turning the key and heading east, into the sunrise.

Putter, putter.

EPILOGUE

*R*eagan Davis, sitting on the third step of the Murphree E dorm entrance, laces up his Nike Airs and zeros out his Casio running watch. He goes largely unnoticed by the passing students, many of whom seem distracted, staring off into space or walking with their faces turned down, mesmerized by some sort of electronic devices.

It is a beautiful sunlit February morning. The temperature is in the sixties, and the wind is blowing gently from the north. The year is 2014. Reagan has been retired for almost six months. He and his wife recently moved to Gainesville and purchased a home in the Duck Pond area.

Reagan will be running the same route that he ran so many times, so many years before. He doesn't expect to beat the record that he and Jackson set on a similar day in 1974, but Reagan has been training, and he hopes to make his attempt somewhat respectable.

Reagan's run through the tunnel and onto the main body of the campus conjures up many memories, some good and some bad. So many things have changed, but at the same time, so many things have remained the same, just like life itself: always evolving, stepping forward and stepping back, hopefully gaining knowledge from alterations or departures that have proven unwise.

Passing the ROTC building, Reagan recalls his first run as a college freshman. He remembers confronting both the marchers and the hippies . . . his generation.

How far apart we were then, and how far apart we are now. We were the sex, drugs, and rock 'n' roll generation, the rebels without a care in the world, the renegades with no need for guiding principles, setting our own values, answering only to ourselves.

And now? Arguably, we have evolved into the most uptight generation in our nation's history.

Those who protested so adamantly against the Vietnam War have led our country into two altercations strikingly similar in nature and outcome. The young

194

hipsters who shouted peace and love from the rooftops now find themselves trapped in gridlock, opinions so diverse and polarizing that our government is virtually paralyzed.

This was an alliance so sure of itself that it threw out the rulebook. But, later, it would legislate the strictest laws, adopt the most obtrusive policies, and implement the tightest restrictions our society has ever known. Who could have imagined that we would allow spying on our own citizens? Who would have guessed that we would fight so vehemently against a gay couple's right to marry? Lord, we even passed a law dictating the type of light bulbs allowed in our own homes.

But, Reagan reasons as he veers onto Fraternity Row, there have also been many accomplishments. Our tolerance for one another as individuals is growing. Our willingness to assist the most unfortunate through charitable gifts and legislative policies is improving. Race barriers continue to be broken down, and most of us truly believe in equality of the sexes. We elected a black man as our president and will more than likely send a woman to that office in the near future.

But most of all, we have nurtured a generation of mostly hardworking, intelligent, and socially tolerant young adults. This fact alone may prove to be our most important achievement . . . our legacy.

Reagan waves to three brothers standing in the doorway of the Sigma Chi house. *How luck they are.* How lucky he was, and still is, to be one of them. How thankful he is that his parents found a way to make that happen.

Both SW 34th Street and Archer Road are now eight-lane nightmares, far from the two-lane country roads of the past. It takes Reagan more than two minutes just to get across the intersection.

The Shady Oaks Mobile Home Community is long gone, having yielded years before to Florida's growth explosion. Now, in its place, there are restaurants, shops, gas stations, and professional offices.

There is still a light pole at the spot at the top of the hill on SW 34th Street, only now it is made of concrete. Trying to catch his breath, Reagan pushes the stop button on his watch, leans against the pole, and says a prayer.

He hasn't stayed in touch with them, but he will always remember the Frisbee ball gang. And, of course, he could never forget Charley. He remembered reading that she had been full of drugs and alcohol at the time of her accident. Reagan had always wished he'd been a better friend to her. If he had only been there when she'd needed him the most, maybe, just maybe. The autopsy had revealed that she had been pregnant at the time of her death. This memory alone had haunted Reagan for many years.

Reagan stops for a drink of water at the old Frisbee ball field. His watch shows that he is far behind his desired pace, and he decides not to record the remainder of his run. He takes a good look around. There are footballs being tossed, dogs frolicking about, and, yes, Frisbees being thrown back and forth. In a way, it is as if life has stood still. In many other ways, however, it is clear that time has flown by.

Memories may fill our minds, but the hopes and dreams in our hearts will keep us moving forward—moving forward with the expectations of making new and, hopefully, joyful memories. With this on his mind, Reagan comes to a stop on SW 13th Street in front of the gingerbread structure, still standing proud after all these years.

Following the demise of Hoggetowne Pizza and Subs in the late '70s, the building has housed many businesses: a pool hall, several restaurants, doctors' offices, even an adult bookstore. Until recently, it had been sitting vacant, overgrown, and almost begging to be torn down. But, not unlike Reagan himself, it had been brought back to life: reinvented, refreshed, sporting a happy facade, and full of hope for a bright future. All it took was the right person at the right time.

Standing there, looking up at the new sign, Reagan decides to leave the rest of his run for another day. There are last-minute preparations still to be tended to. He's sure that his wife could use his help. He knows she will be happy to see him. She always is.

Reagan walks toward the building, but before opening the door, he glances up at the sign one more time.

Molly Davis' Italian Cuisine
Grand opening today 6:00 PM
Red roses accepted